Flame For Two

Raleigh Damson

PRINT ISBN 978-1-7780254-3-3

EBOOK ISBN 978-1-7780254-2-6

Raleigh Damson Books

raleigh@raleighdamson.com

To those who love without condition.

1

CHAPTER ONE - HARPER

Harper's heart pounded so hard against her chest that she heard its roar in her ears, even above the chatter of a hundred other dancers. She took a deep breath, trying to clear her mind, but only inhaled the heavy scents of baby powder and hairspray. She couldn't believe she was going through with it.

She had waited in line for four hours, all the while telling herself that this was a terrible idea. And on the walk over to the theatre this morning, while feeling eyes on the back of her neck, convinced someone was following her, she nearly ran for the safety of her office. Here she was, despite this being a terrible idea. Dancing had been absent from her life long enough. Oh, she had her adult ballet classes, and she kept in shape with her CrossFit training sessions, but it wasn't the same as being on stage. The anticipation made her palms sweat.

Her feet were on the stage floor, and she stood straight and tall as the director marched on stage and welcomed them to the audition for *Canada's Best Dancer*. He split them up into groups. She ended up being in group "C," Then the choreographer came on the stage and showed them the first routine.

Committing the routine to memory was the simple part. Getting her body to execute the steps with some artistry was the challenge because it wasn't in a studio where she spent her days but in an office, following her boss from floor to floor, making sure everyone had what they needed from Team Tech needing special wristbands to Team Stealth having the newest non-military Kevlar coated tactical pants that they could get their hands on, the cost not being an issue. She was good at her job, but it wasn't where she'd thought she would end up.

She had thought she would be like these other dancers here, maybe with an international company, maybe even as a principal dancer or touring in a stage production as part of the chorus. Dancing on stage was all she dreamed about, following in her mother's footsteps.

After they tried out the routine, they cleared the stage for the first dancers to take their turn.

Pushing down the rise of emotion, Harper waited in the wings with the rest of her group. Her work was interesting and challenging and made her happy mostly, but it wasn't what she was born to do. Life had come in like a wicked tsunami, wrecking everything she held dear.

But she was here now, and she threw her shoulders back, kept her head up, and glided onto the stage with her group. There were a thousand reasons she shouldn't be here, like the TV cameras that panned the room for their promo shots. But when the music started, Harper didn't care. Losing herself in the steps of the contemporary routine, her body knew what to do even out of practice.

Before the tsunami of destruction, dancing had made her feel free, a moving part in something boundless, and for the sixty seconds of this first routine, that feeling infused her limbs again.

The music stopped, and the director walked down the rows. "Cut," he said to the girl next to Harper, then "Cut" to the girl on the other side of her. As he passed, Harper exhaled. She was still in this.

"Wave at the camera for me," Came the instruction as Harper took her place in the wings again.

Ignoring the churning in her stomach, Harper flashed a grin.

"How does it feel to get through that first routine?" the woman behind the lens asked.

"It feels amazing! I'm so thrilled." Harper offered the woman a smile, twirling on the spot.

"Thanks," the camera moved on.

Three hours later, she was packing up her dance bag in disbelief. She had made it through to the solo round and gotten to perform her routine. Now she waited for a callback.

Other than feeling slightly guilty about lying to the production people by ensuring them she would be available for interviews, she felt great. For the first time in years, she had accomplished something all on her own.

Coming out of the changing room, Harper smoothed down her sunflower-covered pencil skirt and tucked in her black high collar blouse. Refreshing her lipstick, she pulled her long mahogany hair into a ponytail and exited the theatre into the grey, drizzling November afternoon, turning on her phone as she walked.

Immediately, her phone started buzzing. She was never offline, certainly not for most of the day, and she knew her assistant Claudia could only cover for her for so long without questions. She sped up, work was only a few blocks away, and it was easier to walk there than hail a cab.

Her skin started tingling. She checked the windows of the buildings she passed by, using them as a mirror to glance about her, reassuring herself that nobody was following her. It was all in her head. Years of looking over her shoulder made her paranoid.

Crossing the street, Harper looked over her shoulder, but it was only other people in the crowd going on with their day.

Reaching the street where Axis Management stood proudly, like a contemporary modern art piece, all in black glass and sleek materials, Harper slowed down.

"Harper! Harper!"

Harper turned at the familiar voice. "Josie, hi."

"You walk so fast! Where were you coming from?" Josie stopped, leaning on her crutch.

"I had an appointment," Harper said. "What brings you by?"

"I was hoping to catch Ares, but there is no way into the building. I tried calling him but couldn't get through."

"They prefer it that way," Harper said with a smile. "Ares should be on a plane flying home. Do you want to come up with me?"

"No, if he's not in, there's no point. It's just...." Josie looked away, running her hands through her short black hair. "One business he sent my way cancelled their contract with us, and I wanted to know if he knew why."

"Sorry to hear that," Harper said. Josie was sweet as her catering company's pies, and Harper knew it was uncomfortable for her to ask for help.

"Just so I can improve, if something was wrong, I don't want him to fix this," Josie said. "I can get my own business."

"Your food speaks for itself," Harper said.

"Thanks," Josie said, glancing down. "I'll get in touch with Ares later in the week. You should come over for dinner. My mom would love to see you."

"I will, definitely," Harper said. Josie and her mother, Fleur, were two of only a small circle of people who knew about her personal tsunami.

"Take care," Josie called.

Continuing to the door of the shiny metallic glass building, Harper stopped by the seamless entrance and punched in the code to activate the retina scanner. When the lock flashed green, and the doors opened, she walked into Axis Management's smooth terrazzo main floor, the security firm that did everything from bodyguarding to government contracts and more. The main floor was empty, the curved front desk clear. She passed the conference room before stepping into the elevator and riding up to the executive floor.

"Hello," she said to their receptionist, Viv.

Viv raised her eyebrows at her and pointed down the hall.

Yeah, they'd be looking for her. Harper glanced at her watch.

"Harper!"

Halfway to the office, Claudia flew towards her. "You need to check your messages. Ares's plane is delayed, and there's that fundraiser tonight. My sister thinks the baby is coming but I can stay if you want."

"Go! Keep me updated!" "Thanks!" Claudia smiled and waved.

Harper sighed. She did not need this after the rehearsal; she wanted to go home, curl up with a book and tune out the world.

Entering the executive wing, she smiled. Her desk sat outside her boss's office. His door was closed. Putting her bag away, she sighed. He was going to need a suit.

She waved bye to Viv, who was shutting down her system and walked down the hall, hitting the elevator's up button while rearranging the schedule for tomorrow in her head. When the elevator opened, she strode to apartment number one, the biometric lock opening to her touch. This was a ridiculous hassle.

"Totally unnecessary," Harper grumbled under her breath. From the closet, she took out a suit and folded it over her arm. She made a couple of quick phone calls and returned to the executive wing. Passing her desk, she paused at the door.

But interrupting came with the territory of being the executive assistant to Xander Montague, billionaire and genius extraordinaire. She knocked once. Her phone buzzed in her pocket. If he didn't get a move on, they would be late. He hated being late almost as much as he hated wearing a suit, so she did the whole swipe her hand over the lock thing again.

When the door whisked open, she wished she hadn't interrupted.

"Hey," she said, leaning against the door like it was no big deal she had walked in on her boss getting a blow job at five-thirty in the afternoon.

There he sat on the black leather couch in the lounge area with his head resting back, his curtain of dark hair flowing along his arm, his hand guiding the woman's head, while Harper acted like she was just passing through to drop off a file or wake him from a nap. Like it didn't make her heart twist in a pang of jealousy because she wished it was her between his strong, muscular legs.

Xander's eyes flew open, and the brunette woman between his legs startled. Xander swore, and his hands came around the back of the woman's neck, pulling her off.

"Sorry, Cindy, I'll make it up to you."

"You could tell her to go." Cindy pouted.

"I have business," Xander said, his voice firm. He had already thrown on his boxers, guided Cindy up from the floor, and smoothed down her dress.

"Bitch," Cindy murmured to Harper as she walked past her.

Harper flashed her a smile as wide as her lips could stretch. It didn't matter how many women came, they went, and she stayed.

"Cindy." That tone made Harper feel small. He never used that deep baritone voice on her like that, though she wished he did. His tone of dominance sent a thrill down her spine.

He grabbed Cindy's arm and raised an eyebrow at her.

"Sorry," Cindy mumbled, looking at the ground.

"I'll call you," Xander said.

As Cindy exited the office, the doors swished closed, and Harper adjusted the suit bag in her hands.

"No! Not the suit!" Xander said, with a hand across his face, as if he was a vampire, and the suit bag Harper had draped over her arm was the blazing sun.

Harper sighed. He refused to keep suits in his office, so she had to keep them stashed in a closet up in the apartments Axis Management had above their offices, and they went through this routine whenever she had to get him one. "You know I wouldn't bring it if it weren't for a good reason."

"Nope, I didn't see it. I'm sure I have a meeting somewhere."

Harper shook her head and watched as Xander tapped his keyboard and frowned.

"You locked me out of the system!"

"You gave me executive privileges for this reason. Go shower. The car will be here in half an hour."

"I'm expecting Erik, and there is that meeting with the Martin Group. I have to go paint a wall or fix a fence."

"No way out of this one. I told Erik you weren't available tonight. He's going to see you at one tomorrow. Ares is Zooming with the Martin Group from the hotel." She put the suit in Xander's hands. "And Mr. Montague, you have never fixed a fence or painted a wall."

"Are you so sure?" his voice purred.

Harper smiled. This was the side of her otherwise serious and dour boss that few people got to see.

"*Positive.*"

He had created a popular scheduling app that had made him his first million. He designed a sleeker better satellite phone for military operations that earned him another million and other things, but Xander didn't own a hammer.

"Is there no way he can get here?" Xander pulled back his hair into an elastic band. His rock band T-shirt hit the floor in another second, revealing his tight abs and broad shoulders.

"Ares doesn't like you doing these things, either," Harper said. She turned away as Xander's hands went to his waistband and walked down the corridor with the muted, dove grey walls to her inner space.

When they had been going over plans for this building, Xander had insisted she had a space of her own, and Harper disagreed. She followed Xander wherever he went during the day, and when he was in his office on this floor, she was at her desk, just outside. A wholly separate space for her wasn't necessary, but she loved it after having this retreat for a few months.

She'd had this office done in what she thought of as an "ocean light" theme. The walls were light blue, the curtains in soft pink and framed photos of beaches were scattered around the room. A standing desk and a comfy chaise that doubled as her bed when she worked through the night were the only pieces of furniture in the room. She pulled out a red sparkly gown from the closet next to her bathroom and kicked off her flats, replacing them with heels. She hung the dress on the bathroom door and started her make-up.

"Are you sure he can't get here? We can't send the plane?" Xander appeared in her bathroom doorway with a towel wrapped around his waist.

Harper met Xander's steel eyes in the mirror. The press called him the "Prince of Darkness of the Business World," and with his pale skin, powerful features, and that long black hair, it was a title he nurtured.

"It's a security threat, so the whole airport is closed. He had to do some sweet talking to leave the airport and go to the hotel. He'll be on the first flight out as soon as they have cleared the threat."

While Xander was the Prince of Darkness of the Business world, Ares, his brother and co-CEO, was known as the Archangel, having a reputation for never saying no to a request for a donation or a photo op, never refusing an invitation to a charity function.

"Not this one," Xander said, taking the gown from her and walking out of the room with it in his arms.

As she finished making up her eyes, Harper smiled, being used to Xander's whims. He had a reason for everything he did.

"Wear this tonight." Xander held up a light purple A-line gown. As he dangled it in his hand, Harper saw it was asymmetrical. The front of the skirt would be slightly shorter than the back.

"It's lovely," she said.

Opening a drawer, she selected a pair of earrings and went to put her hair up.

"I saw it and thought of you."

As their eyes met in the mirror, Harper's pulse raced. He continuously surprised her.

"Are you sure there is no way out of this? They don't even feed you at these things."

"Axis Management gave ten thousand dollars to the Firefighters' Foundation. This dinner is to thank their top donors."

"And ask for more money," Xander grumbled.

"Naturally. We'll get through it, and then you can play Zombies till dawn."

"*Outriders*," Xander mumbled.

"Go get dressed," Harper closed the door on him.

"Top donor? That means I need to give a speech?!"

"There's a full bottle of Xanax in the top drawer of your dresser, in the closet."

"Meet you outside in five."

Harper finished her hair and slipped on the gown, running a checklist in her head of everyone she knew who would be there, trying to prepare for the evening, including a plan to get Xander out of there as quickly as possible.

Many competitors and journalists would love to know that Xander Montague, the mighty Prince of Darkness of the Business World, had a severe anxiety disorder. Harper did everything in her power to keep that contained only to people whose fingerprints could open these rooms. Xander was her rescuer and her protector. She owed him a lot. Keeping his secrets was an easy ask.

Before leaving her suite, she admired how the dress fit in the mirror. Xander always chose right. The dusky purple brought out the olive tone in her skin, highlighting her green eyes. The bodice hugged her breasts snuggly. The longest part of the skirt hit just below her calves, showing off her long legs. She touched the *x* pendant at her throat. It was another mark of Xander's protection he had given her. This *x* served as a broadcast in certain settings to talk to her; one had to speak to Xander first. And while only those in the BDSM scene might know what a protection collar meant, it was her touchstone, another way of reassuring herself that she was safe.

She shut off the lights and through the doors to the central executive area. Before she left, she stopped by Claudia's desk, leaving her a few notes for her meeting with Team Tech and telling her she would be in around eight o'clock the following day in case Claudia's sister's baby didn't come tonight.

At the side door of the building, she found the co-CEO of Axis Management, as most of the world knew him to be, pacing back and forth and speaking rapid French into his phone. His raven hair was in its trademark braid, hitting the centre of his back. He had a pair of sunglasses on. He was decked out in a black, light wool suit with a faint but present red pinstripe. Underneath the suit jacket, he wore a high collar black shirt. His black boots shone to a high gloss. His expression was stoic, with no signs of the humour and playfulness that, in private, she knew well. A few feet away from him was the bodyguards for the evening, Asher and Soren; the job was to keep the press away from Xander.

As Harper came beside him, she heard him utter a curse involving a holy sacrament that never translated the same to English. He slipped his phone into his inner suit jacket pocket and stared ahead.

"That good?" Harper asked.

Xander looked at her. Harper stared back, unflinching. "Benoit thinks he has what I want, but he won't give it to me yet." Harper couldn't help but gasp. Xander had been working with their technology competitor for months, searching for information that would lead to figuring out who was responsible for an attack on Team Stealth back in June.

"What does he want?"

"He wants access to the information we might have on upcoming government contracts. I'm not good at sharing."

Harper kept her expression neutral, but her mouth went dry, and her heart thudded hard against her ribs.

"We know that."

She often wondered if he could share if he would. But Xander was a person-to-person type of guy. He kept his inner circle tiny, his outer circle small. Axis Management might be worth billions, but they were a small operation run on threads of loyalty.

"I don't have anyone I can send to him to soothe his feelings."

Xander paced for a moment. Harper waited with her phone out.

"Laurent. Get him in my office first thing tomorrow. He's also the least scary person we have to send."

As the limo pulled up, Carli, their driver, opened the door, and the two bodyguards got into their vehicle, going on ahead. Xander often had a team of their bodyguards follow them to any public appearance he made. Harper settled into the seat while leaving a message for Nick Laurent, a member of Team Stealth, or as the team was better known, Bandit Brothers. Xander slipped in beside her and looked at the ceiling.

"I hate these things."

"It will be over before you know it."

"You're gorgeous in that dress."

Harper smoothed out the skirt of her gown as she looked down. "Thanks."

Xander wasn't the only one who wanted the evening to be over. It was getting harder to hide how she felt about Xander. Harper knew he still thought of her as the not quite legal enough to drink girl she'd been when he rescued her.

"Here we go," she said as the limo pulled up at the hotel. There was a swarm of press and a crowd out front, shoulder to shoulder people.

"Fuck me," Xander said.

As he offered her hand, Harper's pulse raced when she caught sight of a big man, who stood head and shoulders over the rest with his spikey blond hair.

"Logan Marrock," she breathed.

"I'll have someone besides you to talk to," Xander said, and he almost smiled.

"Perfect," she said, but her stomach had tightened, wondering how she would get through the night with these two men. One who she wished would love her back, even as she couldn't stop thinking about the other.

2

CHAPTER TWO - LOGAN

Not for all the world would he admit it, but Logan Marrock didn't mind these shindigs. It amused him to put on the tux, shake people's hands, and watch as they tried to compensate because he stood head and shoulders above them all. He found some men did this by touching him a lot with slaps on the back or putting more strength than necessary into the handshake. Logan smiled and went through the motions, then laughed about it the next morning while he bench pressed 250lbs. He liked being in crowds. Even better, he enjoyed being on stage in front of a packed audience with a naked submissive at his feet, waiting for his rope.

It wasn't the suit or the event or the crowds he minded; it was being here as his half-sister's uncle's right-hand man. Yeah, he couldn't say that five times fast. As a representative of a company with questionable morals, it chafed at him. But he knew how to keep his emotions in check—most of the time.

He sent Hana a quick text, telling her he would call her tomorrow. His half-sister had gotten a raw deal. His musician father had left his mother for the palm trees of Hawaii and then, years later, repeated the same feat, this time after having Hana. And Hana's mom was the heiress to the famous SolCan company. Or she should be, except for Edwin, who refused to update an outdated clause about women inheriting. So, Hana's mom, Paige, did what she could on an art appraiser's salary, and Hana's future wasn't as bright as it could be.

Until Edwin realized that Logan, an accomplished mountaineer, veteran, and ex-search and rescue tech, could be helpful to his benefit, a deal was struck, Logan would do some PR for the company, and Edwin agreed to pay for Hana's school and give the kid access to her trust fund.

Logan gritted his teeth just thinking about it. In the press release for tonight, they splashed all his accomplishments on the pages. He didn't care except for the worry that it would affect his job with Axis Management. Although when Team Stealth went in, nobody saw them. Or at least nobody who would run to the press. Usually. Except for that leak back in June.

He just had to make it through tonight, and tomorrow morning he would be rock climbing, freestyle. If he timed it right, he could catch the sunrise on the bluffs.

Another clap on the back from Mr. Olson brought him back to the moment. He smiled widely and refrained from pushing his arm off of him. It wouldn't look good to manhandle the VP of a major bank.

"So, you can get me in to see Ed next Thursday? I would make it worth your while."

Logan laughed, knowing Mr. Olson meant that would be a prostitute or an insider tip, and leaned down to put his hand on the banker's shoulder. "I'll pass it on. Right now, I'm here to support the firefighters."

"Yes, of course. I need to get in there. My wife doesn't like to be sitting at the table too long without me." Mr. Olson gave him a wave. As Logan moved to follow him, a car stopped and idled behind him. He turned, curious to see the next guests.

His pulse increased as he watched his boss, Xander Montague, give his arm to Harper Blake. "Hey, the party just got interesting." Logan extended his hand to Xander, clasping his forearm, and brought him in for a man-hug.

"Thank fuck," Xander said.

"Ares has the plague?"

"A security threat closed the airport."

"I tried to get him here," Harper added.

"I guess Superwoman is no match for airport security." Logan grinned at her, watching how the flush spread across her cheeks ever so slightly. And he noticed how her gown hugged her bust *just* right and showed off her long legs. Her hair was in some kind of braided knot, and he preferred her mass of long, nutty hair down. If he could change anything else about what she was wearing, it would be to rip off that golden *x* charm that dangled above the hollow in her throat, the symbol that marked her as being under Xander's protection. He would take that off in a hot second and put his collar around her neck.

"Let's get in there and get this over with," Xander said. He offered Harper his arm, and Logan bit the inside of his jaw, stifling down a wave of annoyance. He wanted her on his arm and in his bed. The way she looked at Xander as they walked into the space told him maybe he hadn't made those intentions clear as he'd thought.

When he had signed on with Axis Management, it was a present, gift-wrapped and tied with a bow. It kept him from eking out a living by teaching rock climbing and offered him the adventure his thrill-seeking spirit craved. Plus, he got to do it all with his buddies. From rescuing actresses to gathering intel on threats to the government, the missions varied enough to keep his interest. He owed his buddy, Jordan, for getting him in with the company. That was how he'd met Harper, and from the moment he saw her, he wanted her. He couldn't stop thinking about her.

A server asked for their names, then escorted them to a table in the centre of the room. Logan took the chair on the right of Harper.

"Sorry, Mr. Marrock, your table is across the room."

Xander reached out and deftly removed the two nametags. "There has been a mistake. Mr. Marrock is part of our party. As my brother isn't joining us, we don't need these place settings."

The young man gulped, looked at Xander and quickly cleared two settings, and they all took their places around the table.

"Not bad for five hundred dollars a plate." He was expecting Xander to joke about how that was pocket change to him or not worth the price of the dried chicken they were about to eat. Instead, his boss sat with his hands resting on the table, staring blankly at the front of the room. Harper had her hand on top of his and spoke quietly to him.

For as long as he had known Xander, he had never seen him in a gathering like this, cultivating the idea that he didn't like people. That was true, Xander wasn't everyone's cup of tea, and Logan figured there weren't many people his boss could gel with. For a huge corporation, they kept their teams small, and Xander vetted everyone who worked for Axis Management up the wazoo but watching his paler than regular expression, Logan wondered if something else was up with his friend. The look on his face was one

Logan recognized. Novice climbers were usually sure they could make it up the hill, but their faces got all ashen at the halfway mark, and they froze, suspended between going up and going down. That's precisely the expression Xander wore right now.

"So this should be fun," Logan sat back in his chair, drumming on the table with his palms. Xander glanced over at him.

"You couldn't get out of this one either?"

Logan spread his hands wide, recognizing that his boss had noticed how he was observing him. Xander did not miss a single thing.

"Ed insisted." He stood as the Jensons approached their table.

"Logan! Good to see you. You should come out with me on the golf course."

"My golf game isn't up to snuff," Logan said, returning the man's handshake.

"Please go with him and let him beat you. It would be good for his ego," said Mrs. Jenson.

"I'll consider it."

"Mr. Montague, I saw how much money you donated. The Firefighters' Association is very grateful."

Xander merely grunted at her.

Logan put a hand on Mrs. Jenson's arm. "I think they are going to start the speeches now. We can catch up after dinner."

"I'll have you booking a time with me by the end of the evening," Mr. Jenson said.

"I'm sure you will," Logan said.

The owner of the largest shipping company on the West coast went back to his table with his wife.

"Are you really going to golf with that fucker?" Xander asked.

"They aren't that bad."

"A captain of one of his barges fell asleep on the job," Xander said.

And that kind of behaviour wouldn't be acceptable to Xander.

"Okay, he's awful," Logan grinned.

Harper laughed, her face relaxing and her green eyes twinkling. Xander's lips turned up slightly.

On the stage, a white-haired man in a suit tapped the mic. "Good evening, ladies and gentlemen, and thank you for coming...."

Logan watched Harper take out her phone and furiously text as his speech droned on. He couldn't wait to get her on the dance floor. Over the last couple of months, they had gone out for two breakfasts and three lunches, and one time, Logan had brought her to Club Bandit, the BDSM Club he was a founding member of, for one of the intensive rope seminars he gave to its members. He had hoped to have her in rope by the end of that night, but work called her away.

"We would especially like to thank our top donor, Axis Management, for their generous donation of ten thousand dollars. Mr. Montague, please come up and say a few words."

Xander got that frozen look again and remained in his chair. Harper patted his arm. A few people in the room coughed and stared.

Logan jumped out of his seat, striding up the two steps to the stage. He clasped his hand on the director's back.

"Before we hear from Mr. Montague, I have an announcement." The director nodded and made room for him.

"Thank you for letting me interrupt, and folks, I'll be short. I know we are eager to eat the wonderful food they are about to serve us." The crowd laughed. "The dedication of firefighters is unlike anything else. I want to announce that SolCan will donate one hundred thousand dollars to the Firefighters Association."

There was applause at this, and Logan continued talking about how they all had to support the services and called on his fellow business leaders to match the donation. When he saw the servers wheel out trays, he stopped. "Now it's time to eat! Thank you all, and have a good night." As he made his way back to his table, he shook hands here and there.

"Is Ed Greyson going to be okay with that?" Xander asked quietly as Logan retook his seat. Xander was the only one who knew who Ed was and why he was here. It was the hard part about being on Team Stealth, which they unofficially renamed Bandit Brothers as a tribute to his buddy Jordan. Xander and Ares knew everything about each of the guys on the team.

"Hana's granddad was a volunteer firefighter. I'll make sure it's in his name."

Xander nodded. "Now, I don't get to give my speech."

"You know, this is a rare appearance by the Dark Prince of the business world. I'm sure I could tell them to stop serving."

Xander gave him the finger, and he laughed.

Donating might have saved his boss from giving a speech, but it kept him away from Harper because everyone in the entire room came over and shook his hand after the dessert plates were cleared. A few women asked him to dance, and, not wanting to say no, he danced with every one of them. Just as he was going to take Harper onto the floor, his cell rang.

Good old Uncle Ed, calling to ream him out.

"What were you thinking?" Edwin shouted.

"That you're going to need the publicity when you go public with moving all manufacturing overseas. Can you even use 'Canada' in your name anymore?"

Edwin wasn't the brightest, just the meanest, and he would only do something that cost him money if it benefited him. Bonus if it was for the torture of other people.

"Fine. You make sure it's in Stewart's name, and I want to see you here by the end of the month. It's time for you to come and work for a living if you don't want Paige to live out her golden years in poverty or Hana to lose her spot at university. It's your choice."

Logan gritted his teeth and breathed through his nose. He imagined crushing Ed's neck in his hands. He could easily take the weasel. Ed thought all he did was teach rock climbing. He didn't have a clue that he worked for Axis Management.

"Hear you loud and clear," Logan gritted.

"Good." Ed clicked off.

Logan took a steadying breath before heading back inside. He was boiling on the inside but made sure not to show his anger. He sighed, seeing a tall, board-shouldered man with dark hair approach Xander's table.

"Mr. Montague? I'm sorry to bother you. I'm Elijah Weber. My old man owns a sod company—"

Xander nodded. "Better Lawns, yes. Your father is in the news nearly as often as I am."

Logan laughed. "For different reasons. How is he feeling these days?"

"Better, thanks," Elijah said, giving Logan a stare.

Ace Weber made the news because he'd started a dog rescue facility on the side and reportedly gave over half his earnings away each year. The man recently got into a horseback-riding accident.

"I wanted to come over and ask if the rumours were true. Do you play *Outriders*? You might know me as Zolt182."

"Come sit down here," Xander said, his face lit up.

"Harper, would you like to dance?"

Harper looked at Xander. "I have Carli coming in half an hour."

"Call her and make it an hour. I'm talking," Xander said.

"Okay, done," Harper said, putting her phone down on the table. "Take me for a spin, Logan."

"Yeah, let's do it, Kitten." He offered his arm to her, and her long fingers gripped his biceps. Finally, he was touching her. He guided her to the dance floor as the DJ played a slow beat.

Her green eyes met his. Her cheeks flushed, and he wanted her in his bed with a ferocity he'd never experienced before.

"I've wanted you in my arms all night."

He placed his hand on her back, pulling her close to him. She smiled, exposing the slight dimples in her cheeks.

"You already showed me your moves. Quite impressive, Mr. Marrock."

"Impressive enough to come bouldering with me tomorrow morning?" he whispered in her ear.

"I need to work."

"Even Wonder Woman needs time off."

"I thought I was Superwoman?"

Logan laughed, his hands moving to her waist. "You are Superwonderwoman. Come home with me tonight?"

He meant it teasingly, but the light went out of her eyes, replaced by a deer in the headlights stare. He felt her tense up in his arms, and he pulled her even closer, wrapping another arm around her upper body. He wanted this woman badly, but he would wait.

"That's too fast a move for you?"

"It's not that I don't like you, Logan. I..."

"Need to go slow?"

"Yes." The relief in her voice brought the light back to her eyes.

"Okay. I'll go slow," Logan said. Dancing to the slower beat, his hands roamed just above her hips as she swayed perfectly in time to the music.

Extending his arm, he flung her out for a spin and effortlessly, Harper spun out and back to him without missing a beat.

"You must have had a round of dance classes in your past," He purred.

She glanced away, her mouth pressed in a thin line. Every time he asked her questions about her past, she closed up. He wanted to know everything about her.

"Yes."

She got the word out, and Logan knew it was an effort for her to keep that smile on her face. He cupped a hand to her cheek, feeling her soft skin against his rough hand.

"You can tell me anything, you know."

"You look very handsome in your tux," she smiled.

Logan laughed, his hands caressing her back.

"So, there is this thing at Club Bandit—"

"That's not slow." Harper laughed.

"Slowly think about it?" Logan asked, whispering the words against her ear, feeling her shiver.

"Okay, I'll think about it," Harper said. Her lips were right in front of his. He wanted to slide his tongue in, inhale her taste, hold her, and never let her go.

"Perfect." He danced her around the room while already planning how to get her to open up and land in his bed.

3

CHAPTER THREE - XANDER

Xander surveyed the clutter chaos of Harper's desk, biting the inside of his cheek. The mess irked him. And it annoyed him more that a tiny part of him thought it was endearing because it was one of Harper's quirks. He leaned over the edge of her desk, the only clear part of the surface and waited until she looked up from her screen.

"We need new bodyguards. I want initial background checks on the three new potentials for the Threat Assessment and Personal Security Division. Also, there was an error on page six of the last time allocation report you sent. Resend it."

Damn, Harper was cute when her brow furrowed, and she bit her bottom lip ever so slightly. She furiously tapped her keyboard, found the report, and glared at him. "There is one typo in the fifty-page document. Only you and Ares see it."

"Are you arguing with me?" He raised an eyebrow.

"No. I'm pointing out your request is petty."

Xander gave her his steeliest glare and rapped his knuckles on his desk. "And it was petty when I made you redo the budgets when you were missing the decimals the first year you served as my executive assistant, and it was petty when I made you re-order the carpet for downstairs because it wasn't black enough. I like the details to be correct, or have you forgotten?"

"No, Mr. Montague." Harper glared at him. The keys clacked as loud as they could. "Time allocation report has been resent."

Xander walked past her and into his office, disappearing behind the black wall. He let out a breath, looking toward the mountains out his window. Ever since the night of that benefit, things had been tense between him and Harper, and that annoyed him. He should be happy for her. All he ever wanted was for Harper to come out of her shell and be the confident woman he knew she could be. And now that it was happening before his eyes, it turned out he couldn't take it because he wanted the reason for her coming out of that shell to be him. Not some giant spikey-haired Dom.

Last year, when Logan started spending more time with Harper, he thought it was a passing lark. He was sure it wouldn't go beyond coffee when Logan realized Harper wasn't an experienced sub.

It annoyed him that he hadn't seen this coming.

"Hey, why did you make our sweet HR girl, Gardenia, cry?" Ares asked, opening his door.

Xander picked up the stacks of bound contracts beside his chair and let them fall onto his desk. "Did you know that Axis Management has no policy about interpersonal relationships in the workplace? And I didn't make Gardenia cry. She was flustered because she didn't see a way of doing what I wanted without turning over our 'successful structure.'" He put air quotes around those last words.

"We know what brand of toothpaste every employee uses. Imposing an anti-dating policy seemed counterintuitive to that whole 'trust us, we got your back' approach we were going for. And I dare you to tell Team Stealth they can't date each other." Ares's impressive dimples appeared as he helped himself to an orange juice from the black bar fridge located underneath the counter against the wall.

"That's what Gardenia said. She said the one place we might want it is in our Personal Security and Threat Assessment Division."

"If we just called it 'Bodyguards,' people would know what we were talking about," Ares said, his turn to use air quotes.

"Yeah. I'm going to assign Logan to the Bodyguards." He was only half-joking.

"Nope." Ares wagged a finger at him. "You can't. I'm not dealing with that kind of rebellion. Logan is the leader of Team Stealth, and you know it."

"Quinn—"

"Isn't back yet, and what he wants to do is still up in the air. What's this about, Xander?" His brother plopped himself down in front of the window in his club chair.

It was about seeing Harper in Logan Marrock's arms. Seeing her look at Logan with wide eyes and laugh in response to his words. It was about him wanting to hold on to her and not wanting to let her go.

It was about lying to himself that he didn't want the smart and sexy woman.

"Harper."

His brother smiled as her name left his lips; that slow, sultry smile got him fans every time he uploaded a new video to his social media feeds.

"I can't believe I'm even thinking about her like this. So what if she wants to go out with Logan?"

"You've been her protector for years. I'm surprised it took this long for you to realize you had an attraction to her."

His younger brother was wrong. He had been attracted to Harper since her university acceptance came.

"I moved her out of the house. That's when my attraction grew." Xander moved things off his blotter.

"Five years?" Ares let out a low whistle.

Yes, five years ago because an eight thousand square foot mansion with ten bedrooms and two wings wasn't enough space. He was too old for her and too wounded. He couldn't cross the line of being her protector.

"I don't like her hanging out with Logan."

"Xander, if you won't tell her how you feel, you will have to let Marrock be. You can't keep them apart."

Xander grunted. He could if he wanted to break her heart, cause her pain, and lose one of his best operatives.

"Tell me what Dorian from the Martin group said."

From the look on his younger brother's face, he wouldn't like it.

"What we expected. He doesn't want to sell, but he's happy to keep us as customers."

Xander snorted. The Martin Group was a private aircraft and drone manufacturer, and he wanted that company because he suspected that the aircraft involved in the attack on Team Stealth last June had come from the Martin Group.

"Then we need to up our offer, arrange an in-person meeting whenever he's back in town."

"You need to tell Harper how you feel."

If he thought for one moment that he would be any good for her, he would. But he went through women hard and fast, and when it came to having a submissive, Xander knew that what he required, what he craved, would destroy her. It had destroyed the last woman he'd had a long-term D/s with.

When Harper had graduated from university and asked to be his assistant, Xander thought it was a bad plan. He was a hardass. He wanted everything right, all the details in place. He didn't cut corners. But he saw how his expectations helped focus her mind, and she transformed from the scattered, nervous creature she had been when he first met her, and he began to wonder if Harper could handle his dominant needs. He shook his head. There were things You-Only Live-Once Logan Marrock wouldn't get. The man was a Dom, but from what Xander knew, only during a scene. He wouldn't know that Harper used to cry herself to sleep and wake up covered in sweat from a nightmare, that her favourite weather was the rain, and she hated temperatures above twenty degrees Celsius. He wouldn't get that Harper did best-having someone give her a point of focus. Logan Marrock was one of his best operatives; when he was on the job, he was detail-oriented and the person most clients wanted leading their team, but in his personal life, he was relaxed. Too relaxed for what Harper needed.

The ringing phone brought Xander's attention back to the present.

"Took you long enough to answer that," Ares said with a grin. Xander shook his head at his brother.

"Hey, Nick."

"Sealed and done. Benoit will be happy to let our cyber people try out his new toy."

"Yes! Outstanding job Nick," Xander said.

"Okay, but before you bring out the bubbly, I told him about Jordan. He's an emotional guy, Benoit."

Xander closed his eyes. He didn't want anyone, least of all his competitors, to know his weak spots, but it couldn't be helped in this case. Benoit would want to know what drove the outrageous price Axis Management will pay for his technology.

"I don't want Benoit mouthing off to the press about some deal he's made with Axis Management, Nick. You press the fear of his god into him, got it?"

"Okay, boss," Nick said.

"See you when you get back." Xander hung up and looked across at his brother. They high-fived across the desk. With Benoit's invisible hacking technology, they could send out feelers for anyone who is selling a similar aircraft to the one used in the attack last June, when Team Stealth went to rescue Mulberry Stevens, daughter of actor Grace Stevens, who had been left alone in the desert by kidnappers.

He lost a man on that job. It was their first causality of doing this work, and there wasn't a day that went by that Xander didn't think of Jordan, his first recruit of Team Stealth and the founder of Bandit Brothers.

Xander would find out who was responsible for his friend's death, no matter what it took.

"One step closer."

"Not this time. I still can't piece it together, Ares. Someone had to have known our team was there."

"Or we were tragically unlucky."

Xander tidied his desk, logged off the system and stood up, grabbing his briefcase off the edge of the desk. "If I find out someone in this building leaked it—"

"Our people are solid," Ares said. "We've been over this. It has to be whoever was behind Mulberry's kidnapping, and whoever they were, they seemed to be warned off. She hasn't had a threat since."

Xander knew the facts, as well as Ares, but he wasn't convinced. It was high on his list of things that kept him from sleeping.

"We will sort this out, and I will destroy whoever was behind that attack," Xander said.

"Perfect. Ian and Charlotte are coming by tonight for some drinks, and I have a girl coming over. We can open up our dungeon. Want to bring Harper?"

Xander snorted. "You're not giving it up, are you?"

"She's not Olivia, Xander."

He shook his head, his teeth gritting at the mention of his ex-sub. It wasn't himself he was worried about it; it was Harper, who he had promised to protect.

"Come on, that new scotch is calling my name."

Ares opened the door for him, and he stopped. The other thing that kept him up at night stood right in front of Harper's desk, holding her hand.

"Hey, Logan." Ares slapped him on the back. "Good to see you."

"You too."

The conversation floated in the background as Xander zeroed in on Harper. She had dropped Logan's hand like a cookie from the forbidden high shelf, and her cheeks glowed with two pink circles. Impressive for a woman who didn't blush easily. She was fidgeting with her computer.

"Ready, Harper?"

"Yes, all set for tomorrow morning."

"And will I see you tomorrow night?" Logan asked.

Harper laughed. "I'll let you know."

"Did I just hear you ask a submissive who is clearly under protection—*my protection*—out without my permission?"

Logan spread his hands far apart. "Sorry. I thought I was cleared, considering you know everything about me. And we've been for breakfast and lunch and coffee. And that one thing at Club Bandit."

"Even still."

"How was I to know you were a stickler for protocol? Never seen you around the club."

Xander returned Logan's stare and stopped himself from curling his fingers into fists.

Becoming Harper's protector had outed him as a Dom, but there wasn't much he wouldn't do for her. He had decided the harm it could do him was small and, if anything, would go to his whole Prince of Darkness image. And he thought the only people Harper would likely encounter would be people he knew. Honestly, he thought her interest in BDSM was a passing curiosity.

"That's why you ask," Xander said.

"Xander, it's okay. I never meant to hurt you. You were okay when he took me out the other times. At least...I assumed," Harper said.

"And you shouldn't have."

Harper rubbed her arms, and Xander cursed. He wanted to wrap her and hold her and tell her there wasn't a need she had that he couldn't fulfil. But that would be a lie.

"Xander, I would like to take Harper to a Founder's Night at Club Bandit. Most of the people you've met, the members include people who work for you. I promise no harm will come to her."

There weren't many people Xander had to look up to. Logan Marrock was one of the few men he did, but Xander owned the damn building, so the giant did not intimidate him. He took one look at Harper's face and knew there wasn't anything he could say.

"Xander, surely you trust Logan to keep her safe and have fun. You're her protector, not her keeper." Ares's calm voice broke through their stare contest. What could Xander say to that? He couldn't tell her no without telling her why.

Catching sight of Harper's hopeful expression twisted his heart. He hated this, but he couldn't deny her.

"I've heard your reputation for pushing boundaries. You better adhere to her limit lists."

Harper's face lit up, and Logan grinned. At least he'd made their night.

"You know I will," Logan said. "See you tomorrow." He flashed the peace sign and whizzed out of the office.

Xander's hands clutched into fists. But he caught the small smile around the corners of her mouth as she got her bag out of her drawer and slung it over her shoulder.

"Did Xander tell you we have company tonight?" Ares asked.

"No," Harper said as the elevator doors pinged open.

"Ian and Charlotte are coming by."

Xander noticed her face blanched slightly, and he knew it was at the mention of Ian.

"I have some school stuff to catch up on. Someone's been driving me hard all week," Harper said.

"You like it," Xander said.

"Thanks," Harper said. Her hand on his arm sent a jolt of desire through him. But Ares was right. He was her protector, nothing more.

Outside at the curb, Carli was waiting for them.

"Good evening, Xander, Ares. Harper."

"Straight home tonight, Carli," Ares said.

As he settled into the limo beside Harper. Xander checked his buzzing phone.

"Anything urgent?" Harper asked.

"I would tell you if there was," Xander snapped.

Harper pulled out a pair of earphones and plugged them into her ears.

Ares shook his head at him, and Xander ignored his brother.

And as their ride started across the bridge to home, he texted Cindy, hating himself all the while.

When the limo pulled through the iron gates, with the monogram "M" across them, and stopped at the old staff quarters, Harper unplugged her earphones and gathered her bag.

"Have a good night, Harper," Ares said.

"See you tomorrow," Harper said.

Only when she was behind the door to her apartment did Xander exhale the breath he was holding.

"You're a damn fool," Ares said.

Xander snorted, knowing his brother was right. But there wasn't anything he could do to fix it. He closed his eyes as the limo continued to the front door.

"Are you coming?" Xander asked as the limo stopped. His brother frowned at his phone.

"Xander, one of the alerts I have for Harper just pinged. Someone ran a search for her family."

His mouth went dry, and his heart pounded in his ears. It didn't mean anything; her infamous family got searched a lot. But his instincts tugged at him, telling him this search was more than a casual glance through history.

Damn, he'd almost thought they were behind this, but it cemented his reasons why he had to continue to be her protector and nothing more.

4

CHAPTER FOUR - HARPER

As it got closer to six o'clock, Harper fidgeted, trying to clear her desk. Cluttered spaces were a pet peeve of Xander's, but when she felt stressed, her inclination was to cocoon herself in the clutter. Xander insisted on her space being clear. Usually, the task gave her a method to control her nerves.

She tried to focus on the details of doing it, but her hands were shaky as she moved paperwork and a collection of burner phones the Research and Development Team had dropped off. Harper was just putting those in the safe when the main office door opened, and Xander came in with Cindy on his arm.

Cindy flashed Harper the finger behind Xander's back as Xander opened the door to his black fortress and kissed Cindy deeply.

Harper's stomach fell to the floor. She ducked her head and moved one pile to another on her desk.

"I'll be a moment," Xander said to Cindy, and his door closed again.

"She's a class act." Harper couldn't help but say.

"Tonight, you're going to Club Bandit with Marrock?" Xander leaned on her desk, a frown on his face.

"Yes," Harper said.

"It's your choice," Xander said. Somehow, the words sounded like a threat.

"You could come with me," she whispered.

He raised one eyebrow and strode over to her desk.

"Angel, you know I don't go there." His silky voice sent a shiver up her spine.

"I know," she said. Besides it being too much for Xander's anxiety, who needed a BDSM Club when he lived in a mansion with its own dungeon?

He reached out and stroked the side of her face with the back of his hand, and she nearly stopped breathing.

"If I thought you were in any danger, I wouldn't let you go. I will always keep you safe," Xander said and disappeared into his office.

"Okay," she said. A part of her resented herself for needing the reassurance, but with her past, she would always look over her shoulder. Harper shook herself, finished tidying her desk, and went into her private sanctuary.

After a quick shower, she put on the white button-down shirt and a black miniskirt that Logan had requested she wears tonight.

Over the past week, he had talked to her about limits and how far she wanted to play, and he had told her to be ready with her safeword.

She swallowed hard as she picked up her mascara. "You like him," she said to the mirror as she brushed it on. Yes, she liked Logan Marrock. He was loud, confident, and sexy, cared about his friends, and loved taking risks. He lived for big, showy gestures and having fun.

Harper needed more fun in her life, and though it was Xander with whom she wanted to walk through the doors of Club Bandit, he didn't want her. He had made that very clear. The more she and Logan hung out, the more he distanced himself from her as if to make it clear that it was just a professional relationship between them and nothing more.

She'd had nothing when he took her in all those years ago. No money, no home. Harper didn't even have proper ID. If it weren't for Xander, she wouldn't have finished school. She definitely wouldn't have gotten her business administration degree. There was no way she could repay the debt she owed him.

So, each day, she kept the secrets of Axis Management and did her best to make his life run smoothly. Years of looking after her and keeping her safe couldn't have been easy. Maybe he saw her as a sister, and that was why he had a hard time letting her go out with Logan. Harper brushed out her long hair, contemplating whether to text her friend Kayleigh and let her know where she was going tonight, but that would likely make her friend jealous.

She smoothed down her skirt. It was going to happen. Tonight she was going out with Logan Marrock, and she wanted it. If it couldn't be Xander, then she was happy to be with Logan and explore the heavy attraction between them.

A knock sounded on the door, and wondering if it was Xander, Harper opened the door. Standing there, dressed in black slacks and a black jacket, was one of their bodyguards, Janette Jennings.

"Hi, Janette. Do you need anything?" Harper asked. Peering over the woman's slender 5'3" frame, she saw that the outer office was dark.

"I'm your shadow tonight. Request from Mr. Montague," Janette said.

Harper shook her head. “It’s unnecessary. You’re on tour with the Pho Boys next week. I’m sure you want to spend as much time with Beth and the kids before you’re gone for the next two weeks.”

Janette shook her head. “They know the deal. I will not disobey a direct order, Harper. You know that.” The former British military policewoman stood impassively.

“I’m just going out for fun.” Her heart did a weird dance. Xander sending Janette was overprotective, but it made her feel cared about.

“No need to explain anything to me and no judgement. Are you being picked up here?”

“Yes.”

“I’ll follow in my car and stay close by, but I will not enter the club,” Janette reassured her. “I’m your ride home if you need it.”

Harper exhaled, hating that she needed this reassurance, wishing she could just call an Uber or drive herself home.

“Okay. My date might spot you,” Harper said.

“Doesn’t matter. I’m here for you, not worried about being spotted,” Janette said. “Do you know when he’s picking you up?”

“Half hour,” Harper replied.

“I’ll be ready. And Harper, enjoy the night. You deserve it,” Janette said.

“Thanks.” Harper closed the door.

Her pulse raced in her veins. She touched the *x* pendant at her throat. Even though Xander disapproved of what she was doing, he still ensured she was safe.

Harper had been wondering how to get home because no one knew she lived on the Montague’s estate. She wished she could be as carefree as her friends Gardenia and Kayleigh, but her past didn't give her that freedom.

That was what attracted her to BDSM, the freedom it embodied. After a couple of years of living with them, one night, she had been walking near the wine cellar and passed a door that was slightly ajar. She'd peeked in and discovered the dungeon. The chains and whipping posts had scared her. If Ares hadn't been coming down to grab a bottle of his favourite chardonnay at that moment, she would have packed her bags that night.

Ares gave her a very dull book about BDSM, answered all her questions, and stressed that nothing happened without consent. Harper couldn't imagine agreeing to be hurt or tied up in the name of fun, and the book didn't answer all her questions. Wanting to learn more, she'd slipped out with no one knowing and gone to a club downtown, the Rude Bar.

It was an old, converted warehouse; the music was too loud; the floor was sticky, and the volume of people was overwhelming. But everywhere she looked, people had this air of freedom around them.

Then a creepy guy hit on her, and she'd gotten out of there as fast as possible, running right into Ares. Because, of course, they knew she had gone out.

"Love, what the hell are you doing in this place?" Ares asked, his face filled with worry and concern.

"I wanted to see what it was like," she said.

Ares took her by the arm and brought her into the car where Xander was waiting.

"What were you thinking?" Xander thundered.

"I was just curious."

"Angel, there are better places to explore than that poor excuse for a club," Xander said.

"How did you find me?"

He raised an eyebrow at her. "Locator on your phone."

She wouldn't have expected anything else, but at this time, the distance between her and her past had lengthened, and she felt cooped up. She had Xander remove the locator, and he did on the condition that she would always let him or one of their bodyguards know where she was.

The next week, Ares took her to Club Bandit and introduced her to the owners, Zee and Ella Riddell. Xander and Ares knew the Riddells from a charity poker game.

Ella had started monthly submissive nights, where subs would get together to talk, and then afterward, there would be demonstrations on everything from bondage to high protocol. It opened Harper's eyes, and her curiosity grew. The more she learnt about kink, the more she wanted it, and she started going to a few public demonstrations. When Doms began to ask her to play, it became too much. Xander presented her with his protection collar, and word quickly got around that she was untouchable even if they didn't know which Dom it was that put that *x* on her throat. The Bandit Brothers did know, though, and it was an extra layer of protection that the guys made sure no other Dom came near her.

As she watched people play, the freedom they experienced reminded her of how she felt when she danced, free and unencumbered. She wanted to experience it for herself, but other than attending workshops, she hadn't played with anyone.

Her stomach was a twisted ball of knots when her phone chimed with a text. Logan was here. Smoothing her hair one last time, Harper locked the office and found him in the hallway.

"Hello, Kitten." Logan kissed her cheek. "That outfit hugs your just right. Beautiful."

He looked like an advertisement for a kink club. A leather vest over a black silk T-shirt showed off his tight abs, leather pants hugging his sculpted muscular legs. He smelled like leather. His height and breadth swallowed her up, but Harper felt safe with Logan.

"Thanks," Harper said.

"I'm happy to have you on my arm tonight. Let's go," Logan said, extending his arm.

Harper's pulse raced as they took the elevator down to the parking garage. *You're okay,* she told herself. *You've wanted this for years.*

But now that it was happening, she wondered if she could handle it. Logan held the door of his Range Rover open. After she settled herself on the seat, he buckled her in.

On the drive over to Club Bandit, Logan drummed his fingers on the steering wheel in time to the bass beat of the rock music. Logan Marrock, Harper, had noticed, was almost always in motion.

"Founders Night is only open to the founding members of Club Bandit and their guests. We won't do anything you don't want to, and we'll take it slow. Are you excited?" Logan put a hand on her thigh.

Harper smiled. "Yes." The warmth of his hand sent a current through her, making her squirm.

"Good." He flashed her a grin of perfect white teeth, and they drove through the open black iron gates onto the private property. Behind gates, that's how she spent her life.

To her surprise, he parked around the back of the mansion. Harper tried to see Janette's car but couldn't spot anyone behind them.

He opened the passenger door for her, took her hand, and helped her out of the car. He keyed in a code, and the back doors swooshed open, revealing a long hallway lined with dark wood and a row of closed doors. Most of them, Harper knew, were hotel-style rooms and a few theme rooms.

Logan tugged her hand and pressed her against the wall. The textured bronze wall felt hard on her skin. Harper yelped, and Logan grinned. The heat of his body engulfed her.

"Before we go further, I need to kiss you," he said, placing his palm on the side of her cheek. His hand slid down the curve of her hips, around her waist, and he pressed her against him.

He pressed his immense body against hers, enough to make her aware of him, to feel his muscled legs touching her. She flushed, her stomach dancing with excited butterflies. His hands cupped either side of her face, and his mouth slanted over hers. His tongue caressed hers, she immediately opened her mouth wider, letting him in deeper, and he kissed her, his passion and intention clear; he was going to consume her. He nipped at her bottom lip, pressing his hips into her body. She shivered as he tilted her head, his tongue in her mouth, his kiss deep and driving. She knew she could be swept away by him, with his passion and energy and a part of her wanted it, while a part of her feared what that'd do to the carefully constructed self she had built.

"Are you ready?"

"Yes," Harper said.

Logan raised an eyebrow at her, trailing his thumb over her lips. "Sir. Tonight, I am your 'Sir.' Got it, Kitten?"

"Yes, Sir," Harper said.

The word felt natural on her lips, and Logan's answering grin sent her heart racing.

"Let's head on in." He took her arm, guiding her up the curved staircase.

The sounds of Club Bandit met her ears: the moans and gasps from people playing, the sharp sound of leather slapping skin. A woman cried as her Dom put a pair of clamps on her. The play stations were around the perimeter of the room. Some members lounged on the sofas or chairs by the bar, looking at the violet wand demo onstage at the back of the room. Harper flushed.

A few months ago, she had been in the crowd and watched Logan perform a rope suspension, rigging a submissive tied to a chair. Harper had watched, fascinated, as Quinn, Logan's friend, used a remote-control vibrator and the submissive orgasmed in public.

"Good evening, Logan. Harper," Ella said, coming out from behind the bar.

"Good turnout Ella! Zee must be happy."

"He's thrilled." Ella's eyes sparkled. She took Harper's hands in hers. "It's nice to see you out. Have fun tonight."

"Thanks, Ella," Harper said.

"And you be good, Mr. Marrock," Ella said with a grin.

"What's the fun in that?" Logan replied.

The older woman smiled, and Logan brought them over to the bar, signalled for two bottles of water, and then led her to a seating area.

"Here, sit. Let's talk," Logan said, handing her a bottle of water and gesturing to the two armchairs that were a little away from the rest of the seating.

"Thank you, Sir," Harper said.

"I enjoy hearing that from your lips," Logan said.

He brought a chair right in front of her and put his hands on her thighs, rubbing them up and down.

"I like saying it," Harper said.

"I wanted to go over your limits list one more time. No marking, no sex in public, no leaving you alone, and no rope?" His eyebrows raised. Logan loved rope.

Harper swallowed. She hoped he would understand.

"I'm sorry, Sir. I've been to rope workshops, but I'm not comfortable with it yet. I'm trying to work up to it." She bit her lip and stared at the floor.

Maybe she wasn't ready for this. If she couldn't do what Logan wanted, what good was she?

"I know you have been patient with me, waiting months for this, having to go through Xander—"

His lips on her mouth made her swallow her words.

"First, never apologize for a limit. I want you to let go with me, Harper. I want to get under that veneer you show the rest of the world, and you can only do that if you feel safe. Second"—Logan leaned forward and flicked the *x* charm—"I can deduce that he's important to you, that you two have some kind of relationship outside the office, but I don't want to hear his name. Tonight, that's my rule. Clear?"

He didn't ask for much, but it was hard not to say Xander's name when he meant so much to her. His grip tightened slightly over her legs as if he was cementing his expectations with his touch. "Yes, Sir, that is clear."

"Good. What about soft restraints? Would you be willing to try?"

A shudder of fear ran through her before Harper could stop it. But she was safe with this man, and she was tired of her past dictating her every moment.

"I'll try it," she said.

"And no whips?"

"On the try list," Harper whispered.

"I'm not picking up my whip tonight, but I want to. And unless you tell me no, I will have you naked and under me before the night is over. What do you say to that, Kitten?"

His attention and his words sent her squirming on the chair. Could she handle this? She didn't know, but she was here because she wanted to try.

"Sounds great, Sir," Harper said. The room was filled with the murmur of conversation and soft cries from a submissive tied to a bench in the corner while being flogged. Across from them, a big muscled Black Dom was petting the short hair of a petite woman as she laid her head in his lap.

So much in this room was life, and she wanted to be a part of it.

"Take your necklace off," Logan commanded. He stretched his hand out, waiting.

5

CHAPTER FIVE - LOGAN

"My necklace?"

Her dark pink rose lips formed a sensuous pout, and Christ, how he wanted that mouth around his cock.

"Yes, Harper. I'm not going to scene with you while you are wearing another man's mark. I want that chain off you." He didn't like explaining himself, but this was her first time playing, and he was trying to be gentle.

Glancing over her shoulder at the play going on behind them, she licked her lips. "Okay," she said.

Tonight, he would show her how serious he was about those months of whispered intentions.

She unclasped the necklace and put it in his palm.

"Good girl," Logan said. "I know it means a lot to you. I'll keep it safe and give it back." Though he wanted to crush it.

The smile he got for praising her lit up the room. "Now, what is your safeword?"

"Nijinsky," Harper said, with perfect inflection

"Okay. Wow, not going to mistake that for a pleasurable sound."

Harper giggled.

He extended his hand. She put her slender fingers in his, and as she started walking, he tugged her back. "No."

"Sir?"

"Dance for me, Harper."

The woman moved like water. When he'd had her on the dance floor at the benefit, he'd thought about seeing her dance ever since. He was tired of being stonewalled by her each time he asked about her past. It was loud and clear she had something to hide.

"Here?" Harper asked.

"Is there a problem?"

"No, it's just no one else is dancing." Harper frowned.

"I didn't ask them," Logan said. He swallowed up her personal space in three steps. "You look beautiful when you dance. I want to show you off tonight. Now dance, Kitten."

He took a step back, crossing his arms over his chest.

Harper put a strand of hair behind her ear, closed her eyes briefly, then, with one sweeping motion, she stepped to the left. Swayed her body in the most sensual, smooth way. Her arms made a half-circle as she swooped down, her palms touching the floor, and swayed to the right, ending with her hands under her chin.

"Beautiful," Logan said. He grabbed her arm, his lips finding hers. He stroked her hair, his fingers trailing down to her hands. "This way," he said.

As he walked over to the last play station, he nodded at fellow Doms and paused, watching his friend Soren tie a voluptuous woman to a post at the station beside theirs.

"Do you like this?" he asked Harper, sliding his hand around her waist and bringing her against his chest.

"Her expression is so peaceful," she said, but he caught the hitch in her voice that told him it wasn't for her. The sub was kneeling on the floor, her arms stretched out behind her, lashed to the post.

"My goal tonight is to put a similar expression on your face, Kitten," Logan said. Against his chest, he felt her shiver and heard her breath catch. "Over here, and we'll get started."

He led her down the step. A medical table with restraints sat empty, a small stool on wheels and a counter behind them.

"Here we are." He set his bag down on the counter.

"Logan—" Harper began.

"Kitten?" He took out a thin disposable painter's plastic cloth, spread it on the medical table, then laid down a cotton sheet on top.

"Never mind," Harper said.

"I want you to tell me if you are concerned about something. If something feels unsafe, or you have questions about it, talk to me. Tell me what you need. But I want you to trust me. I know restraints aren't your thing, but I like this table and the soft lighting in this space. I want to make you into a wax-covered painting. What do you say?"

He watched as her eyes dilated, her tongue licked her lips. "Yes."

He helped her onto the table, pleased at her response, thrilled that he had guessed correctly she'd be brave and explore wax play.

"Lie back," he said. "Gorgeous, Kitten," he said, running his hand along her neck, seeing her full breasts underneath the short-sleeved white button-down shirt.

From his bag, he took out a pocketknife and flipped it open.

"How far do you trust me, and how far can I push you? How much fun will we have while discovering those limits, challenging those boundaries?" He pressed the knife flat against the buttons on her shirt.

She smiled, her eyes wide.

"Do it, Logan."

Damn, the sultriness in her voice caused his cock to twitch. He leaned over her, so close he could see where her mascara started on her long, thick eyelashes.

Slowly, he slid the knife under the buttons on her blouse, starting at her throat. Her hips jerked off the table as he pressed down with the knife, cutting the buttons off nice and easy.

"Just warming up," Logan said, putting a hand on her side, reassuring her with his steady touch. "What's with the bra?"

"I like it," Harper said.

"I didn't tell you to wear it." Logan grinned. "Going to take you shopping."

With a slight twist of the knife, he cut through the closure in the front. She gave a soft yelp, and he smiled. He kneaded her breast, cupping his fingers around the fullness. His fingers pinched her nipple, eliciting a cry from Harper as she twisted on the table.

"Easy, Kitten," he said, slapping her thigh lightly. "Now, what do we do about this?" He slid the knife under the waistband of her skirt.

"Maybe you can just take the skirt off...Oh!"

He grinned at her soft exclamation and brought the knife down gently, tearing the skirt in half.

His hand slid down to her panties. He circled her clit. Her hips arched to meet his veiled touch.

"Later, if you decide," Logan said.

He wanted to fuck her so badly, but he wanted it to be on her say so. He dragged the edge of the knife along her mound. She wiggled under him.

"Can't have these getting in the way." With the knife's edge skimping her mound, Logan cut the silky material off, revealing her smooth and shaved pussy.

"There, now you will feel every hot drip of wax that lands on your smooth skin," Logan said.

"I've always wanted to try this," Harper said.

Her arms were relaxed at her side, but the slight tremble in her tone said she had doubts.

"What's your fear, Harper?" He dropped a soft kiss on her, pulled the rolling stool over, and gestured for her to sit up from the table. He slid his gigantic hands along her back, loving how she leaned into his touch, closing her eyes slightly as he massaged her shoulders.

"Too many to count," Harper murmured.

Stilling his hands, he cupped her cheek. "Here, right now, what is your fear?"

"That you'll burn me."

Turning her chin to him, he ran a finger along her lips.

"I'm asking for a lot of trust, I know. The candles I am using are specifically made to be safe for wax play. Here." He rolled back to his bag and took out purple and blue candles. "Feel how soft they are. See my thumbprint? That tells you they have a lower burning temperature." He put the candles in her hands.

Harper rolled them in her hands, pressing her thumb into the blue one. Shaking her head, she handed them back.

"You need to vocalize. I don't accept shakes of the head."

Damn, he wanted this woman, and the fiery flame of desire that shuddered down his spine seared him.

"Okay, let's do it, Sir."

Her sultry grin sent the blood rushing to his cock. He pushed the stool away and grabbed the torch from his bag. He grinned, seeing a small crowd of people in front of their station.

"Yes! You know I love a good show. You're going to find out if you like being watched, Harper. Lie back down, and let's colour you, beautiful."

He knew he was smiling like the wolf that caught the deer.

"I'm excited, Sir," Harper said.

"Are you really?"

"I feel warmed up," Harper said.

Leaning the candles against her thigh, he rummaged in his bag for a moment.

"How do you feel about this?"

The purple black blindfold was typical of what you would find in sex stores. He had everything from a gimp mask to a hand-tooled leather eye mask, but sometimes simplicity did the job.

"Yes," Harper said, her green eyes sparkling.

Gently, Logan brought her up to sitting, held up her long thick, abundant hair and settled the mask over her eyes. It was enough to cut the light and the people and keep her in the scene with him. Taking a moment, he settled her down on the table.

"Cup those breasts for me," Logan ordered.

With a small smile playing about her lips, Harper lifted her breasts, her nipples beaded, asking for attention.

"Here we go," he said.

Picking up the blue candle, he flicked the torch on and lit it. Holding the candle high above Harper, he slowly tipped the wax over, and as blue circles of melted wax poured over her breasts, Harper moaned.

"How does that feel?"

"Good," Harper said. "Slightly warm."

"Yeah, you're going to love this." He placed his hand on her breasts, playing with the wax between his fingers. He tugged on her nipple. Her hips jerked off the table.

"You look so sexy." Logan kissed her mouth hard, wanting to make her a melted puddle of bliss by the night's end. "And more."

Holding the candle close to her ribs, he waited a minute and let the wax pool before tipping it over her.

"Ow!" Harper cried out, squirming on the table.

"Hold still," Logan told her, slapping her thigh playfully.

Taking the purple candle, he flicked the torch again beside Harper's ear.

The wax pooled quickly, and he let the melting candle fall, drips of wax hitting her toned abdomen. Harper giggled, twisting to the side.

"Found your ticklish spot," Logan said.

He kept alternating the blue and purple candles until her body was covered in wax.

"Yeah, girl, you love this, don't you?" He ran his fingers through lines of wax on her legs.

Damn, this was so satisfying, to coat her from breasts to thigh in wax, the designs of blue and purple all over her body. Holding the candle high above her, he held the wick to the torch. She mewled as he brought the candle closer to her skin, then he held it above her, watching as the drip of wax flowed down from the candle, hitting her smooth stomach. The softest, most lustful sound escaped her mouth, her shoulders coming off the table. Logan rubbed the back of his hand along her ribs lightly, giving her his touch of reassurance. He got fully immersed in the scene as he continued working on her, moving the candle from different high points, covering her legs, and her shoulders. The people watching faded away, and his eyes were glued to every microexpression that crossed her face. He held the candle over her breast, lit it and felt the drip of wax as it cascaded off his finger, flicking it onto her nipple. "Ahh! Hot." "Yeah, you so are." Logan kept working, seeing where she licked the wax the most, on her lower stomach, near her beautiful pussy.

She looked stunning, her toned body covered in his crafted designs. Every time a drop of wax hit her, she made those delightful sounds, long past being shocked by the heat of the wax.

He watched her eyelids flutter close, her hips jerk off the table as he ran his hands through the warm droplets of wax. He lit the candle, this time holding it right above her, letting the wax drip around her thighs. She jumped and flinched. He dipped his finger into her folds. Damn, her juice covered his fingers.

"Going to cover your pussy now," Logan said.

Her eyes opened, her mouth made a delicious "o," but she nodded. "Yes. Sir." He held the purple candle high, her legs trembled slightly as he brought it closer to her mound. "This wax is going exactly where I want it, Kitten." He took his time, hearing her sharp intake of breath. He brought his knee up beside the table, nudging against her thigh, offering her reassurance as the drops of wax fell off the candle. She screamed at the moment the rivulet of wax hit her pussy lips.

"God, no! Logan!"

She bit her lip, shaking her head.

He laughed softly. He rubbed the wax over her clit with his thumb, with the tiniest touch and her hips arched into his hands. "How are you feeling, Kitten?" "So good."

Leaning down and keeping his tone low enough for her ears only, "I want to take a picture of you, is that okay?"

And he might have as well have thrown cold water in her face. Her stomach muscles clenched, and she shook her head back and forth.

"I'm a security operative. You can trust me." Running his hand up and down her wax-coated skin until her body relaxed. "I'll send it to your phone and delete it from mine."

Harper's body still, her protests stopped. "Yes, I would like to see what I look like."

After clicking a few photos, Logan hovered over her. "Now for the fun part," he said, flicking open his knife. "Let's get this wax off you."

"I was hoping you were going to clean me up."

"I always clean up," Logan said.

Using the knife's edge, he laid it flat on her thigh and slowly scraped the purple and blue wax off her legs.

She tensed as his knife ran over the wax on her collarbone. "I got you, Kitten."She exhaled and closed her eyes.

He was so damn proud of her.

When he got to her stomach, as lightly as possible, he used the blade's tip, sending Harper giggling.

"It tickles. Stop."

"Stop isn't a safe word," Logan said. "Hold still, Kitten."

This was a good way to test her fortitude, to see how much she would follow his direction. A moment later, her face fell into that composed expression he knew so well, and with exacting care, he scraped off every bit of wax, Harper holding entirely still until he got to her ribs. Then her hips came off the table, wiggling under his touch.

He put his hand on her, holding her still. "Aw, Kitten, I'm going to punish you for that," he said.

"I couldn't help it!" Harper insisted.

"That's what they all say," he said, running his hands through her thick hair. It was so shiny and thick. Why she ever tied it up, he didn't know.

Quickly, he moved the knife to her breasts and with sure upward motions, he got all the wax off her and flicked her nipples with his index finger.

"They were begging for attention," he said as he flicked the other one.

Harper moaned. "It burns a little. I like that."

"Yes, you do."

Her hitched breathing had spelled that out to him.

Laughing gently, he turned to his bag again and brought out a soft purple robe.

"We need to clear the space, Kitten," Logan said, noticing Nick with his hand on a dark-haired woman, waiting.

"All right," Harper said, reaching to take off her blindfold.

"No, you don't," Logan said. "Close your eyes." He eased the covering off her and captured her mouth, his tongue demanding she open under him. The sweet taste of her flooded his system, right to his cock. Damn, he wanted to be buried in her. He slipped the robe over her shoulders and helped her off the table. He sat her on the stool. "Stay there."

He went to pull the sheet off the table, and one of Ella's club helpers stepped in to help.

"I can help," Harper said.

Logan shook his head. She was leaning forward on the stool, a slightly dazed look on her face. She needed space.

"We got it."

He put his torch and candles securely back in his bag.

"That was sexy as hell, Kitten," he said.

"Was it?" Her voice was small.

"Yeah," Logan said, pulling her close to his chest. He ran his hands through her hair and pressed her close to him, kissing her hard.

"That scene was hot. Thank you for your trust."

"You're welcome, Sir," Harper said.

Taking her hand in his, he passed Nick, giving his friend a nod and led her back to the bar.

"A blowtorch, Marrock?"

Zee, the grey-breaded owner of Club Bandit, did not look impressed.

"Nothing in the rules about using open flames." Logan shrugged.

"Now there will be," Zee said.

"Got to break them to make them," Logan said, his eyes on Harper the entire time. She fidgeted next to him. He put a hand on her arm, reassuring her.

"Your scene has sent the place buzzing," Zee said.

"My intention," Logan said. He loved a good show that got people talking.

"What are we going to do with you?" Zee said, clapping him on the back.

"Book me for another demonstration and up your insurance." Logan grinned.

Zee laughed. "Have a good night."

"What made you uncomfortable there?" Logan asked Harper, putting his hand on the small of her back. She shrugged a shoulder and flipped her hair behind her ear.

"Hey Victor, an energy drink and another bottle of water," Logan called. "Kitten, look at me." He spoke low, right above her.

"I didn't know what to do," Harper whispered. "You didn't tell me what to say to Zee or if I should have said something."

Yeah, he thought, being ignored might unnerve her. That's why he'd tried that small dose of it.

Victor passed him his drinks, and he uncapped the bottle, holding it out to Harper. "Drink," he said.

She took the bottle and lifted it to her lips.

"You don't have to be on with me here, Kitten. In life, out there, you are laser-focused, never missing a detail, always taking notes. Alert to what your boss needs and wants. You can disappear into the background with me unless I want otherwise. That scene built trust between us, and I was giving you a breather. Zee took his cue from me."

"Okay," Harper said.

But his insides twisted because she looked hurt.

"Now, we can end the night here, or I can take you down the hall into a guest room, and we can try something more. Your call," Logan said, tangling his hand in her hair, and tilting her face to him.

6

CHAPTER SIX - HARPER

With me, you can disappear into the background.

It was exactly what she wanted, but she found it challenging to do. His words sent her pulse racing.

Anticipating Xander's needs, keeping up with work and taking classes, she was always doing something. It was the way she wanted it. Sensory input and being occupied kept the memories from clouding her present.

"Let's go to the room."

Lying on the medical table, not having to think about anything other than feeling where the wax hit her skin, had turned her brain off. All she had cared about was the next sensation. And she wanted more of it.

Logan tugged gently on the sash around the robe.

"Perfect," he said.

Taking her water bottle from her, he put it down on the bar and took her by the hand, his cool touch calming the butterflies in her stomach.

At the top of the wide curving staircase, a thick burly man with glasses, stood beside a table.

"Hey, Max. Any rooms open?"

"Number three is all yours," he said, clicking something on his tablet.

"Thanks."

With his fingers on the small of her back, Logan guided her down the steps, stopped at the third door closest to the stairs, tapped in a code, and the doors swished opened.

"That has impressed every other girl," Logan said, grinning.

Harper laughed. "My retina gets scanned every day. Xander keeps asking our R&D about using droplets of blood, but so far—"

Logan pulled her into the room so fast that her breath whooshed out of her as he pushed her against the closed door.

Her stomach fell to the floor, and she gulped. Never, ever, would she have talked about the inner workings of Axis Management with anyone. Yes, Logan was a trusted member of Team Stealth, but certain things didn't leave the executive space.

"Do you remember the one rule I stated at the start of this night?"

"Yes, Sir."

But she'd let Xander's name slip.

"Did you agree to keep that rule?" He raised an eyebrow. The intensity of his glare immediately had her looking away.

Cupping her face with both of his palms, the heat from his body seared into her flush. Harper wiggled under his grasp.

"Yes, Sir," she whispered.

"That's the second time you didn't do what I said tonight. Are you willing to submit to punishment, or do you want to leave?"

It was ironic how much she prided herself on self-control, and yet, she had failed to follow simple directions with Logan.

Trying to sort her thoughts, her eyes roamed over the tufted grey headboard, the Queen bed with the fluffy pillows, the padded bench at the end of the bed and texture grey panelling on the walls. Sound barriers, she thought. The room had an air of being calm and luscious.

No, she didn't want to leave.

"I'll stay," she said.

"Good." Logan's hands slid over her shoulders, down her sides, and stopped at the slash of her robe. With one quick tug, he pulled it open

She bit her lip as his hands went through her hair.

"When I said I wanted under your veneer, I meant it. I want to bring you to stillness, to turn off your mind and for you to trust me with those emotions you work so hard to conceal. Kneel."

A team of highly trained private operatives obeyed this man, and she couldn't help but do so. Harper sank to her knees, the coolness of the wooden floor seeping into her warm body.

"Open your legs, wide as you can, there." Logan put a hand on her shoulder. "Does that feel comfortable?"

"Yes, Sir." What was he going to do to her? She knew he loved his whips and ropes, and both were off the table.

"Good. Stay like that, silent for two minutes," Logan said.

This wasn't what she'd expected. Harper bit the inside of her cheek, swallowing down her retort. Willing her hands not to move, she stared straight ahead.

Letting out a shaky breath, Harper tried to stay still. *What if this isn't for me?* She had wanted this so much, but she found it hard to maintain her stillness against her racing heart after merely a few seconds. Forcing herself to breathe deeper, she tried to rely on her dance training; she picked a spot and focused on it.

The memory of her mother's studio rose from the dredges of her locked past. If only she had done more. The next moment, she closed her eyes hard, remembering how her wrists felt stressed as they were lashed behind her, her aunt's menacing voice telling her she wouldn't be good for much booming in her mind.

"Harper." Logan's calm voice interrupted her memory. She opened her eyes to see him squatting in front of her. "You're doing this because I asked you to focus on pleasing me."

He could read her so well. The big showy man had asked her to be quiet, to be still.

I'm here because I didn't follow his request.

A weird knot of desire mixed with shame formed in her womb, and she licked her lips.

With an effort, she picked a spot above the headboard and focused on it, telling herself her Dominant asked this of her, and she wanted to please him. So, she took another deep, steadying breath, stared at the wall, determined not to move.

The heat from his palms cupping her face startled her out of the headspace she found.

"Good girl. I know you found that challenging. Where did you go in your head?" Logan asked, crouched in front of her.

That smooth timbre sent a shiver of desire through her spine, but his words halted it. Harper couldn't tell him about her past.

Seeing the desire in his eyes, she launched herself forward, her arms coming around Logan's neck. She kissed him, tugging at his lips softly with her teeth. Shamelessly, she threw herself at him as if she could absorb his energy, his easy way of handling life.

"Kitten," Logan growled low in his chest, but he returned her kiss. "God, woman, you are so tempting." He broke off the kiss, and his vast hands cupped her face. "But I'm not going to let you get away with that. We've got to communicate, or this will not work. When I ask you a question, I expect an answer."

How could such a gigantic man be so controlled, so gentle? Harper leaned into his touch, nodding her head. "Yes, Sir."

"Tell me," Logan said.

Gasping for breath, Harper shook her head. The idea of telling him. Her chest constricted at the thought. "I want to," she said. His amber eyes bore into her as his fingertips touched her lips.

"Then speak."

How long did she wish to be with this man? And tonight had been perfect. But this she couldn't do. "But I need to work up to it," Harper said. "Tonight, can we just be together?"

"Whatever you tell me, stays with me, Harper. You can trust me." The silk in his voice brought tears to her eyes.

"I do. I haven't shared my past with anyone. But when I slow down when I don't have something to do, it's in my head. I can't talk about it, not yet."

Logan kissed her softly, gliding his hand down her face to her shoulders. "For tonight, I'll leave it. But I want in, Kitten, all the way in."

A shiver raked her body at his touch.

"I'll work on it." Her throat tightened. What if that wasn't enough for him?

"How I love a sub who is aware they need work," Logan said.

And his mouth was on hers, his passionate kiss telling her it was okay for now. Harper felt the tension leave her body, and she returned his kiss. It was ten, no twenty times better than she could ever imagine. His hands slid down to her waist. In one smooth motion, he lifted her from the floor. She inhaled an outdoorsy scent mixed with the aroma from his leathers, and she clung to his powerful shoulders. Now his teeth were on her lips. He bit down on her lip with that controlled gentleness, and she let out a moan; her pussy clenched.

"This is going to be so damn good."

"Yes," Harper said.

Gently he pushed her down, so she was on her back. Logan braced above her, and she melted as he captured her mouth again, his tongue dominating hers. She couldn't let him into her mind, but her body was all his for the taking.

He broke the kiss and ran his palms down to her thighs, pulling her legs wide open.

"Does your cunt taste as sweet as it smells?"

She threw her head back, wetness pooling between her legs.

Gripping her thighs, Logan placed each leg over his muscular shoulders, and Harper squealed as he slid her to the edge of the bed.

"Sir!" The warmth from his circling fingers on her clit made her squirm.

"Let's see," he said as he placed his hands under her hips and brought her closer. It was an odd time to feel embarrassed, but his gaze, staring at her intimate parts, made her want to cover up.

"Stop thinking," he commanded.

"God!" Harper cried as the warmth from his tongue sent shivers through her. She lifted her hips higher to him as his tongue slowly glided from slit to seam.

A low whimper came out of her mouth from somewhere deep within her. All her nerve endings were humming with desire. Her fingertips dug into him, trying to make the slow glides of his tongue quicker.

He slapped her thigh, and that little bit of pain almost sent her over the edge. Harper dug her fingers into his shoulders and closed her eyes, lost in the sensations. Gasping as she felt his firm lips pulling on her clit, she yelped, and as she felt his finger deeper within her, Harper's head came back, her eyes lifted to the recessed ceiling. An exploding burst of pleasure spun her head. The orgasm kept rolling through her. She drummed her heels on the top of his shoulders, her legs trembling.

"Perfect," Logan said, his hands lifting her farther back on the bed. Harper smiled at him, trying to keep her heavy lids open as her legs still trembled with the aftershocks of pleasure.

"That was intense," Harper whispered.

"Kitten, we've only started," he said. Moving her gently so her head was on the fluffy pillows, he slid his hands down either side of her, spreading her legs open. Taking her hand, he put it right on her swollen clit. "Keep yourself wet for me."

Her legs trembling slightly, she rolled her head back and forth. It was too much. Her clit was super sensitive.

"Look at me, Kitten."

With an effort, Harper fought through her cocoon of bliss to see Logan standing at the end of the bed, slipping off his leather vest. Swiftly, he slid his black T-shirt off, revealing his musculature.

He's so perfect. What does he want with me? Harper's finger lazily made a circle on her clit as Logan's hands unbuttoned his leather slacks, sliding them off over his tight ass. She licked her lips, her throat bone dry. Logan Marrock was big everywhere. His thick, long cock was standing up straight, pulsing with need. Like the rest of him, it was huge.

The want in his eyes clear as glass. Harper's head buzzed, excitement and nerves mingling together.

From his bag, he took out a condom and glided it on.

Kneeling on the bed, settling right between her legs, Logan cupped her cheek with his palm. "Kitten, I have wanted you since I first set eyes on you. Remember?"

It was the first meeting of Team Stealth, and they were working out of the main floor of an old house.

"I was wearing a turtleneck," she said.

It was November, and an unexpected cold snap had her ordering space heaters.

"That clung to your curves," Logan said, his hands running up and down the length of her. "You were confident, walking into a room full of arguing alpha men, setting the box of donuts down. You said, 'Only take one if you can shut up long enough to eat it,' You had us quiet before your bosses came in."

Her face flamed at the recollection.

Three weeks earlier, she had finished her degree, and after asking and asking Xander for a trial run as his executive assistant, he had finally said yes. His first order was to "go in there and shut them up," and she had, with the only thing that came to mind. She couldn't outyell those guys, but she thought maybe she could feed them.

"I had no idea what I was doing." Harper laughed.

"Yeah, you did." Logan's mouth was slightly rough on hers as he kissed her, long and deep, his tongue tangling with hers. He balanced his weight on thick arms, but she arched to him, wanting to feel his cock against her sensitive flesh.

The warmth of his hands spread under her as he raised her hips. Harper cried out, and his eyes bore into her.

"Let's take this slow, Kitten."

And using gentle movements, he eased into her core, little by little, until she gasped as his cock stretched her, burning her slightly as his length filled all the space. With exacting slow strokes, he slid in and out of her.

"Logan, I can't," Harper said.

"Yes, you can, Kitten." Logan pinched the nipple of her right breast, making her moan low in her throat. He slid his hand up behind her, bringing her chest to his. "Wrap your legs around my waist. There. Damn girl, you feel like hot magma. I'm going to combust in you." His smile made her laugh. She gripped him as hard as she could with her legs, his ridged cock pulling out of her.

"Sir!" she gasped as he brought her hips up and down on him, harder as he increased the rhythm. That burning sensation multiplied by a thousand. Harper bit into his shoulder, hearing Logan laugh in her ear.

"Let go so we can both burn, Kitten," Logan said.

He pumped into her slowly as if he had all the time in the world to keep her tightly wound.

"Sir!" Harper shouted. She wanted more, dammit.

He laughed. Cupping her ass, he brought her down on his cock. She screamed as he drilled into her, the burning exploding into a hot tidal wave of pleasure.

And right at her scream, his muscles strained against her chest, and she felt his sheathed release deep in her core.

"Damn, Kitten." Logan ran his hand on her hot skin, and for a moment, she couldn't grasp her breath, the room spinning on her.

With absolute gentleness, he dislodged from her, and in the absence of his warmth, she felt a little more level. He walked over to the far wall, opened a mini-fridge and took out a bottle of water.

"Drink."

A tiny thrill went through her at hearing the huskiness in her voice. She got to this man.

Coming back to bed, Logan wrapped his arms around her, nuzzling her neck.

"That was so good."

"Yes," Harper said, closing her eyes as his comforting warmth seeped into her.

"Now you have three choices," Logan said, nibbling her ear. "We can spend the night here. I can drive you to wherever you want to go, or you can shower and get in the car with your bodyguard."

Her heart thundered. Of course, he knew. She twisted away from him, panic shooting through her veins.

"Nope, no running," Logan said, pulling her back. "You don't have to explain. I'm only giving you choices."

"Stay with me, here, please," Harper said.

"You got it."

As he brought her head to his chest, Harper threaded her fingers through his, basking in how safe she felt being in Logan Marrock's embrace.

7

CHAPTER SEVEN - XANDER

Xander riffled through Harper's desk, disparaging at the mess the clutter had become. Doing this bought him a couple of moments because he wasn't looking forward to the meeting.

"Damn it." He took a file from the pile, and other paperwork fell to the floor.

"It would be easier if you waited for her to come back from a dinner break," Ares said. "You're making work for yourself."

"Her desk has been a mess all week!" Xander glared at his brother.

"She knows where everything is in this mess. What are you looking for, anyway?" Ares said, leaning against the door.

"I want to find the hard copy of the report from last week on Mulberry's detail. An inconsistency is bothering me."

"There haven't been any new threats?"

"No, but she has had a couple of hang-ups, and after reading today's report, something rang off to me about it. I can't find it!"

With annoyance, Xander pulled the paper off the desk. Since Harper's date with Logan, her work had been less tidy, her attention somewhere else. A dreamy look on her face. He'd caught her looking at pics on her phone, giggling over texts.

"Let's go before we're late," Xander said, marching out the door.

"You know, the man didn't put a ring on her finger," Ares said, catching up just before the elevator doors closed. "You've got to cheer up."

"She went out with Logan to a BDSM Club, Ares. I think her choice is clear," Xander said, fixing the cuff on his suit jacket. God, he hated wearing suits.

"You didn't give her a choice, Xander. Here, take these and ask Harper out. Tell her how you feel about her. Then she *can* make a choice." Ares reached into his jacket pocket and passed him an envelope.

"Tickets to the ballet?"

"It's Stravinsky. She'll love it. It's box seats. You go in the stage door and exit the stage door." Ares shrugged. "Easy. You could try out our new bodyguard hires as part of their probation."

"You got it all worked out."

"Always do." Ares grinned.

Xander shook his head at his brother. All week, there was a lightness to Harper. She was happy, and Xander should let her be. She put up with him enough at work. He couldn't help but notice that she had worn her hair down all week instead of her usual pulled back in a braid or a twist, and Xander knew that was Logan's influence.

He put thoughts of Harper aside. They had this meeting to take care of. He tried to focus his thoughts during the drive over to the restaurant. This wasn't his favourite part of their business, but he wanted to see Dorian Martin's face.

"I guess the view is okay," Xander said dryly. He would have preferred the bar to this private dining space, but the stained-glass windows and the impressive grounds of the art gallery weren't bad to look at. A waiter rushed into the dining room, dropped off their drinks and scurried out.

"He will not sell, Xander," Ares said, coming up beside him.

"I want to know what it would take for him to consider the idea," Xander murmured over his glass of scotch. "He rejected our offer. The man almost closed his doors last year."

Dorian's family had been in the aircraft business going back generations, creating military aircraft, helicopters, and now drones. The man was hungry for more wealth. Xander's business was knowing people. Something raised his hackles when Dorian rejected Axis Management's group to buy his rumoured stealth aircraft, and Xander wanted to know why. He couldn't accuse Dorian of the attack on Team Stealth because he didn't think there would be any benefit to him, but he was sure it was Dorian's aircraft used in the attack.

"Here he is now," Ares said.

Xander threw the rest of the amber liquid back and put the glass down on an empty table.

"Dorian, you're looking well," he said, shaking the older man's hand.

"Yes, and it's nice to see you out of your cave. Shall we sit?" Dorian gestured to the middle table. Ares sat first, twirling his wineglass in his fingers.

"Thanks for meeting with us," Xander said.

"I couldn't pass up dinner," Dorian said. "But I got to tell you I haven't changed my mind. How is your business going? It must be so mucky with all those people you have."

"That's why I only hire people I can count on. I hear your staff turnover is high these days."

"Everyone wants to be paid more for less work." Dorian waved at him dismissively.

"Axis Management wants to diversify," Ares said. "We thought aircraft would be a good way to do it. Would you sell your rumoured prototype stealth aircraft?"

"And what makes you think I have that?" Dorian said.

"Like we said at our first offer, rumour."

"I'm not interested in selling unless you would trade me something. Like shares in Axis Management? "

"Come on, Dorian. We are a private company. We don't have shares. Not on the table," Ares said.

"Too bad. My great-grandfather started this business, and I can't part with the latest advances. My shareholders would frown on me selling."

"You had an eight-point-nine million loss last quarter," Xander said.

"You know how it is. You run at a loss."

"No, I wouldn't, Dorian. We have never run at a loss," Xander said, trying hard to keep the smugness of his voice. He didn't like this man.

"You know, if you could hook me up with what you got, I might be interested," Dorian said.

"We have bodyguards and a highly-skilled tech team. If you want to contract with us, we could come to an arrangement." Xander knew they couldn't keep what else they did at Axis Management a secret forever. Still, for now, few knew about their private security operatives, aka Team Stealth, their research and development department or the government contracts they'd taken on. The fewer people who knew about those, the better.

"No, that's not what I meant." Dorian leaned forward. "I heard you had a live-in hooker."

Xander looked right at Dorian, ignoring the pounding of his heart.

"That's nonsense, Dorian," Ares said, laughing. "We don't have to pay for sex."

"I don't know. If one of you is practically an agoraphobic, having a little sex trophy hidden away where the press can't see her might be perfect. And one that speaks English. I could pay for a whore too, but that's not what I mean. Do you have a contact with someone who provides modern-day courtesans?"

Ares leaned back in his seat. "Dorian, I don't know what you think we are, but you sound ridiculous," he said.

After a moment, Dorian relaxed and came into a smile. "It was a rumour. Nothing more. Now I've got to go. I don't need dinner after all. You gentlemen, have a good night."

With an effort, Xander moved. Taking out his phone, he sent a message to two of his people from different teams to get to the office right the hell now.

"Xander, I'm sure—"

Xander glared at his brother. He hadn't set up this meeting, and he didn't know if they paid the nearby staff to spy on them. Maybe that was a paranoid thought, but that's how his mind worked.

"I'm sure there'll be another opportunity to meet Dorian. I have a full day tomorrow. Let's call it a night." Ares stood.

Xander took a deep breath and followed his brother. His heart was going double time, and he could barely breathe.

Fuck. He knew Dorian was somehow connected to the attack on Team Stealth, and his insinuation had just confirmed it.

But jumping to conclusions wasn't Xander's style; seeing patterns were.

"He can't know. He's just talking," Ares said as soon as Carli closed the limo door.

"Pretty specific talk," Xander said, punching in two numbers on his cell. "Only Ian and Charlotte and that excuse of a man Talbot know about Harper."

"The Tech Team needs more time with the new toy," Ares said.

"We hire the best minds in the country. They are going to work all night if they have to, but we will find out who was behind that attack on Team Stealth."

"Why did you call Erik?" Ares asked.

"I need him to check Ian's ex-wife. It's the only person who knows about Harper that I haven't spoken to in the last couple of years." He forced himself to take deep breaths, reminding himself Harper was safe at the moment and there were no threats to her. Dorian might have just been making shit up, but it was too close to the truth, and he had to check it out.

Ares pressed his lips together, and Xander knew his brother held back his opinion on how he would have treated the matter.

In the elevator, Ares reached out, hitting the button for the lower floor.

"Going to get a workout in, and I'll be up in an hour."

"Fine."

He took his suit jacket off as he walked out of the elevator. He couldn't wait to change into his usual T-shirt and jeans.

"Harper?"

The doors to the executive suite were open, soft light spilling onto Harper's desk. She smiled, looking up from tapping at her keyboard, the ends of her long hair brushing her arm.

"What were you looking for? I came back, and my desk was hit by a tornado."

"The latest report on Mulberry. I need the hard copy."

Shaking her head, Harper reached into her drawer and passed Xander a red file folder. "Here you are."

Damn, she was so poised.

"What are you doing here so late?"

"Claudia's sister went into labour, this time for real. I'm going over her schedule to make sure I cover what she had this week," Harper said, her eyes on the screen.

"Harper." Xander threw his suit jacket down on a chair, watching her brow furrow. He waited until she looked away from the screen.

"Yes?"

"Hire another assistant. I don't want you to burn out," Xander said.

She tucked her hair behind her ear and nodded. "I know. It's okay if I just do it for a while. Claudia wants to get back as soon as she can."

"Nonsense," Xander said. "Let her take the time she needs. Speak to Gardenia about getting you another assistant." Hiring good people and keeping them by rewarding their loyalty and giving them what they needed, like time off, was how Xander kept a tight lid on what went on in Axis Management.

"Okay," Her voice sounded small. "How was your meeting?"

His hand reached out, taking a long strand of hair in his fingers. "It was fine. I'm meeting with our tech people tonight. What are your plans?"

"I was going to grab a bite with Logan, but I can stay."

Damn it, yes, he wanted her to stay. "They are going to be working through the night. I would appreciate it if you can arrange a midnight food delivery and breakfast," Xander said, letting her hair fall through his fingers.

"No problem," Harper said, reaching for the phone on her desk.

"Thanks."

She smiled at him while talking on the phone. His chest twisted. Keeping her safe had been his number one priority for years, but now, when he looked at her, all he wanted to do was take her in his arms and hold her.

And he wouldn't stop there. He would kiss those perfectly shaped lips until they were swollen and make her scream his name as he brought her to climax over and over. The blood rushed to his cock at the thought.

In his office, he quickly changed. He hung up his jacket and remembered the tickets to the orchestra. Damn Ares, he wouldn't give up.

Xander ran a hand over his scruffy face. So many reasons why he shouldn't pursue Harper. He was too old for her; he didn't want to ruin the relationship they had now. But one night at the orchestra, and maybe it would end his longing for Harper. He scoffed at the thought.

"Harper?"

"Did you need anything else?" Harper turned from packing her bag.

"No, I was wondering—"

"Hey boss," Erik Knight said.

Xander returned the man's fist bump.

"I'll talk to you later," he said to Harper, giving her a nod. He gestured for Erik to go into his office.

"Thanks for coming in. Did I interrupt your evening too badly?"

"No, I was running security for Zee's place, but I got someone to cover."

Xander pursed his lips, taking in the built like a brick wall man with shorn hair. Erik Knight was the guy he went to when he needed it done fast. He was the best at reconnaissance and did his job well. Though he served at the same time as the Bandit Brothers and was one of them, he wasn't tight with the group, and he never got the story as to why. But Jordan brought Erik to him. Xander smiled, thinking of his friend. I'm not the only one with strays.

"I want you to get me everything you can on this woman, Nadia Albu. I want to know it all," Xander said. He had to check out Ian's ex-wife. It was a hanging thread.

"This is a full-time job. Why don't you quit your other jobs if it's a question of money," Xander started.

"No, it's not the money. I like being busy," Erik said.

The man had his demons, that was for sure, and he always came through, so Xander didn't have an issue.

"All right, thanks, Erik."

"You got it."

Xander followed him out on his way down to meet with Team Tech.

"You're still here," Xander said.

Harper looked up from scrawling through her phone.

"You wanted to talk to me."

Her face was so open and trusting.

Xander took a deep breath. "Do you want to go to a show with me on Friday? It's Rite of Spring."

A slight flush coloured her face.

"It's all right. You're with Logan."

"No, Xander. I would love to go with you," Harper said. "Thanks."

The big grin he knew he had on his face made him feel like a dope, but he didn't care. "Great. Wear your hair up?"

"Sure," Harper said, coming around her desk.

"I like seeing your neck."

Damn, what a creepy bastard you sound like.

Harper laughed. "Okay. Good luck with tonight."

He walked down the hall, waiting for the elevator doors to open.

"Mr. Montague, what is going on?" Meg Carlson asked.

"Let's go into the conference room on the first floor," Xander said. "I have a new challenge for you."

8

CHAPTER EIGHT - LOGAN

Logan rechecked his phone, striding up and down the sodden pavement outside the restaurant. He wished Harper had agreed to let him pick her up from Axis Management or her home, but she'd insisted on meeting him at the restaurant.

But it wasn't okay in his book. He wanted to push her boundaries; he knew it was a delicate line to walk. He didn't want to beat her into submission or force her trust. Instead, he wanted to cup his hands full of sugar and have her willingly eat out of them after giving her what she needed to feel comfortable.

It took time, Logan understood, to establish that kind of trust, and even though the last scene they'd had at Club Bandit broke some ground, the walls Harper put up around herself were thick. He had to be patient.

Seeing her come around the corner, Logan let out a low whistle. Her hair flew behind her back. She walked with the confidence of a runway model, the navy blue trench coat hugging her curves just so, and the smile she gave him in return pulled at his heartstrings. He glanced around to see if he could spot a bodyguard and saw the shaved head of one of their new recruits duck into a shop doorway.

"Good evening, beautiful." He took her hand in his and kissed her cheek. "Shall we?"

He opened the door of the surf and turf restaurant, one of his favourite downtown spots, housed in an old building, with exposed wood and high ceilings.

"Have you been here before?" Logan asked while waiting at the hostess desk.

"Once for lunch when Axis Management first opened," Harper said. "They all know Xander by name and gave us the rooftop patio to ourselves."

Her face flushed slightly, and she pressed two long slender fingers to her lips. "Sorry, it slipped out."

Logan put an arm around her and drew her close to his side.

"Don't sweat it, Kitten. I asked, and you answered. It's hard not to talk about our shared boss. I'll let it go when we're outside of a scene."

"Thank you, Sir," Harper murmured as the hostess flashed a smile at them.

They followed her to their booth in the corner, and after taking their drink order and giving them menus, the hostess left them.

"How was your week?" Logan asked.

"Trying to catch up on school," Harper said. "How was yours?"

"Work for me was pretty light, as you know, but I had a couple of night classes over at the climbing centre. I love teaching rock climbing."

"I've got to come to a class sometime." Harper smiled.

Taking her hand in his, Logan smiled. "I would love to teach you the ropes and have you in them."

Harper looked down. A small smile played about her mouth, and God, that was sexy.

A server interrupted them, dropping off their drinks. "Ready to order?"

"Yes, I'll take your seafood Cioppino," Logan said. "Harper?"

"Oh, I didn't know, I thought—" She started playing with the cutlery on the table, shifting in her seat. Something had made her uncomfortable.

"Hold off on my order and come back in a couple of minutes, please," Logan said to the server.

"Not a problem. It's a big menu. Take your time," the server said.

Leaning across the table, Logan put a finger under Harper's chin. "What's going on, Kitten?"

"I thought maybe you were going to order for me, and I got thrown for a moment when you didn't."

Caressing her jawline, Logan raised an eyebrow. "I've seen you order everything from coffee cups to furniture to a fleet of computers while typing with one hand. I didn't think ordering dinner is hard for you."

"It's not. I just... I thought because we're doing this." Harper gestured between them. "I guess I assumed you would order for me because you're an alpha—a Dom."

"I'm happy to open your door for you and carry you over a puddle, Harper, but I wanted you to have a choice. You said you had been here before. I thought maybe there was something you liked. While I always want respect and courtesy, unless we are in a kink environment, I'm not going to tell you what to do. I'm a Dominant, Harper, not a control freak."

"Okay. Sorry. I shouldn't have assumed." Harper fidgeted with her napkin. She bit her lip.

Something pulled at Logan, and he wondered if there was something she wanted that wasn't his thing, like being a 24/7 Dom.

"No, you shouldn't have."

Her face flushed, and he rubbed his thumb over her knuckles. "But darling, we could have talked about it before. What were you going to order?"

"I wanted to order steak, but it feels weird because you ordered stew," her brow furrowed. Logan wanted to ease her anxiety. He took her hand, holding it lightly in his.

"I had dinner with Nick last night and had steak. I'm a red-meat-once-a-week guy, part of my weight training," Logan said.

"Okay, so you don't mind if I order it?"

"Here in this seafood and steakhouse, no?" He raised his eyebrow at her. She smiled, relaxing slightly.

"Their food is amazing,"

Harper laughed and ducked her head. "Okay, I feel silly now."

"I'm proud of you for communicating, Kitten," Logan said. "Good timing. We're ready now," Logan said to the server.

Harper ordered her steak, laughing.

"For the record, I am thrilled to be doing this with you. Try to relax. If I want you to act a certain way or do something, I'll tell you, but let's have fun together."

"I'm happy to be here with you," Harper said.

"So, what do you think about coming to my class on Friday? It's for beginners, so you would fit right in."

At her startled expression, Logan wondered what he had said to throw her off. For a confident woman, she had a lot of minefields, and God, did he seem to hit them all. Then again, you got to hit them to get through them.

"I can't this Friday," Harper said.

"What are you doing on Friday? Has anyone told you that you work too much?" Logan said, keeping his voice light.

"Yes, Quinn tells me that all the time," Harper said. "Have you heard from him lately?"

"Answer the question," Logan said, trailing a finger along her arm, noticing how she shivered slightly at his touch. "I think I mentioned how you not answering my questions tries my patience. You could consider that under the umbrella of the respect I mentioned."

She fingered the petal of the carnation in the vase. Finally, she met his eyes.

"So, Xander had tickets to the ballet, and he asked me to go with him. It's not anything serious. I love Stravinsky, and he knows that" she glanced down at her hands.

"The man asked you on a date." It was irrational for him to be jealous, so he tamped that down quickly. He took a breath, covering her hand with his. "Have a good time."

"You're not mad?"

As an icy grip clutched his chest, Logan shook his head. "Exclusivity is something we didn't talk about."

He felt suddenly uncomfortable. Though he said it with his usual ease, he couldn't help but feel irritated. For years, he had tried to get her to go on a date with him.

But he wasn't a long-term commitment type, and a spike of jealousy ran through his veins at the realization that Xander *was* a 24/7 type Dom, at least that's the impression Logan had of him.

He smiled at Harper while his emotions played ping-pong inside his head. Maybe if she went on this date with Xander, she would get him out of her system.

Or maybe she'll decide she doesn't want me, and the billionaire has more to offer, but life was all about playing the odds, and he liked his.

"That's true. You're still doing demos at Club Bandit?"

"Yes, I have one on Saturday night. I'm going to tie two girls together and attach them to a pole," Logan said.

Harper giggled as the server coughed beside their table.

"Consenting adults, I promise," Logan said, raising his eyebrows.

"Lucky girls," their server commented as she put the food on the table. "Enjoy."

"Does it bother you if I tie other girls up? Have you seen my channel?"

Looking up from slicing her steak, Harper frowned. "I haven't dated much, and you're my first D/s relationship. I'm not sure if it would bother me at some point, but right now, it doesn't. And everyone has seen your rope demos on kinkTube, Mr. Marrock."

"If it ever does bother you, we can talk about it," Logan said. "And if you want to take this further to something more serious, I'm in for that."

"I know," Harper said around a mouthful of food. The intense gaze in her eyes made his cock as hard as a stone. He couldn't get enough of this woman with all her facets. Nothing was boring or standard about her, and Logan couldn't wait to see where they ended up. It'll be with my *collar around her neck*, he grinned.

"Three choices," Logan said when they finished their meal. "I can take you home, we can go to Club Bandit, or you can come back to my place."

"You like giving choices," she smiled.

"Yes, I do," Logan said. "Which is it, Kitten?"

Harper put her coffee down, reached across the table, and grabbed his hand. "Show me your home, Mr. Marrock."

"Here's my ride."

She flashed him the biggest smile. Logan reached out and tapped the seat. "Yeah, she's pretty slick," he said, petting his Kawasaki Ninja bike he'd bought after he left the army. His buddies joked that it looked like a toy with his big body over it, but he didn't care. He liked how it drove.

"Sweet! A college friend of mine had a motorcycle and used to give me rides. Does it go fast?"

"Oh yeah. Safety first," He handed her a helmet.

After Harper put it on, Logan put on his and swung his leg over the bike. Harper followed suit and snugged herself against his back. "Now hold on," he said, starting the ignition. The feel of her hands grabbing his waist made him want to drive up into the mountains, and Logan took a long way around, passing the harbour before taking the ramp into the underground parking of his condo. Through the doors, into the elevator and down the hall, Harper stayed silent, and he let her be, sensing that she needed a few moments.

"Welcome to my home sweet home," Logan said, opening the door for her and gesturing for her to go ahead. "Let me take your coat."

He put his hands on her shoulders and slid the coat off.

"Wow."

"Yeah, the view is great."

Harper shook her head at him and gestured to the living room corner. "You have a *stripper pole* in your living room."

"Yes," Logan said, hanging up his jacket beside hers in the closet. He undid his boots, grabbed the pole, and flipped around it.

"Super impressive."

"I try," Logan said. "I needed some variance in my workout routines. This checks the box. Wine?"

"Yes, please," Harper said, wondering over to look out the window.

Seeing her in front of the windows, walking around his apartment, infused him with pride. He wanted this woman to be here, and he wanted her in his bed before the evening was out. And in the morning. He shook himself. This wasn't anything serious.

"Wow. That's a wall of you," Harper said, gesturing at his wall of fame.

"I like to show off my accomplishments," Logan grinned, handing her the glass of wine. On the back wall beside his fireplace were pictures of his friends and him on climbs.

"Who are they?"

"Those are my search and rescue teammates. And that's Quinn, Jordan, and me right before we left home."

"You all looked so young," Harper mused. "You were on a magazine cover?"

Logan set his wineglass down on the coffee table, took her hand in his, and led her to the low black sectional.

"How about this, Kitten? I'll tell you about that magazine cover if you answer a few questions for me. And if you answer them all, I'll reward you." He nuzzled her neck, her sweet scent bringing back memories of the night at Bandit Brothers. Lightly, he smoothed her furrowed brow. "You can safeword, if any question is too uncomfortable or tell me if it's too much."

Harper's face relaxed, and she looked up from her thick lashes. "And what would be my reward?"

Gliding his hands down to her slender hips, he lifted her onto his lap. "I'll do a pole dance for you," he nuzzled her ear.

She giggled, the sound sweet, and Logan grinned at her.

"I would like to see that," Harper said. "I don't know if it's worth my answers, though."

"You wound me," Logan said. "Okay then, how about a spanking?"

Those brows furrowed again. "Aren't spankings supposed to hurt?"

"Not all of them. I prefer giving spankings as rewards to subs for stretching their boundaries," Logan said, trialling fingertips along her neck. Under his touch, she shuddered and squirmed on his lap.

"I have wondered what it would be like," Harper said. "Okay, I'll try."

"Good," Logan said, pulling her beside him. "Now, to tell you about that magazine cover, they took it after I climbed Mount Robson."

"That's incredible," Harper stared at him. "Really?"

"Yeah, it's a nice achievement," Logan said. His hands ran up and down her side. He pulled her back beside him so he could see her face. "But it gained a lot of attention. And that's how my half-sister's wicked uncle has me around the balls."

He put a finger on Harper's lips, stalling her questions.

"Hana's mother's family is religious and controlling, and when Hana's mother, Paige, met my dad, he gave her a ticket out. They ran away and had Hana. When my dad left again, she returned, but her family had disowned her, and Hana couldn't access her trust fund to pay for college. But Edwin saw my mug in that magazine, and we struck a deal. If I used my little fame that climb brought me for the good of his company, he would give Paige and Hana what is rightfully theirs."

"That's horrible," she bit her lip.

"Yeah, but I don't like horrible people, and if I can do something for my kid sister, I will." Logan shrugged. "That's her."

Logan picked up a framed photo of a younger giggling Hana and him on a Ferris wheel.

"Cute. You're very generous and loyal to do that for them."

"Loyalty is what makes me a Bandit Brother."

Harper stared at him for a moment and shook her head.

"What?" Logan replaced the photo on the shelf and rubbed her shoulders.

"It's the trait Xander values the most. I was just thinking you two had that in common, sorry." When he said nothing, she continued. "What about your mom? What does she think?"

"She doesn't know about this deal," Logan said. God, his mother, would fly into one strong current of rage if she found out. "She loves Hana, too, though, so it would piss her off."

"Even though Hana is your father's child from a different mother?"

"Yeah. She invites my dad over for dinner whenever he's in town."

"I'd like to meet your mom and Hana. How did Edwin's family get so much money? Solar panels are new, right?"

"Yeah. Grandad was an inventor, made a new scratch restraint cover for wristwatches, and sold it for a mint. When solar panels gained popularity, they took his interest. He invested in one of the early solar panel companies, modified the coverings, and then created SolCan. We all have a past, Kitten. It's how we choose to deal with it that matters." Logan ran his hands over her back, massaging her gently.

"I know, but mine is hard to talk about."

"Not talking about it gives it a lot of power, darling," Logan said, brushing her face lightly with his fingertips.

Harper closed her eyes and leaned into his touch, and Logan wanted to purr.

"You like this, showing me that you are relaxed with me? Brings me a lot of pleasure." He kissed her delicious mouth, tasting her. He broke off the kiss with a gentle nibble on her bottom lip.

"What about an easy one? Where are you from?"

"Grew up over on Vancouver Island," She wrapped a piece of hair around her fingers.

Logan dropped a sweet kiss on her lips.

"That wasn't too hard. Now tell me about motorcycle man," Logan said, adding a touch of command to his voice.

"I met him in the first year of University, and I lost my virginity to him," Harper said, blushing.

"Any other conquests?" Logan asked, dropping kisses along her jawline.

"None worth talking about," Harper said. "What about you?"

"This isn't an equal exchange," Logan said, tugging on her hair slightly. "But I've never had a long-term relationship between the military and work. I play a lot at the club. I like kink, and I like putting on a show, but I don't always go to bed with them, despite what you may think."

"I have thought nothing like that," Harper said. "I've watched you tie. You seem so intense with those girls."

"Yes, it's like an art. I want the experience to be good for them. I want to give them what they need and make it beautiful. But right now, I want to give you what you need."

His hand slid around her neck, and his tongue caressed hers, making her open for him. His hand slid down around her breast through her silky shirt and then to the other one.

"Let me show you something." Logan tore himself away from her, but he wanted her reaction to his toy chest. "Come with me," he said, extending his hand.

9

CHAPTER NINE - HARPER

It was how his eyes raked over her, from head to toe, taking her all in, that made her skin flame with desire. Harper swallowed. Being asked questions about her past had been uncomfortable. He'd kept his word and didn't push her too far. But she liked how he prodded her and how she felt when she opened to him. His enormous presence and his warmth caught her.

"Yes, Sir," Harper said, putting her hand in his.

As she followed him down the hallway dotted with framed pictures of his travels, Logan stopped at a doorway, leading her into the bedroom.

"Mr. Marrock, you keep surprising me," Harper said, taking in the charcoal walls, the enormous bed with navy blue pillows and accents.

"Good," Logan said, opening two doors to the closet. He gestured for her to walk in, and Harper couldn't believe what she saw. Against the wall, hanging neatly, were floggers and whips, every colour and size. Rope and lots of it neatly wound, took up an entire shelf. Hanging on the side wall, were paddles and canes and a few rubber implements that made her shyly curious to see them.

"And more," Logan said, opening two drawers.

She couldn't help it. She sucked in her breath to see nipple clamps and the array of blindfolds and gags.

"You have everything," she said.

"I'm always adding to the collection," Logan said. "See anything you like?"

Yes, she did, but was she brave enough to voice it? There was a distance between wondering about it and doing it, and Harper didn't know how far she could go to cross that distance.

"A few things," Harper said, running her hands through the trails of the floggers.

"Which one?" Logan asked.

"I like you," Harper said, running her hands over his thick biceps. Standing on her toes, she kissed his thick, soft lips.

He returned her kiss, then wrapped his hand through her hair, tugging her away.

"Kitten, are you not answering my questions again?"

"Sorry, Sir. Had to think about it."

"Pick something."

That commanding tone made her stomach drop slightly. Reaching into the open drawer, Harper retrieved a pair of nipple clamps with a chain between them. "These," she said.

"And?" Logan said, raising an eyebrow.

"What is this?" Harper reached out and ran her hand under an implement that looked like a tube covered in leather.

"Ah, it's a jack. It has a leather core and is wrapped in leather, like a small leather bat, but it's squishier."

"It looks like it would hurt."

"Like anything, it can, but I would have to swing quite hard. It's thuddy." Logan passed it to her, and Harper gripped it by the handle, swinging it lightly in her fingers. It felt lighter than she expected.

"Can we try it?" Harper whispered, her eyes not quite meeting his.

The heat in Logan's eyes as he cupped her face, pulling her in for a kiss, sent a flare of desire through her. For years she had been curious about this man, wondering what gave him his ease of life, his big personality, she might have fantasized once or twice about seeing him naked, and now that she was here with him, in his bedroom, it made her feel out of her head with desire.

"Yes, Kitten, we can," Logan said, taking her hand and pulling her to the covered bench at the end of his bed. "But first, a couple more questions."

"Okay," Harper said, shifting on the bench.

"I told you about my family. What about yours? Are you close to yours?"

Harper closed her eyes and fisted her hands. She hated thinking about her family. She took her head and reached for Logan's hand.

"It's hard to talk about," she said.

He took her hand in his and sat down beside her, pulling her over onto his lap. He ran those enormous hands along her shoulders again, and Harper felt his warmth seep through her muscles. A massage from him would be great after cross-fit training.

"I'll always listen," Logan said. "Share one thing."

"Both my parents were ballet dancers, and I thought I would be too." How she managed not to choke on those words, she didn't know. His hands worked over her knotted muscles, and she closed her eyes.

“I can’t see how you had much choice,” Logan said against her ear.

He rubbed slow circles over her lower back, his fingers going to the waistband of her pants.

“It has a button,” Harper mumbled.

“So complicated,” Logan said, but she felt his fingers unsnap the button after a moment as he nibbled her neck.

“I didn’t really, but I loved it. They had a studio built at the back of our house, and I spent every moment I could in there.” Harper closed her eyes. Before the fire, before the safe world, her parents created had crashed down all around her.

“It’s okay. You’re safe with me.” His lips firmly against her melted away her anxieties and brought her back to the present moment.

“Thank you for trying to answer my questions. I know it’s hard for you.” His hands slid over her black lacy panties. “I might make it a rule not to wear undergarments when we’re together.”

Harper laughed. He shuffled her around as he eased her out of his pants. “My lingerie is getting wrecked with you.”

“Careful, Kitten, I might take that as a challenge,” Logan said, and with that, he grabbed her panties, and Harper heard the fabric rip.

“Sir!” she protested, laughing.

“It will be a fun shopping trip,” Logan murmured. His big hand cupped her right butt cheek, and gently he brought it down on her with a snap.

She felt the searing heat from where his hand had been radiate deep within her core, and the pooling wetness between her legs made her want more.

As his hands ran circles around her bottom, Harper tensed. Logan pulled her hair, giving it a gentle tug.

"Relax, Kitten," he commanded.

Her face felt warm as her hands grabbed his legs for support. She took a deep breath and gasped as Logan trailed a finger along the inside of her right thigh, continuing until his fingers found her pussy. Harper moaned, closing her eyes.

He rubbed lightly over her clit, making her sway on his lap, but his big hand came down on her, keeping her from moving.

The sharp snap of his open palm stopped the stirring of desires, and as he landed the slap on her bottom, she whimpered across his lap. Quicker than she could keep up with, he alternated left, right, and the spark of desires climbed deep within her core again.

"Do you like this?" Logan asked, his voice sultry, making her open her eyes.

It was hard to admit that she did like this, but she wanted more of it. "Yes."

"Good," Logan said, increasing the rhythm of his palm hitting her ass.

It could have been moments or hours or half the night. Harper lost sense of time, lost in the sound of his palm landing on her behind. Harper found her hips rising off him to meet his hand with each slap, urging for more.

"Are you still with me?" Logan asked.

He slid a finger deep inside her, slowly coaxing her to arousal.

Mewling, Harper arched off his lap. "Logan!"

"Shatter for me. I'm here to pick you up," Logan said.

She believed him. Maybe she couldn't let him in all the way, but she knew he would catch her and take care of her. She felt his fingers curl from deep within, pressing on her G-spot. Her muscles contracted around his fingers.

"Perfect," Logan said. He gathered her to his muscular chest and held her.

Gasping for breath and in the next, sobbing, she clutched his arms. That was a release she hadn't known she needed

"Sir," Harper said in his neck, his fresh scent familiar to her, a touchstone of comfort and warmth.

"You make my cock so hard, Kitten. Want to go further?"

She couldn't help glancing over at the thumper and the nipple clips on the end of the bed. Logan laughed, running his hand through her hair.

"Yes!" Harper said, her hands reaching for the button of his dress shirt.

His mouth came around hers, his hands running along with her shirt. Harper's fingers wet to the enclosure of her demi bra.

"Yes, let me see your gorgeous breasts."

Harper knew her face was flaming as she cupped her hands under her breasts for him.

Logan's firm hands came around her waist, and he set her on her feet.

Logan picked up the nipple clamps and ran them along her neck, over her breasts.

The coolness of the metal made her shiver.

Bringing a hand around her waist, he pressed her to him, his muscles rippling under his smooth skin. This man was gorgeous.

His fingers skating along her ribcage made her giggle, and she moved to swat him away.

"I remember how ticklish you are," Logan said, grabbing her hands.

"God, you're beautiful." He was kneeling in front of her the next moment, his mouth hot on her nipple.

His tongue swirled around her pebbled point. She moaned, her legs feeling wobbly as he sucked her nipple in long rhythmic pulls.

"Sir!"

Her hands pressed down on his shoulders as he switched to the other nipple, the nipple clamps hanging from his other hand ominously.

"Now, we decorate these beautiful breasts," Logan said. She threw her head back as the clamp bit into her sensitive skin.

The bite of pain triggered a cascade of pleasure. "They have to match," she whimpered when the cold teeth bit into her nipple.

"How does that feel?" he asked.

"I like the pressure." She liked all of it, his intense glaze on her, the bit of the metal, how wet she knew she was for this man.

"Good," Logan said as he pulled on the chain.

She stood on her tiptoes, feeling the sensation of the clamp spread.

"You tell me if they get too much," he said.

"Yes, Sir," Harper replied.

"Turn around, Kitten, and keep your hands at your sides," Logan said, picking up the thumper.

Willing her muscles to relax as she pressed her feet hard onto the floor, Harper focused on a black and white framed photograph of a mountain above the headboard on the wall.

"Ouch!" she yelled as Logan swung the thumper at the back of her calf. But it was the surprise that made her cry out. It wasn't pain but a delicious thud. "*More* please," Harper said.

"You got it."

She could hear the smile in his voice.

The strike of the thumper on her other calf took her by surprise. And she squealed as Logan reached around and tugged on the chain between her nipples.

"That's...good," she moaned.

Laughing, Logan struck her ass with the thumper, each blow coming on the middle of her ass, and as he got into a rhythm, that floaty feeling began to consume her.

The repetitive, thudding sensation was almost better than his hand spanking her. Each time it contacted the backs of her calves, under her sit spot, the pleasure built in her, almost bringing her to an orgasm.

"I want to be deep inside you, Kitten." She barely heard him, lost in the feel of the thuddy leather against her skin. It sent heat through her, low in her pelvic floor.

He struck the thumper across her ass. Harper closed her eyes. The only thing she heard was leather on her flesh. She felt like she was floating away beyond her usual crowded thoughts.

A hand on her back urged her down, and she grabbed the bedsheets, feeling the leather bench under her stomach. So delicious, the thumper hitting her was like the slightest little impact. It was almost gentle, but the thud as it struck her skin was sharp enough to have pain. Exactly what she was craving. She closed her eyes, lost in the sensations of leather, and his warm touch on her back. Lost in the thud, the warmth of the thumper against her skin, the coolness as it was taken away. All of her limbs started to feel heavy.

"Come back, Kitten," Logan murmured in her ear. He stroked her hair, holding her for a moment. And she wanted to cry.

The tears were there, and why did she have to cry every time she had a scene with this man? She turned her face in his wall of thick muscles and gulped in air.

"I got you." She knew. She felt it deep in her bones that this man would catch her.

He held her for a long moment, his hands brushing her arms.

"Thank you."

"Whatever you need, Kitten. You good?""Yeah."

Spinning her around, so she was in front of him, Harper melted into him. "Ready? Going to take these off," Logan said.

She tensed but still was unprepared for the sharp bite as the blood rushed back to her nipples. His mouth was on her in a flash, lapping the nipple as he flicked the other clamp off. Her hands threaded through his short silky hair, her head rolling back as his mouth eased the soreness of her tingling nipples.

Her hands reached out to his chest as her legs wobbled underneath her. Logan led her to the bed, settling her against the pillows.

He shucked his pants smoothly, then tossed them on an armchair in the corner. Reaching into a nightstand drawer, he pulled out a condom and then held it out to her.

"Put it on for me." The heat in his eyes turned them darker, and knowing she was the one to cause that to happen made her pulse race.

Harper rolled forward on her knees. His cock was standing erect, big and beautiful, and ready. She couldn't wait to have it deep inside her.

"I would love to," Harper said, but before she ripped open the packet, she took his length in her hands and brought it to her mouth, taking it as deep as she could.

It was so big, she couldn't get it in all the way.

"You can take more," Logan encouraged, grabbing her head. He controlled her, guiding her up and down his shaft.

This was more than she could have ever imagined, but his cock in her mouth was so good, and as he controlled her movements, so different from any other time she had given a man a blow job, she knew Logan wouldn't lose control here. No, it was plain he was still in control with every tug of her hair, every flick of her nipples, every slow back-and-forth motion he made.

Harper breathed through her nose and swallowed around him.

"God, Kitten," Logan said, pulling her head back, so his cock slid out of her mouth. "Wrap me up before I lose it in you."

Slowly, Harper ripped open the condom, running her fingertips up and down his cock, before putting the rim of the rubber over the tip of his shaft, cupping the stiff muscles of his backside; as she finished rolling it on, she smiled as he let out a long hiss.

Then he was kissing her collarbone, kissing the tops of her breasts. His mouth made her skin so hot that she didn't know how she could move. But she did as he positioned her. He brought her hands over her head.

"Let me know if you're uncomfortable with this," he said.

In response, she arched her hips to him. "Please, Sir."

"You make the sweetest little sounds." He let go of his hands, trailed his fingers between her legs, and she spread them wide for him.

"Now, Kitten."

As he pressed his thumb to her clit, the barrier to that pleasure that had been growing, coiled low in her belly blew apart, and she shrieked, fisting the sheets in her hand.

"Open your eyes," Logan said.

With an effort, because it was hard to wrench herself away from the cocoon of pleasure, Harper did, meeting his smouldering green stare.

"Yes, Sir?"

"You are so willing, so ready," he said, his finger circling her nipple. "Going to take this nice and slow."

Watching as he eased back so he was between her legs, he stroked his sheathed cock before pausing at her entrance.

Slowly, he glided in. He rocked in her core as her hips rose to meet him. Her body felt so hot, so ready for his hard cock. He circled his hips, then eased out.

"Logan," she bit out.

"Slow," he repeated, easing the tip in again and then pulling out. He did that several times before sliding into her. She mewled, reaching for his arms. The man was lighting up each nerve ending of her body. She was swimming with need and heat. Reaching up to grab him, Harper moaned, the low sound vibrating through her body.

As Logan thrust deep in her, his hot mouth came over hers, his teeth grazing her lip. Under him, she purred, watching his muscles flex and ripple as he went deeper with every stroke.

"Wrap your legs around me," he gritted out.

Without hesitation, Harper did. Logan's hands eased back above her knees, pressing down on her as he increased his pace, stroking hard in her.

Harper felt her muscles contract around his penis, felt the slick sweat on their skin glistening in the soft light of the bedroom, and arched forward, trying to get that orgasm.

So close.

"Now," Logan said,

Harper cried out as he dove deep into her. As his body went rigid, his face tensed. God, his beautiful, chiselled face, so dear and familiar to her. He relaxed as his orgasm washed over him with a shudder. He slowly brought himself down next to her, the gentle giant so careful to keep his weight off her.

"You're delicious," Logan said, wrapping his arms around her.

"You're pretty tasty yourself."

The vibration of his deep rumble against her back sent a ripple of pleasure through her. She enjoyed making this man laugh.

"Bathroom?" she asked.

"Through there." Logan gestured to a door at the end of the bed.

Sliding out of his hold, Harper eased off the bed.

Stepping into the bathroom made her feel like walking into a spa. Black tiles lined the wall, huge soaker tub, two sink vanities and a vast walk-in shower.

After washing her hands and splashing water on her face, Harper took a washcloth from a stack on a shelf and ran it under the warm water.

"I can get used to this sight," she said as she re-entered the bedroom.

Logan was stretched out on his back, his hands under his head and a grin across his face.

"Yeah? Me too," he said, tugging her hand at the side of the bed.

Harper smiled, easing the condom off him and tossing it in the wastebasket she spotted near the bed. Then she slowly wiped him up

"That feels amazing. Did motorcycle boy teach you that?" Logan asked.

Giggling as he lifted her on the bed, Harper shook her head.

"No, that one I thought of all by myself."

Logan took the washcloth from her, putting it on the nightstand.

"You have good ideas, Miss Blake. What happened to motorcycle boy, anyway?"

"It didn't last. Xander didn't think I should continue taking in-person classes."

She hadn't meant to let that slip. She snuggled against Logan's chest, kissing his neck, trying to distract him.

His fingers trailed the side of her face. "I didn't realize you've known Xander that long. Why would he have that much say in your life?"

There wasn't going to be an easy way out of this. His tone was thick with command. She pressed her body against the hard plane of his chest, kissing his lips. He tugged on her hair.

"Kitten..." he growled.

She couldn't give him everything, but she could share this. Her heart raced wildly.

"Xander helped me out of my unpleasant situation. I have lived with Xander and Ares since I was sixteen."

She held her breath as Logan's hand stopped stroking her hair.

"Sixteen, Christ."

"There's been nothing sexual about it. I mean, I might have wished for it, but he's been nothing but a gentleman to me, a protector, an older brother."

"You don't wish for something sexual with your older brother," Logan said.

"No, that came later, I swear when I was of age. And still, nothing happened. He doesn't notice me."

"Kitten, he notices you," Logan said. "And now he's asked you on a date, and you trust him. He knows everything about you, and you won't let me in."

"I'm trying, Logan," Harper said, running her hand along his jaw. "It's difficult for me. I do trust you! I have had little practice talking about what happened to me, so it's hard. Would it be better if I didn't go on a date with Xander?"

Her stomach twisted in a knot at the thought of cancelling on Xander, but she wanted to show Logan she was serious. She wanted him. She loved being with him, and she was unconvinced Xander's invitation was a date.

"I'm not being fair. I asked you to talk about your past, and when you did, I overreacted. Come here, Kitten," he said, kissing her head. "Go to the ballet, but just know I'm here for you, and I want more than a few dates."

His heated gaze sent a thrill through her, and she snuggled next to him, in moments feeling her whole body relax into a deep sleep.

It took a moment for her to realize where she was in the semi-dark. A loud buzzer had stirred her from her dreams. Logan paced in the hallway, the phone to his ear.

"Yes? Okay, be there in twenty."

"Morning," Harper murmured.

"That was Xander, calling Team Stealth in, telling me to grab my go bag and get there. Going to shower," he said, pressing a kiss on her mouth.

"I better get up too," Harper said, and on cue, she heard the trill of her phone from the living room. Walking through naked, Harper found her purse and fished out her phone.

"Sorry to wake you, Angel, but I need you this morning. Sending Team Stealth out on a job." Xander's silky voice brought her mind back to reality.

"Okay. I'll be in soon," she said. "What do you need?"

"Team Tech is going to set up for us. Cancel all appointments for today. This afternoon, I want the new bodyguards in my office," Xander said.

"Okay, you got it."

"Angel, where are you? I noticed you weren't at home this morning."

"I'm with Logan," she whispered.

"See you both soon," Xander said after a long pause. His tone was dry, and Harper knew he was holding back.

A weird wave of guilt crashed through her, but she knew she wasn't doing anything wrong.

10

CHAPTER TEN – XANDER

Twenty minutes after making the call, Logan stormed into the office, like a barely contained storm, ready to let loose. His fists clenched at his side.

Xander leaned against the window. He sensed this was going to be an explosion.

"What the hell, Xander? Harper's been living with you since she was sixteen? I didn't think you were into young girls."

Not the explosion he was expecting. Xander breathed through his nose, focusing on taking steadying breaths because he felt like throwing the giant out of the building. Where the hell did Marrock get off talking to him like that? The man should damn well know better, and it pissed Xander off that he came in with this bluster of anger after giving him what he wanted. But Xander wasn't going to rise to his bait.

"If Harper told you that much, then she *trusts* you," he said, keeping a tight rein on his temper. "I wouldn't misplace it."

Logan put his hands on his head and turned away from Xander. "That's no way to care for someone by keeping them locked up."

"She's *never* been locked up," Xander said, working to unclench his jaw. "Did she mention the degree she got? That's she's working on the next one? Did she tell you how I looked out for?"

Logan slammed his hands on the desk, sneering at Xander. Xander stared right back at him, unflinching. He had no problem with the quiet.

"So, what did I miss, guys?" Ares said, entering the office, looking from one to the other.

"Logan's mad at me for keeping Harper safe."

"Ahh. Maybe he's mad that he doesn't know why you needed to," Ares said. His younger brother came and stood next to him. "Logan should get over it."

Logan glared at them, spun away, and leaned against the wall, the furthest he could get from them. Xander couldn't help but smile; it seemed the giant man was at a loss for words.

An alert on his phone told him the others had entered the building. It amazed him that this team of highly trained former military men he and Ares had put together always came through.

The purpose of Team Stealth was to go in and do those jobs they wanted out of the press, to take on those dangerous assignments. When Xander had thought Axis Management would only be a security company specializing in personal and cyber protection, he'd never thought such a team would exist.

But these men had come through for him every time.

"Good morning." Nick Laurent had contacts in today, and his curly hair was slicked back, but usually, he looked more like a librarian than a seasoned former military officer.

"Morning, Nick," Ares said. "Thanks for coming in."

"It's about time something happened around here." Nick grinned. He also spoke several languages and couldn't help but have mad computer skills because of his father. He was the calmest of the bunch and a whiz at dissolving conflict.

"Thinking of working for the old man?" Xander asked.

He pointed a finger at Xander and shook his head. "Never."

Xander smiled, knowing the dig would get his blood pumping.

"Where are we going?" Gabe Arthur was the next to enter the office. He looked more like a sprinter than an army vet, but he knew his way around a dangerous situation. When Ares approached the medical technician about being part of Team Stealth, he wasn't done in the military, but he couldn't ignore the offer they made and recruited him to the private sector.

"It's a plane ride," Ares said.

Gabe pulled a face, and Xander smiled to himself, knowing it wasn't his favourite.

Erik Knight strolled into the office, nodding at the others. He was a valued person on the team—when they didn't hate on him.

"Morning, Erik," Ares said.

Erik gave them a crisp nod. Xander depended on Erik for anything that required discretion because the man could blend in seamlessly with any crowd, and he knew a thousand different ways to get the scoop on someone.

"Hey, all," Logan said, flashing his buddies a smile and fist-bumping them as if his feathers hadn't been ruffled a moment before.

Damn it, that's part of what made Marrock so likeable.

He saw Harper taking off her jacket outside his office and hanging it in the closet. Logan caught his eye and looked away. Damn, he wished she hadn't told Logan anything. "Just waiting on Meg to get started," Xander said.

It wasn't yet five in the morning. The entire room reeked of testosterone, humming with anticipation. "Sorry!" Meg, barely five feet, hustled into the room, dropping a tablet as she skidded to a stop in front of Xander's desk.

"Thanks," she said as Nick handed her the tablet. "Thank God for bumper cases, right?" She flashed a grin at the men around her and blushed to the tops of her ears.

"Thanks for coming, Meg. I know you're tired," Xander said.

"I am, but it's okay. Can I...?"

"Of course," Ares, always the gentleman, cleared a stack of folders off the club chair in front of the desk and took Meg's heavy bag from her. "Take a seat."

"Thanks," Meg mumbled, looking down at her screen.

The office was a tight fit for them, and he knew they should take over the empty conference room on the main floor, but they never used that room for Team Stealth. He liked them all here, in his black fortress of an office.

"Let's get started," Xander said, glancing at his watch. "Meg's team worked all night long on implementing the technology we bought from Benoit. Thank you, Nick," Xander said. The guys all clapped Nick on the back, except for Erik.

"It was no big deal," Nick said, but his eyes showed how pleased he was.

"And they tracked down a lead on the invisible aircraft used in the Mulberry attack. They found out through conversations and emails that an aircraft that sounds similar is up for sale tomorrow morning in Latvia," Xander said. "Your job is to intercept that sale. I want that aircraft brought to a hangar here, where I have a team waiting to examine it."

"Why bother?" Logan gritted out the words, tension radiating off him.

"I want to know who was behind the attack on Mulberry because keeping our clients safe is our job," Xander said, struggling for calm.

"Let's go do our job," Gabe said. "What do we need to know?"

"Here is the area we think the sale is taking place, from a group who is connected to a cartel. In this village, in an abandoned church," Meg said.

Xander watched Erik's eyes as he scanned the room.

"Problem, Logan?" he asked, crossing his arms over his chest.

"This is a new technology, and I don't think it's accurate. What kind of criminal is going to show up at an abandoned Latvian church to sell an aircraft? It makes little sense."

"It's a lead, Logan. We have to follow it," Nick said.

"I trust my team," Meg said, her brown eyes wide behind her glasses. "Maybe no one suspects the church."

"Or maybe your fancy new program got it wrong. Come on, Nick, you don't buy this, do you?"

Nick shrugged. "I go where I'm told, same as you."

The thing about Logan was that he was always moving forward, and he didn't like going backwards. It made him feel cornered, and when he felt cornered, his instinct was to fight. Each of these men had reacted differently to losing Jordan; each of them reacted differently to a new job. This was how Logan responded.

"It appears I'm late to the party," Quinn Walsh said, walking into the room, Harper right on his heels.

"You're right on time," Xander said. "Either go or quit, Logan. I thought you would want to know why your friend died and who caused the attack. Maybe you aren't the operative I thought you were if you can't keep your cool."

He noticed Logan stepping forward, curling his fingers into a fist as his nostrils flared, and Harper's gasp of breath at his words.

"Come on, let's cool off," Gabe said, taking Logan out of the room. "Meg, send us the details to the encrypted server."

"Already done." Meg nodded

Nick and Gabe, and Logan left after clapping Quinn on the back. Erik stayed by the wall. Quinn walked into the room and extended his hand. "Happy to be back, I think."

"Perfect timing," Ares said.

"Thank you, Meg. Harper, can you set Meg up in one of the apartments?"

"No, that's unnecessary. I'll just go to a hotel."

"Meg, that's why we have apartments upstairs," Ares said, coming around and putting an arm around her. "Harper will get you sorted. I keep telling you to move closer."

"I like my house," Meg mumbled.

"He's pissed," Quinn said when Meg and Harper walked out of the room.

"Yeah. Not everyone dealt with Jordan's death the same way you did," Xander remarked dryly. Quinn's mouth quirked in a smile. Losing his best friend had eaten away at him, and Xander preferred Logan's angry outburst when he was reminded of it. "Want to talk about it?" Quinn asked.

"Not yet," Xander said. "Go catch up with them. We'll have drinks when you get back."

"Sounds good." Quinn fist bumped him and glared at Erik on the way out.

"You two are speaking?" Xander asked.

"We won't ever be friends. But we'll get the job done."

"I thought of keeping you back because I need you to continue to stay on, Nadia, but I need everyone on this job."

"Whatever you need."

Xander nodded. He knew his team would pull together. That's what they did.

"This is an impeccable way to end the week," Xander said, sliding next to Harper in the limo. She gave him a small smile.

"Anything from Team Stealth yet?"

"Not since noon. I'm not worried, Harper. They'll be home tomorrow night."

He wanted to take her slender hand in his, but he resisted.

"I know. Kayleigh told me she could be my assistant today," Harper said.

The thought of Quinn's loveable but high-strung sister being in his office made Xander's blood pressure rise. He shook his head back and forth.

"Yeah, I told her she had to know how to use a spreadsheet and needed math skills, and that deterred her," Harper said.

"I need to take her to lunch soon."

"You're free next Tuesday," Harper said. "So far."

Xander smiled at her. Kayleigh had become a little sister to him after she stormed his office in a fit of tears last year after learning about Jordan, who she had considered family. Fortunately, Ares had been there, ready with a hug and comforting words. Ares told her they couldn't replace her brother, but she had two more now.

"That's a date then," Xander said.

At the faint flush on Harper's face, he wished he had chosen better words.

"So tonight, we are trying out Luis and Talon. I want them to blend in seamlessly and only step in when someone gets too close. Hopefully, nobody pesters us."

Her rich, melodious laugh made him relax, and she put her hand on his thigh.

"They come with good references, and we're sneaking in the loading dock, cutting through the staircase from the orchestra level of the theatre and going up to the box seats," Harper said.

It was too much, he knew. But he wanted a night out with her where he could pretend they weren't just work colleagues. He could pretend that he wasn't her protector but merely a man out on the town with a woman he adored.

"Sorry about all this, Angel. I wish I could just walk into that theatre with you on my arm."

"You are," Harper said, patting his thigh.

Carli pulled up at the loading dock, and a guy in black from head to toe was meeting them.

"Let's see your favourite ballet." Xander extended his arm to her.

From the moment they were settled in their seats, at the orchestra side, straight from view to the stage, Xander was hyperaware of Harper how she flipped through the program, how her fingers played with the *x* charm at her throat and how she almost reached over to touch him but refrained.

Damn it. He wished she would reach across and take his hand or casually put her hand on his thigh. Her floral scent imprinted on his brain, and he loved watching how her eyes sparkled at the modern take on the ancient ballet.

"I'm sorry you never got to dance it," Xander said during intermission.

Harper glanced away, smoothing out the dress of her skirt. "It's okay."

"What is it, Angel?"

"Nothing. Just being here brings back a lot of memories."

"Some good, I hope?"

"Yes," Harper said. "I need the washroom. Can I get you a drink?"

"No, thanks," Xander said. "Let me know how Talon does."

Harper smiled and exited the curtained space, and he exhaled when she was gone. Taking out his phone, he scanned for any updates. There was none but a text message from his friend Ian saying he and Charlotte enjoyed playing and could they do it again soon?

In the middle of writing a text message, Xander's hand stilled. Seven years ago, Ian was still with his first wife, Nadia, and was there the night he took Harper home. Though Xander had sent Erik to do a full workup on Nadia, he had left Ian out of the equation. He bit the inside of his lip, cursing his oversight. He considered Ian a friend, but he wouldn't leave a stone unturned when it came to Harper's safety. He made a note to have Erik look at him when he got back.

"Just in time," Harper said, coming through the curtain.

"Good," Xander said. He couldn't help it. He reached out and grabbed her hand as she settled in the chair. "The second half is lively, isn't it?"

Harper smiled at him as the lights dimmed, and his heart pounded fast and heavy.

The door to their box opened while the dancers were taking their bows. "Mr. Montague, if you come now, we'll get you out of here before the crowd," the tall, tanned bodyguard Luis said.

"Certainly," Xander said, holding his hand out to Harper. Walking between the bodyguards, they exited the lobby, with no camera flashes or anyone asking them questions, and right into the limo.

"That was a fun night," Harper said. "Thanks so much for taking me."

"You're welcome. Would you like to come back to the house for dessert? I have your favourite cake."

"That sounds great." Harper smiled at him.

As they rolled by her apartment, Harper grinned at him.

"What did you tell Logan?" Xander asked.

"I didn't tell him about my past, but it came out that I've lived with you and Ares since I was sixteen."

Xander swallowed hard. It was a lot of pressure on her, he knew, for her to be someone else, never revealing all of her. Damn, she's lasted this long without getting close to anyone.

"Harper, you should be able to talk freely about yourself. It's okay. I was only looking for an explanation because being accused of liking them young, as Marrock said, was the highlight of my week."

Harper closed her eyes, and he couldn't help it. He reached out and cupped her chin. "Come on in and eat cake."

Xander led her up the three steps, then opened the door and allowed her to walk ahead of him into the ample, vast space. The house was Ares's choice. It was bright and modern, with vaulted ceilings, big open spaces, a formal dining room at the back, and an informal living room out front, and beyond were the mountains and ocean views.

Harper followed him through to the kitchen. "Do you mind?" she asked, taking a water glass.

"Of course not," Xander said. "I'll be back."

Ducking into a hall closet and Ares's downstairs office, he changed out of his dress shirt and into a black T-shirt.

"Now I feel overdressed," Harper said upon his return, gesturing to the silver gown she was wearing.

"You're fine," Xander said. "When's the last time you ate cake in a fancy grown?"

"Never." She smiled. His heart raced.

"Want to go out on the patio? It's a warm enough night."

"Sure. I can carry plates."

Xander nodded, grabbed the cake, and let Harper take the plates and utensils. They had a housekeeper and a cook that came twice a week, and otherwise, he and his brother got along fine. He wanted as few people around as possible.

The fairy lights gleamed on the patio, giving an excellent view of the spiral pool, and Harper settled in against the patio furniture.

"Josie's cake is the best," Harper said.

"She's very talented."

"She's been struggling a bit."

"Has she?"

"Yeah, I ran into her last week." Harper stopped abruptly.

"Angel, what is it?"

Harper looked away and down.

"Nothing. Forget I mentioned it." She bit her lip, not meeting his eyes.

She was keeping something from him. Putting the plate down on the table, Xander leaned over, tugging on her arm. "Tell me."

"Xander, I can't," Harper said.

"You can tell me anything, Angel."

"Maybe I can, but I don't want to. Can I not have one secret?"

For her safety, no, she absolutely could not.

"No secrets, ever. You know that. What else do you want?" Xander said, passing her a plate.

"You," Harper said, putting down the plate and launching herself onto his lap.

Her lips met his, and he couldn't help but respond, his hands coming hard around her neck. Her soft lips, her floral scent, and her long eyelashes seared into his brain.

It was like walking through quicksand to pull himself away, but he had to.

"Harper."

"Why don't you want me?" she said, her eyes downcast.

"Angel, you have no idea how much I want you. But it's a fantasy you have," Xander said, easing her off his lap.

"No, it's not a fantasy. I know what I want, Xander."

Oh, that look of steel in her eyes. It was the reason he loved her.

"It's impossible to keep my hands off you, Harper. But for both our sakes, I have to," He stood, turned and walked away from her with his heart in his throat.

"Is this because of Olivia?" Harper said.

He shook his head, breathing resolutely through his nose and easing out a slow breath. “Goodnight, Harper.”

It took every ounce of his strength to walk back inside, up the curved staircase to his side of the house and shut his bedroom door.

11

CHAPTER ELEVEN - HARPER

He left.

Stunned, Harper wiped furiously at the tears in her eyes. Maybe it was time for her to do something else. He didn't want her. He would never want her, and being here was too painful.

"Hey, love, I didn't expect to see you here."

Harper peeked out from her hands at the familiar warm tone, seeing Ares with his suit jacket open, his dress shirt untucked and unbuttoned, revealing a smooth chest. His curly hair was in disarray. His eyes looked puffy and red.

"I didn't expect you to be here. What happened?" Harper smiled at him.

Ares strolled over to her, lifted the fork from the plate, dipped it into the slice of cake on Xander's plate, and closed his eyes as he popped it into his mouth.

"Heaven help me, that woman can bake," Ares said when he swallowed. "I had a date."

"And it didn't work out?"

"Oh, I was enjoying myself a lot. She's a musician." Ares held up four fingers, and Harper giggled.

"Four cats?"

"Yep, I got out of there as soon as I could. How was the ballet?"

Harper shook her head, rubbing her eyes. "That's my favourite piece, and it was so nice to be out with him, and I thought something would happen, but it didn't."

"Ah, Harper, he cares about you a lot."

"I know, but I'm never going to be more to him than the scared girl he rescued. Ares, it hurts so much. He doesn't even notice me."

Ares reached out an arm and brought her close to his side. "He does. My brother loves you. He's too stubborn to admit how he feels about you."

Harper shook her head, but her heart leapt. No one was closer to Xander than Ares, and if he thought Xander had feelings for her, maybe there was hope.

"I should change, get to bed. I have to hire an assistant. I'm meeting with Gardenia early tomorrow."

"You could go or hang out with me in the movie room, and we can eat a bunch of snacks and finish this glorious cake," Ares said. "We haven't had a hangout night in a while."

Ironically, it had been Ares, with his groomed looks and his light-coloured business suits, who scared Harper. That first night Xander had brought her here, she would yell every time he got close to her, even if she saw him walk by. The poor man had avoided the first floor entirely for a good month. It was Xander, with his big shoulders and his dark, cool vibe, who had made her feel safe. Xander, who slept outside the guest bedroom door, held her when she woke drenched in sweat from a nightmare. Xander, who brought her to all the doctor and psychologist appointments, even though he hated going out and could have had someone else do it. He was her protector, and maybe it was selfish of her to long for anything more.

"Okay, but no trilogies."

"Let's get this cake in."

Picking up the plates and utensils, Harper followed Ares back into the kitchen. He took down a bag of microwave popcorn and handed it to her.

"It's just a button." Harper grinned and slid open the panel that concealed their microwave.

"It tastes better when you do it," Ares said, his brown eyes crinkling.

Shaking her head, Harper put the bag of popcorn in the microwave and took out a bowl.

"Going to change and rinse off the cat dander, be back in a few."

"Meet you downstairs," Harper smiled. Ares always lifted her mood.

When the popcorn finished popping, she shook it into a bowl. The melted butter sizzled as she poured it over the top. She grabbed a few chocolate bars from the freezer and headed down the back staircase to the basement level. Walkout patio doors led to the pool, and light from the lanterns reflected off the glass. Though vast, it was the most relaxed part of the house. Passing the laundry room and the workout room, the door to the wine cellar and the dungeon door, Harper walked into the rec room with the bar that hugged the wall, a large sectional, a huge TV, and then turned left, opened a pair of French doors into the movie room.

Leather reclining couches and the screen filled the room. She set the snacks down and filled water glasses at the bar.

"Here, love," Ares said, breezing into the room in a white T-shirt that showed off his ripped muscles and black shorts with the Axis Management logo on the side.

"Thanks," Harper said, taking the clothes from him. Disappearing into the bathroom off the hallway, she changed out of her dress, folding it up on the shelf, and threw on a black T-shirt and a thin pair of track pants; she had to roll over the waist twice.

Looking at herself in the mirror, she frowned. Her make-up was smeared, and the skin around her eyes looked tight. Time for a spa day with Gardenia, she thought, splashing water on her face. She undid her hair, releasing the tension as she shook it loose.

"Really?" Harper asked, smiling as the brightly coloured characters flashed on the screen.

"What's better than some comedy?"

"Good choice," She snuggled against him in the love seat. *If only my heart wanted Ares, it would be less complicated*. But Ares was like a big brother to her, and she couldn't imagine desiring him.

Ares grinned, threw his arm around her, and she snuggled next to him, trying to forget about Xander's rejection.

12

CHAPTER TWELVE - HARPER

Halfway through the movie, Harper gently untangled herself from Ares's weight, tossed the throw blanket over him, and stopped the movie.

The smart thing would be for her to go to her apartment. Logan's words rang in her mind as she carried the popcorn bowl upstairs. "He notices you, Kitten," and she recalled the look in Xander's eyes. Maybe she had to prove to him she was serious about being his submissive. Maybe she could show him she wasn't the scared girl he'd rescued all those years ago.

Harper threw her shoulders back, pretended she was on stage and marched up the curving staircase to Xander's side of the house. Her heart thundered, but she had to take a chance and show him how much she wanted him.

Her fingers trembled as she stepped out of her clothes, leaving them beside the door. She pushed open the door and sucked in her breath. God, he was so beautiful. In the moonlight, his creamy skin glowed and his long black hair caught in the light. He was sleeping on his back, his chest rising and falling gently, with one forearm flung across his face.

The soft black sheets were cool on her skin as she gently perched beside him. Harper ran her fingers down his hard chest. He didn't stir. She stretched out next to him. Her throat dry, she nudged her foot against his leg. Her hands flowed down the plane of his muscles, almost on their own. Before she could stop herself, her fingers lightly reached around his thick long cock. Harper's fingers skirted down the length of his cock, to the head and back again, cupping his balls in her hand.

"Xander," she said. "I want you."

Her hand massaged his balls. She kissed his lips. His hand came down in a nanosecond, strong fingers gripping her neck.

"It's me," Harper said, trembling a little.

From the moonlight streaming into the room from the vast windows, Harper could make out his stony expression as his eyes opened.

"Harper, what the hell are you doing here?"

"I came to tell you, to show you... I want you."

"Angel, you're playing with fire. Go now."

His tone boomed a higher note than his usual smooth speech.

"I *want* to play."

She kissed him. Xander shook his head. "This is a bad idea."

But he didn't push her off or tell her to leave. Instead, he cupped the back of her neck and crushed her lips to his, kissing her with such intense fervour that his lips blistered hers.

"I want you," she whispered.

"Angel, I want you *every* hour of the day, but you aren't for me. I would destroy you," Xander said, his voice thick.

"No, you wouldn't. I don't believe that. You're the one who told me we are the hardest on ourselves. Let me show you." Her pulse racing, she swung her legs over his muscular hips.

"Damn it, Angel. You don't understand..."

But his mouth was on her again, his hands threading through her hair. His touch blazed a trail of desire right down to her toes.

"Enough! Get out before I hurt you." His tone cut, but Harper stayed right where she was. His firm hands gripped her sides as he set her on the floor. Standing up, he pointed at the doorway.

"You won't hurt me," Harper said.

"I would want to know where you are *every* hour of the day."

"You already do," Harper said. "Anything you want, Xander, I can be for you. I've learned a lot of things over the years. Stop seeing me as a little girl."

"Oh, Angel, I want you." Xander stalked towards her, his eyes flashing.

"Then why can't we enjoy each other?" Harper asked, putting her hands on his chest.

She gasped as he gripped her wrists.

"Kneel, now." His voice, like a thunderbolt, sent gooseflesh prickling along her skin, causing a fiery trail of shivers to wrack her body, but she knelt at his feet, keeping her eyes on the plush black carpet below.

"Because I would want you tied to my bed every night and you eating at my feet every morning," Xander said, his foot sliding between her legs, nudging them apart. "You don't understand what I require."

"I don't because you have never told me this. I've seen you with all those women, Xander. What do they have that I don't?" She didn't want to cry, and she hated the desperation in her voice.

"I did not tell you to speak." Xander pulled her hair, his steel eyes shooting laser beams of command into her.

She gasped, swallowing thickly.

"You can't handle my wants, my needs," Xander growled. He let go of her hair and nudged her down with his foot. She followed his touch until her head was on the floor. "I would want you under my foot." His foot pressed down on her back.

God, why did this make her so wet? She wanted to clench her legs but breathed through the impulse with her forehead pressed to the carpet. His foot moved to the centre of her back. Her nipples hardened to stiff peaks.

"Every single day, no exceptions. No time off. Do you think this is what you want?" Xander moved his foot around her side. He slowly caressed her with his heel. Harper let out a gasp, and tension coiled low in her belly.

His foot glided around in between her thighs. She moaned low in her throat. God, this was awful and so damn good she didn't want it to end. His toe pressed down on her clit. Harper's fingers clawed the carpet.

"Show me," Xander said, his voice a quiet lash against her last remaining inhabitations. "Show me you can be the submissive I need. Grind, girl. Get yourself off on my foot." He moved his toe an inch to the right, and Harper bit her lip.

Her hips ground against his foot, though she wanted his toe back on her clit. She ground down and whimpered. A mix of shame and lust coursed through her body. She was soaked, so damn wet, her skin on fire. Lifting her hips up and down, she mewled. Harper gasped as her clit contacted his toe, and she pressed down on it hard. Tears leaked from her eyes, and a blast of heat poured into her centre as Xander circled her clit with his toe.

"Yes!" Her heart pounded out of her chest. Behind her eyes, she saw black. God, she felt a mess. All the air whooshed out of her body, and she lay flat on the floor, shaking.

"You know what those women have, Angel? *Nothing*." Xander's crouched down by her face. "They are nothing to me. They aren't like you, and that's the problem. I can't use you and hurt you and break you. So, leave now, and we can pretend this never happened."

"Doesn't it matter what I want? What if I want to be this for you?"

"Harper, you are topping from the bottom. You aren't the woman, the submissive I need." Xander gritted out.

"You made me who I am today, Xander. Are you telling me you don't like the woman I've become?"

"Get up and go, Angel. Before neither one of us can recover from this," he snarled at her.

"I might never get a chance again. You might send me off to Latvia." Harper scrambled to her knees. "Please, Xander."

Xander laughed darkly, his hands on her hair. "If only I could send you away. You're going to regret this."

"No, I'm not." Harper glared at him.

His eyes darkened, and his mouth was on hers again, his lips and tongue possessing her, screaming his passion. God. The feel of his mouth was so much better than she had ever imagined. He held her chin roughly, deepening the kiss. He held her, pinning her, exactly where he wanted her. She gasped. He swirled his tongue over her lips and bit her lower lip hard enough to make her jump in shock.

Xander broke off the kiss. He palmed her breasts roughly.

His mouth clamped around her areola, his teeth dragging across her nipple.

Under him, she moaned, arching towards him, running her hands through his silky dark hair.

"I should stop this," he said around her nipple.

"But you won't," Harper whispered.

"No, I won't. Goddess, help me." Xander's mouth was rough and fast on her neck, his teeth nibbling her ear, his hand pinching her other nipple, tugging it so hard the flesh burned.

"I can take it," Harper said, her nails digging into his shoulders.

"On your hands and knees. Now."

The steel in his voice sent fear down her spine, and she palmed her hands into the carpet, bringing her knees under her.

"Wider, spread, Angel," Xander said.

Harper did, crying out as his hands gripped her hips and he settled between her. His rough fingers circled her clit, but didn't touch it. Harper cried, wanting his touch, even with the aftershocks of the orgasm still humming in her body.

"Is this what you wanted when you snuck into my room?" Xander pulled her hair.

"I wanted to show you how much I wanted you."

His pure intensity of touch through his fingerpads seared her. She'd asked for this. She wanted this; she was determined to see it through.

"I would make you wear a butt plug every day. Is that what you want?" Xander said, his voice harsh.

"Yes," Harper said. She closed her eyes as she felt his hot breath on her ass. The scratch of his whiskers against the sensitive skin of her bottom sent shivers coursing through her.

"Damn it, Angel." She yelped as his hot tongue slid between her ass cheeks. Heat flared all along her skin. He smacked her behind, hard, his palm striking her right under her sit bones. The slaps rang out loud in the voluminous room, one, two, three, four, and they stole her breath, but she bowed back against each one.

"I'm going to fuck you so hard," Xander said. "Tell me you want it."

His fingers glided to her centre and found her clit. He pinched it, pulling on her sensitive flesh. Harper fought to stay upright. Her muscles trembled, and she gasped for breath.

Xander ran his cock along her back entrance. She shuddered, wondering if he would penetrate her there without any warm-up. The thought sent shivers all over her body.

"Yes, I want you to fuck me," Harper said.

"Have you ever had anyone here?" Xander pressed his thumb to her anal hole. Harper arched into his touch.

"Yes.""But not me. Not like I would take you. What if I fucked you here, Angel, so hard I tore your skin?"

"You wouldn't," Harper whispered. "Xander, you spent years protecting me. No matter the angry words you say to me, I don't believe you'll hurt me."

"That's why this is a horrible idea," Xander said. "But I like the view from here, how your ass looks. I should demand you leave, but your pussy is begging me to enter it, isn't it?"

She moaned as his fingers circled her clit. She rocked back towards him, trying to urge him on.

"Yes, Xander. Fuck me, please."

His hands were cool as they held her hips. He slowly pushed his cock into her and then dragged it out.

"Yes!" His fingers touched her pussy lips, circling everywhere except her aching clit.

"Spread your knees wider," Xander ordered. She adjusted, pushing her palms flat on the carpet. Xander cupped her cheek, a gentle touch against his harshness. She closed her eyes.

"Spit." He held a palm to her mouth.

His fingers kept moving, but his eyes sliced her, his steely look conveying that she better do what he said.

Every muscle contracted in her, Harper half-moaned, half-shrieked but spat in his hand.

"Again."

Without hesitation, she did, fighting those sensations that threatened to burst her open.

His expression still, his eyes never leaving her, he took his cock in his spit-covered hand and stroked it.

She cried out in protest as he removed his fingers from her. He moved, so he was behind her.

He gripped her hips, his fingers pressing into her sides. "I want you to push back on me with every stroke."

"Yes, Sir," Harper murmured.

Without another word, Xander thrust into her core. Harper pushed back against him. He drove into her again, and Harper pushed back against him, feeling his solid muscled torso. "God, Xander!" His hard cock drove into her, searing her pussy. The sound of her wet pussy against his hardness was everything. It was all her imagings come true. With his cock, he stabbed into her quicker than she could take a breath, but she pushed back on him with each stroke. As he asked. "Damn you, Angel." Xander slapped her ass and pounded into her with one fast stroke, and Harper pushed back on him, feeling the carpet rub her nipples.

His cock filled her so perfectly. He pumped slowly, his hands holding her hips effortlessly still.

"More," Harper cried out. She would prove to him that she could be what he needed.

And with that, he pounded, fast and uncompromising, slapping her ass in time to his demanding rhythm.

His energy flowed into her, in his confident touch, the tilt of his hips. As sweat poured down her and wetness pooled between her thighs, satisfaction infused her. This was better than anything she had dreamed of, beyond anything she had ever hoped for.

"I said to wear your hair up," Xander growled in her ear. He gathered her hair, tugging it hard in his hand, and with one long deep thrust, she felt his hot seed release deep within her. For a moment, he stayed like that, rocking in her, slapping her ass again, then disengaging.

Breathing hard, he shook his head with his hands on his thighs.

His eyes hardened, and she knew there was no refuting that look. "This was a mistake, Harper. It can't happen again."

"Xander, please. It wasn't a mistake. I can be what you want."

"And you would hate yourself for it. I won't let you do it. No. Get out of here, Harper."

"Xander, give us a chance. We can work it out," Harper said, hating the pleading in her voice.

"I said *go*."

Harper stared at him for a moment, but he raised an eyebrow and made a shooing gesture. She bit the inside of her cheek. She wouldn't give him her tears. Not like this. Silently, she got up and exited the room, leaving him sprawled out on the floor.

13

CHAPTER THIRTEEN - LOGAN

"Can you believe this bullshit?" Gabe Arthur clinked his glass of whiskey against Logan's before throwing it back in one swallow. "Too many people in here."

"Are you playing tonight?" Logan raised his eyebrows. Since Gabe's break-up with his long-time sub, Ivy, he's been a secluded, grumpy bastard.

"Nope, just here to watch. But I didn't expect it to be so packed that I'm inhaling the other guy's aftershave. If this is how Zee will run the place, I want my membership fee back."

Logan disagreed. He liked a crowd and seeing new people, and he felt Invite-a-Friend night was a great idea. In a way, the public event was more formal and organized than with the twenty-five founding members of Club Bandit. Tonight they were checked in at the door, where one of Ella's helpers asked them what station they wanted or if they wanted one of the rooms, then given a time slot. They also took his toy bag, and Ella told him it would be set at the station when it was their time.

"We'll vote on opening the club to new members next week."

He stretched out his long legs. His eyes roamed over the hunched shoulders of his Kitten, kneeling beside him on a plush silver cushion. A sharp cry from the direction of the stage made her jump. With her head bowed, her hands clasped in front of her; she looked like many other subs in the seating area. But Logan noticed the tension between her shoulder blades, the stiffness in her neck, and her struggle to keep her stare down. Something was eating at her, keeping her from letting go and staying in the moment with him.

"You know what my vote will be," Gabe said. "Think I'll get another. You?"

"I'm good." One drink was his limit while playing, and as he saw Harper visibly sigh, he grinned at his friend. "Harper, go with Gabe to the bar and ask Victor for a bucket of ice."

Gabe slapped him on the shoulders and gave him a grin. As she unfurled herself from her kneeling position, Logan bit his lip. He might make her do that several million times. The graceful, effortless way she unfolded her body and rose to her feet was downright sinful.

"Of course, Sir."

Logan exhaled as Harper walked through the crowded club, Gabe at her side. Ever since he got back from Latvia, she had been withdrawn. That damn mission resulted in little being accomplished. If the sale of stealth technology had happened, they were too late. A broken shipping crate beside the church gave Nick the opinion that they had missed the deal, but Logan had his doubts. They spent three days in cold, wet conditions before searching the outer corners of the town, trying to ask people if they saw anything suspicious in the village in the last week and then their ride out of there had been delayed, so they'd slept in the forsaken airport for a night.

There were worse jobs he had been on, but it annoyed him this one didn't go through, and he felt annoyed at Xander for sending them.

Jordan died on a job. Logan hated that and missed his friend. But even if Xander tracked down who was behind it, it would not bring their buddy back. They were short-staffed and in high demand. Logan knew they could help people, not going across the planet searching for mysterious technology that was maybe used months ago.

"Going to stay to watch your scene," Gabe said as they came back.

"Good," Logan fist-bumped, his friend.

"Here you go." Harper passed him a pail of ice cubes.

"Hold on to it."

Harper sighed.

Logan frowned. He'd had enough of his Kitten's attitude.

When he had returned from the mission, he'd taken Harper out to lunch and watched as she pushed food around her plate. Later, he took her to dinner, where she checked her phone every two minutes. Back at his place, a phone call from his Uncle Ed had killed his mood. Logan knew he was on borrowed time before his life imploded, and he had to take on working for the bastard full time. It made him feel jumpy and brought his patience level down.

When Logan had asked Harper what was wrong, she'd shrugged, claimed she was tired and switched the topic.

He had thought they'd made progress, but it wasn't enough if she couldn't confide in him.

Logan wanted in under her skin, he wanted in behind those thick walls of hers, and tonight, he was going to bulldoze right through them.

While he was in that sodding field in the middle of nowhere, all he'd thought about was coming back to see her. To her smile, her warmth, her quick wit. He remembered how she tasted when she came on his tongue, how the climax painted her body, making her all soft and boneless. He wanted this woman with everything he had, and Logan needed to show her, no matter what it was. He could handle anything, and she could trust him.

From across the room, he watched as Dev's sub, Liz, finished wiping the station he had reserved. As soon as Liz moved away, his toy bag was whisked over and set on a side table.

"It's our turn, Kitten." He placed a hand on her elbow.

"Okay," Harper said.

"Okay, who?" He pressed his fingers into her elbow, holding her gaze.

"Okay, Sir," Harper's eyes flashed with annoyance.

"Feeling ornery, are we?" He crushed her to his chest, the pail of ice between them. He pulled on her bottom lip with his teeth. "You'll feel differently by the time I'm done with you, Kitten."

Her shoulders hunched up, and her green eyes went wide in surprise.

"I'm *fine*. Let's play," Harper snapped.

She took two steps ahead of him, her shoulders flung back.

As he reached for her, a sub with long black hair and light brown skin, with her arms trussed behind her in rope, stepped in front of him.

"Sir, please use my nipples?"

"Hello, Sasha."

Harper turned to look at what was going on. Logan glanced over at Finn, the sub's Dom and husband. He raised an eyebrow, looking Sasha up and down.

"What did you do now, little brat?" Logan asked as he took a dark nipple in his finger and thumb, pinching hard.

Sasha grimaced. "I might have taken off the nipple clamps."

"And that's what led you to be in this predicament?" Logan pinched the other nipple, then squeezed both, rolling the tender nipples against his palm.

"Yes, Sir. Master Finn said I can't play until I have asked every Dom in here to use my nipples."

"I guess you'll learn your lesson," Logan said, catching sight of Harper's face as his hands roamed over Sasha's breasts.

"I doubt it, Sir." Sasha grinned at him.

"You're lucky your Dom enjoys a challenge." Logan smiled, releasing her nipples from his grip.

"Thank you, Sir," Sasha said and scampered off to the next available Dom.

"You liked that." Logan clasped Harper's hand, bringing her to his chest.

"Liked what?"

"You enjoyed watching me play with another girl's nipples. You thought it was hot."

"No." Her green eyes flashed angry.

"Is that so?" he whispered in her ear, ear, sliding a hand around her ass underneath her short skirt. His fingers traced her clit in a slow circle.

Logan laughed as her breathing hitched.

"Good girl for not wearing panties. I'll go easier on you for that. But your lies have to be dealt with." Logan smacked her ass, playfully.

"Lies?" Her face drained of colour.

His heart twisted. Didn't she know by now that he kept his word?

"I don't mean your past. You can tell me what's going on with you now, or I can drag it out of you." Logan cupped either side of her face. She rested her forehead against his chest. He breathed in her light floral scent and ran his hands along her body, liking how she trembled ever so slightly. "That was our agreement, remember? Your past is off-limits, but your present is not. Spill it, Kitten."

As she lifted her head off his chest, it was like curtains closing on a sunny day. She didn't meet his eyes and looked away. He wanted to ease her against him, make sure she knew he was her safe place to fall.

"You can tell me anything."

"I don't think I can," Harper whispered.

He took her by the arm and guided her down the one step to the empty station. She slammed the bucket of ice down beside his bag.

Time to try a different tack. "I think you are in entirely too much clothing. Strip, Kitten."

With a sigh, Harper threw off her white mini skirt.

"All of it," Logan said, crossing his arms over his chest. She was wearing on his patience. With a sigh, Harper undid the buttons on her shirt, threw it on the floor, and unsnapped the closure on her bra. Logan bit the inside of his cheek.

Her gorgeous full breasts needed attention. Logan strode over.

"Under the ring, now," Logan gestured to the O ring hanging from the ceiling.

As if there were weights attached to every limb of her body, Harper stood under the ring, her hands at her sides. The music from the speakers changed to a techno beat, and Logan danced over to her.

"You want to try with some enthusiasm?" Logan grinned as Harper glared at him.

"Are you feeling up to trying a little rope?"She glared at him, lifting her head. "Sure, whatever."Logan laughed. He reached into his toy bag for a length of rope.

"I like pushing your boundaries, but this was a hard limit. Are you sure?"She licked her lips. "It's fine."Oh, this woman. She was using her anger to push past her fear. Logan wanted to hoist her on his shoulders and take her around to high-five the crowd.

"If it's too much, what do you say?" Logan took her wrists in his hands.

"Nijinsky." Harper bit out the word.

"You can also always say 'red' or 'yellow' if you want to slow down and check-in."

"I'm cold. Are you going to get on with it?"

Logan couldn't help but laugh. She was trying so hard to push away the emotions. Her surface annoyance was almost adorable.

"Going to go gentle and easy. You with me?" Harper bit her lip as he grabbed her wrists to start tying a single column.

"Yes." Logan tied her wrists together, tightly enough to be secure and safe but not tight enough to bite into her skin. Harper stared at him, her expression stoic. With the rope's end, he brought her arms over her head, ran the end through the bight of the tie he had made and tied it off, giving himself a lot of slack in the line. Harper's arms were tied above her head, and it was a comfortable position for her to maintain.

"Nice and easy, Kitten," Logan ran his hands through her abundant hair. He massaged her scalp, and she exhaled a shuddering breath.

"How was your week? Did anything happen at work to upset you?"

Harper shook her head and kept her gaze averted.

"I see how this will go, but don't worry, I have ways of making you talk." He nibbled her ear, feeling her tighten at his touch. Whatever was going on with her, she was broadcasting clearly with her body language that she didn't want Logan to know what it was.

He reached into his toy bag and snapped the ball chain flogger against his thigh. Harper turned her head and stared over her shoulder, her eyes widening. He snapped it again. The long metal strands of silver balls jingled as he flicked it gently against the side of the leg of the spanking bench.

"That looks scary."

"It does, doesn't it?" Logan ran his hand through the strands of metal. "But it depends on how it's wielded."

Standing at her side, he flicked his wrist and slowly brought the flogger around her ribs, under her breasts.

"Ah! It tickles!" Harper screeched, her nails digging into the rope, her weight shifting from foot to foot.

"You never know what to expect with me, Kitten, but you can count on me being here for you. I'll hold you in my arms as you come apart."

Harper bit her lip, shaking her head.

Logan moved, so he was behind her and flicked his wrist, letting the metal strands fly through the air before they landed with a soft snap on her shoulder blades. The metal strands clanged as they landed on her back. He flicked with his wrist. The strands struck once. And again. And she jumped. He increased the tempo until her head lowered, her skin becoming rosy pink.

"How was the symphony?"

Her shoulders bunched forward. He flicked his wrist, sending the shiny strands to catch the side of her ribs.

"Fine," Harper snapped.

Damn, she was pushing him. He shoved the ball chain flogger into the pail of ice cubes, rattling it, so it clanked together.

He snapped the metal flogger hard on the top of her buttocks.

She squealed. "Ow, that hurt. And cold."

He flicked it again on the opposite butt cheek. "God, ouch!"

"Don't make me repeat myself." Logan grabbed her hair from the root and pulled her head towards him.

"I've had better nights." She glared at him.

"It'll go easier for you if you tell me. But you want to keep stalling. I can swing this flogger all night long."

He let go of her hair, gave the flogger a flick against the top of her thigh, took three steps back and swung it, the metal balls clinking together. He threw the flogger, so it came down hard on her back, and with each stroke, she gasped as it landed. Her fingers curled, but her head dropped. All those signs told him she was battling herself, not letting go.

He worked it in figure eight, sailing it through the air, landing it on her ass, liking the shade of red her ass turned.

And the tension finally left her body. A sob escaped her lips. Logan moved to her front.

"Look at me, Kitten. I want to see your face."

With her hair head forward, her arms tied above her, she looked, she looked compliant. But Logan saw the effort it was costing her to hold on to her walls, and he wouldn't let her.

"What about the night made it bad?" He struck her nipple, and she bit her lip and glared at him. Still too much fight in her for his liking, Logan strode up close to her and grabbed her chin. Her breathing hitched.

"Have I ever done anything to make you question my intentions?"

"No, Sir." Her voice was quiet.

"Have I ever done anything to make you feel unsafe?"

She shook her head from side to side.

"I didn't hear you."

God, those eyes bore right into his damn soul.

"No, Sir." Her voice caught in her throat.

"Remember that."

Logan stepped back, waiting until Harper looked at him, then threw the flogger.

When her breasts turned a shade of deep rose, he took a step back and lightly, as if he was tossing feathers in the air, brought the metal strands along her spine, slowly drawing the motion out. Harper's shoulders shook. He kept up the pace, stepping in front of her, wrapping the strands over along her sides.

She gasped and whimpered.

And for once, he wished her hair was up, so the dark curtain of hair wasn't hiding her expression.

"Let go, Kitten."

He sailed those metal strands through the air, throwing them with absolute accuracy, so they came down around Harper's side, and she giggled.

He stepped closer, moving his wrist ever so slightly, trailing the metal strands over her ribs, over her breasts, again and again, watching as she slowly lost control.

Christ, it was beautiful to see how her determination fell to the sensations Logan created through her body. She laughed, straining forward, fighting to stand.

Logan smiled. "Don't!"

Harper leaned back as far as she could.

Logan stepped closer, flicked the flogger over her right side and kissed her, swallowing her giggles.

There was his Kitten, without the staunch shelf of defiance she had at the beginning of the night.

He traced her perfectly shaped eyebrows and kissed her forehead. He returned the metal flogger to his bag and took out two more items.

"What else happened?"

"It doesn't matter."

"I know. Tell me anyway. Honesty, remember?" Logan laid a soft flogger beside the other items on the table. He kissed her neck and her collarbone. Harper closed her eyes against his every touch, then his fingers travelled to her folds, around her clit. Harper shook her head, and Logan withdrew his fingers.

"You had chances, Kitten," Logan said, and with one smooth motion, he placed a clit sucker on her pussy. He flicked it on for a minute, smiling as her body folded over itself, straining against his ropes. Yeah, this is precisely how he wanted her.

"Too much!" She screamed. He felt her muscles tighten against his legs. Her beautiful face scrunched for a moment. Logan spanked her ass as he pressed the little vibe harder against her clit. She screamed, swaying against him.

"Yeah, that's better, isn't it, Kitten?"

Logan switched the clit sucker off, and her eyes opened. She glared at him.

"Your ass looks beautiful red. Let's see if this loosens your tongue more."

Picking up the red-handled flogger with the broad strands, he stepped behind her and threw the flogger.

"Sir! Too much," she said.

Logan threw the flogger, hitting her shoulder blades in a slow, sensual wave on her back, working a steady rhythm.

"God, Logan!" Harper screeched.

"Yeah, it's good," Logan said. "You deserve to feel pleasure, Kitten."

He kept up a steady pace, alternating right, left, right, and left until Harper screeched.

"Feeling frustrated?" He set the flogger to the side and again picked up the clit sucker.

"No! Too much," her protest was hallow.

"Give me another orgasm," Logan said, nuzzling her neck, setting the vibe in her soaked pussy.

"No, I can't," her voice caught on the word.

"You can and you will." Logan kissed her, swallowing her moans as the powerful sonic waves rolled through her body. He kissed her like he wanted to take all her hurt away. His tongue glided over hers as her body shook as the orgasm crashed over her. Tears leaked out of her eyes, her mouth opened, but no words came out. She trembled from head to toe. Logan held her body close to his chest, turning off the vibrator.

"Good girl."

He rubbed her back, her shoulders. He kissed her soft lips and held her until her breathing became steady again.

Then gently as he could, he untied the ropes from her wrists. He bundled up all the rope and shoved it into her bag,

"I got you, Kitten."

Standing there, under the ring, she looked so small. She stared into space, her expression frozen.

With one arm slung around Harper, holding her against his side, he packed up his toy bag, one of Ella's helpers stepping in to help him.

He'd wanted her to let go, shatter, and now he had to pick her up and put her back together again.

"It's all right, darling," he said. He gathered her in his arms and passed the small group of onlookers who had watched their scene, weaving through the crowded club as Harper tucked her face into his chest. He brought her to a private nook off to the side of the bar and settled on a low, black chaise.

"You're safe with me, Kitten."

Her teary face pulled at his heartstrings, and he hugged her tighter. "Anything. You can tell me anything, and you're safe with me."

She shook her head against his shoulder, and Logan rubbed her back.

“I can’t tell you.”“Yes, you can,” he said as gently as he could.

“Xander… I had sex with Xander,” Harper sobbed.

His chest tightened, but he held her closer, pouring his strength into her. “That’s okay. You did nothing wrong.” The words were true, but they felt like glass in his mouth.

14

CHAPTER FOURTEEN - HARPER

As his powerful arms encircled her in his pure masculine strength, Harper exhaled a shuddering breath, her hand on the smooth plane of his chest.

He tucked her head under his chin. "Shh, Kitten. I got you. There was no agreement between us."

He sounded so sure.

Harper wanted to believe him, but it felt like she had done something wrong with Xander. And she had. She had thrown herself at him even after he told her no. She had stubbornly refused to give up hope. Even when he made it crystal clear, there was none.

But remembering what Ares said, a part of her couldn't give up entirely. She still thought Xander might come around.

God, what was wrong with her? Here she was cuddled in Logan's powerful arms, breathing in his familiar scent as he wiped away her tears and her heart still lurched, wishing Xander was nearby. Wishing that he hadn't closed her out.

She jumped as the music volume increased and held on to Logan's chest tighter. She felt the hot streak of tears and wiped them away.

"Kitten, I'm going to take you home. What do you say?"

When he had walked through the office doors on Monday, Harper wanted to launch herself into his arms, but she couldn't. She didn't know how he would react. Even though he talked about not being exclusive, Harper feared it was another thing when it came to Xander. Things had seemed tense between those two ever since Xander said she could play with him. And all week, Xander barely muttered a word to her, and when he did, it was clipped, and artic and Harper couldn't take it.

She feared she had wrecked their friendship. The thought of that sent off a fresh wave of tears.

"I got you."

He kept saying that, and she believed him, making her feel worse.

In her peripheral, Harper saw Ella drop off their stuff. Her friend smiled at her and Harper's head felt so fuzzy that she couldn't form words to say anything.

"I'm so proud of you, Kitten."

She shook her head against his chest.

"I am. You were brave tonight, trying rope. And you were strong tonight for letting go."

"This is stupid. I'm sorry."

"You're allowed to fall apart, Kitten. It's okay."

But she didn't deserve him. She laid her head against his chest, letting the tears fall.They stayed like that until the music lowered and the crowd's noise faded. Logan stroked her back, kissing her cheeks, letting her cry.

She came away from his chest, his soaked t-shirt and nodded. "Ready?" "Yes." Logan helped her dress. She felt a little wobbly on her feet. He took her hand in his, leading her through the hallway out the back exit.

She kept her head down until they were outside, in the fresh air of the parking lot.

"Are you hungry?"

"Yeah."

"Yeah, who?" The look he gave her made her squirm uncomfortably.

"Sir." Harper choked out the word over the tightness in her throat.

Logan opened his Jeep's door for her, reached across her, drew the buckle, and snapped it in place. Before he pulled out, he punched in a few numbers and ordered Thai food. In silence, they drove to his condo.

"Stay here, one more minute," he said after he parked.

"Okay," Harper said.

She watched in the review mirror as Logan tapped on the bodyguard's car window. After a few minutes, the black car drove off.

"All clear. Come on, Kitten, let's get some food in you," he said.

"What did Tallon say?"

"I'm trusted to bring you into work safely tomorrow morning. I informed them you're staying the night."

"Okay," Harper said. She knew if it had been anyone else and not the new hire, they wouldn't have left. She didn't like the bodyguards on her. They were short-staffed enough at Axis Management, but Xander wouldn't budge on them. She knew it was far-fetched, but she took that as further proof Xander wouldn't cast her aside entirely.

For a moment, her head cleared, and she checked her phone, thinking about the audition. She sighed. Maybe she shouldn't have done that because it was another thing to worry about.

"What is it?"

"Nothing," Harper said. "Just thinking about the night."

"Not all scenes end how you want them to." Logan squeezed her hand.

Once inside his condo, Logan hung up her jacket, dimmed the lights, and spun her around to face him. "You and I will talk, but first, you need a bath. Come on, Kitten." He held her hand, leading her through to the master bathroom, where he turned on the taps, poured something from a jar into the tub, and lowered the lights.

"Logan, you don't have to look after me like this."

The heat of his hands matched the blaze in his eyes as his soft lips met hers. "Yes, I do. Get in the tub, Harper."

She obeyed, soaking into the steamy bubble bath, feeling relief as the hot water eased her muscles.

"Thank you," she whispered.

A chirping melody rang out, and Logan grinned. "Food. I'll be back in a few."

How could she have thrown herself at Xander? Logan had shown her repeatedly how much she meant to him. He treated her with exquisite care and made her feel safe and cherished. She swallowed another sob and leaned back against the tub. Her eyes closed after a minute as the residual emotions left her.

She opened her eyes to Logan, stroking her cheek with the back of his hand. "Feel better?"

"Yeah, thank you. I can't believe I broke down like that in the club."

"You're not the first submissive to do so. You won't be the last."

"It wasn't even an intense scene."

"Tonight, it was for you. You never know what emotions a scene can bring out."

She nodded, the scene playing behind her closed eyes lids. The man had brought her to orgasm and forced her to have another one. She let him tie her up with rope. She shuddered in the bath.

"Are you all right if I leave you for a few minutes?"

"Yes. I'm fine." Harper smiled.

"Okay, Kitten. Call if you need me."She laid back in his tub, trying to sort out her thoughts. With Logan, she felt so cared about, so cherished. With Xander, she felt cared for in a whole different way. He pushed her and made demands on her. Logan handfed her tidbits until she got where he wanted her to be. Both methods worked for her so damn well it scared her how much these men saw her. How much her heart wanted both of them. She closed her eyes, swirling the water gently.

"Hey, ready to come out?"Harper nodded. The water had gone cold. Logan helped her out of the tub and dried her off with a big fluffy yellow towel, kissing the back of her neck.

"Thanks," Harper mumbled as she slipped on a silky black robe, he held out for her, wondering if he had a drawer full of them somewhere.

"Let's eat." He laced his fingers through hers and led her into the living room. A fire glowed in the fireplace. The dishes were laid out on a low coffee table, and the Thai food smelled amazing. Cushions rested on either side of the table.

"You eat on the floor?"

"Why not?" Logan said, grinning at her. He brought out a bottle of red wine, uncorked it, and passed her a glass.

Taking a sip of wine, Harper steadied herself. Logan was always full of surprises.

"I'm creating a mood here, Kitten," Logan explained, lowering to the floor. "I want you to feel safe and comfortable."

"I do," Harper said. She sat down across from him.

"Then why aren't you letting me in behind those walls? Every time I think I climbed over one, you throw up a new one in its place."

"Logan, I'm sorry. I don't mean to." Harper twirled food around with the chopsticks.

"I didn't ask for an apology. I asked for honesty," Logan said.

The piercing look he sent her made her blood race and her pussy throb.

"You and Xander had sex. That's what's upsetting you?"

"I know, but it... didn't go well," Harper said, biting her lip.

"Spell it out for me, Kitten, before I come to my own conclusion." Logan danced his fingers along her arm.

Harper took a deep breath and told him the story of how she threw herself at Xander. Logan listened to every word, his face expressionless. When she finished speaking, she covered her eyes with her hands.

"He could have marched you out of there. He chose not to," Logan said quietly. He reached over and took her wrist. "Come on now, no hiding."

Harper shook her head. It sounded so simple coming from Logan, but it hadn't been in the moment. "I don't think either one of us wanted to stop. I was dumb, Logan. He told me to stay away, and I didn't. He fucked me and told me to go, and ever since then; it's been icy between us. I feel strongly for him, and I can't change that."

"You are not 'dumb,' and if I hear you talk like that about yourself again, you won't sit for a week. Got it?"

Nerves fluttered in her stomach. "Yes, Sir."

"He chose to fuck you, and he was an asshole for not walking you out and not looking after you."

As the events of that evening played in her mind, Harper gasped and dropped the chopsticks on the plate, her stomach in knots.

"Harper?" Logan leaned over and flicked her hair off her shoulder.

"He fucked me without protection."

The fierce look in his eyes made her lean back. He clenched his hand into a fist and shook his head.

"I'm going to kill him."

"Logan, no! This is what I didn't want, to come between you and him. And I'm to blame too."

He reached across the table, gripping her shoulder. "No, you're not to blame. He is supposed to be in charge. It's his fuckin' job to look out for you, Harper, and he didn't."

Harper stared down at her plate, wishing the floor would swallow her up. That was true, and he hadn't looked after her that evening. But he had for all the other nights.

"If something comes from that night, we'll cross that bridge when we get to it. He's an ass for giving you the cold shoulder after the fact. Obviously, you feel strongly about him. He got you out of a dangerous situation, and you've depended on him for years. Let me ask you this. Are you ready to move on?"

"What do you mean?" Harper asked, trying to swallow.

"Move out of their house, find a new job, commit to me."

Harper shook her head. "I love my job. But the time probably *has* come for me to move out." She stared at Logan, his beautiful, strong jaw, the love in his eyes. Her pulse raced, but she made her mouth spit out the words. "And Logan, I want to commit to you, but that would be unfair to you, knowing I have feelings for Xander. He told me I am not the submissive he needs. He..." her voice trailed off, seeing Logan's eyes turn a shade darker.

"I think you need to walk me through it, Kitten."

Not meeting his gaze, Harper told how Xander made her kneel, the things he hurled at her and how she insisted she could be all those things and then how he'd fucked her and afterwards told her it was a mistake.

"Harper."

The sharpness of his tone caused her to look up. She wiped away the fresh track of tears that had fallen on her cheeks.

"Yes?"

"You deserve better than that. Xander doesn't know if you could be the sub he needs because he's been clear about not giving you the chance to show him. I want to throttle him for how he treated you."

That was what she had feared most, that Logan would react so badly, leaving her to come between them. And as much as she hated it, his words sent a flare of hope through her. Is there a way she could show Xander she could meet his needs?

"Logan, I was to blame, too."

"He took advantage of you, Kitten, knowing how you feel about him and then sent you off into the night alone. Tell me, what is it you do want?"

Shifting on the cushion, Harper set down the chopsticks and pushed the plate in front of her.

Both.

Logan's enthusiasm, infectious energy, and Xander's stoic, careful, calculating mind were a heady combination. Logan, with his spiky blond hair and Xander with his cap of sleek black. Two men, opposites in so many ways, and she wanted them both.

The thought of not having Xander in her life crushed her, and the thought of Logan rejecting her made her heart feel like it was ripped in two.

She gathered the dishes, bringing them to the kitchen, feeling Logan's potent glare as he tracked her across the room.

"I don't want anything to change," she said.

"Really?" Logan strode across the room, his fingers gripping her shoulder as he turned her to face him. "Nothing?"

"No," Harper shook her head firmly.

His lips crashed on hers, his tongue dominating hers as she parted her mouth open for him. He pinned her against the counter, his knee between her legs. "What about wearing my collar around your neck?"

Harper shuddered as his blazing hot fingertips circled her neck. Her heart thumped against her chest. God, she couldn't believe he was asking her this. She had thought about this, longed for it, and she could feel another onslaught of tears as she felt the relief from not being rejected by him.

"You're not mad at me?"

"No, Harper. I told you I wouldn't be, and I'm not. When we were in Club Bandit tonight, and I saw you watch me as I caressed Sasha, a switch went off in my brain. I can commit to the right person, someone who doesn't mind me doing demonstrations, tying up other girls. I can commit to you." He brushed his hand through her hair.

Harper shook her head. "My feelings for Xander aren't resolved."

"Everyone wants to pretend life doesn't happen by getting 'closure.'" Logan air quoted the words as he said them, "but Kitten, life is messy. I know your feelings are unresolved, but wearing my collar might give you the security you need. You can count on me."

"Yes, Sir," Harper said. "Yes, I would love to wear your collar."

The grin split his face into a sunbeam, and Harper laughed as he picked her up, carrying her down to the bedroom.

"Good enough for me," Logan said. "Let me show you how much I adore you, Harper."

She giggled as his breath tickled her neck, and she clung to his shoulders. Being in his embrace felt so right. He tossed her on the bed, placing his arms on either side of her.

"The whole time I was away last week, all I could think about was you." Logan kissed the column of her throat, pressing down on her. She felt his hardness through his slacks, and her hips rose off the bed.

"I missed you too," she said. Her hands went to his waistband. "Sir, may I please you?"

He ran his hands through her hair, bringing her forward. "You do please me, Kitten."

The low drawl in his voice sent pinpricks of pleasure through her. Wrapping his arms around her waist, he brought her to the edge of the bed, lifting her smoothly. "And yes, you may."

She smiled, her hands working quickly to unfasten his button, pulling his zipper down. Logan helped her slide off his slacks, and a moment later, his glorious cock was free.

She lightly ran her fingertips on the underside, then slid between his feet, flowing to her knees. As her mouth closed over him, Harper closed her eyes. There was comfort in being between his legs, in being wanted. His hand fisted through her hair, and she moaned around his cock.

15

CHAPTER FIFTEEN - LOGAN

Logan stifled a groan and leaned back, hissing at the pressure of her fingers around his balls. "Your mouth feels so right. So damn good."

He placed a hand on the back of her neck.

Her long hair curtained her face as she moved her head up and down. The feeling of her mouth around his cock was hot velvet heaven. Her tongue rolled to the top of his shaft, and Logan kissed the top of her head, tensing as her tongue worked up to his balls, her mouth pressed down on them. He grabbed her face between his hands, moving her. She moaned low, vibrating around his cock. He guided her head down to the tip. Her wide jewel-toned eyes held his as a current of red hot desires flared between them.

"Kitten, I want you naked and spread eagle on my bed," Logan murmured, currents of desire running up his back. He would come down her throat if he didn't have her now.

With her usual grace, Harper stood and looked at him from under her long lashes, a small smile playing on her mouth.

"Make me," she said and stepped out of his reach.

"Oh, it's on, Kitten." Logan launched himself from the bed as Harper ran down the hall. Her giggle, a sweet sound filling the space. As he chased her into the living room, Logan's fingers grasped around her wrist before she moved out of the way. The woman was quick.

"Harper," Logan growled.

Her eyes flashed with merriment, and his heart burst. This was the woman he knew, the playful side of her emerging after the emotional storm. She wasn't being bratty or defiant, more like she wanted him to work for the victory.

And he would have victory.

His fingers barely grazed her. She moved fast. She grabbed onto the stripper pole, lifted herself and spun around, and twirled before dismounting. "Hot damn, woman. I'm going to make you dance on that thing.""Have to catch me first."

He let her race by him through the kitchen, her long hair flowing behind her.

She ran around the stripper pole, back through the kitchen, her long hair flowing behind her.

Logan stood ready at the kitchen door and wrapped his arm around her as she tried to dart past.

"Caught you. Now, what are you going to do?" Logan nuzzled her neck.

She panted against him, giggling.

He held her against him for a moment, loving the excitement in her eyes.

She kicked against him, and he wrapped a leg around hers, pinning her.

"Nope, I caught you fair and square. One of these days, I'll devise a chase and capture scene."

At his words, her body went lax, her nipples drawing to tight peaks.

Logan chuckled. "Someone likes that idea." And effortlessly swung her into his arms, carrying her back to the bed. She sat there, supreme satisfaction on her face, as Logan threw off his shirt. From the nightstand, he grabbed a condom and rolled it on."Now I'm going to have my way with you."

"Yes, Sir." The glow in her eyes was enticing, filled with heat, and her hands came up, cupping the side of his face.

She opened her mouth to him, and he slid in his tongue, dancing with hers, kissing her with all the possession he felt.

Gently pressing her chest, he hovered over her. He traced her jawline with his lips, moving down to the column on her throat, sucking one pert nipple into his mouth, dragging his thumbnail across the other. Her legs wrapped around him, and he ran his hand along her muscular calf, tickling under her knees. Her head threw back, her long burnished strands flowing over her breasts.

He swirled his cock's head at her entrance, fingering her clit as he eased in.

"You *are* ready for me," he purred.

"So ready," Harper said, her hip arching to him. Reaching for her, he cupped his hands under her ass, sliding her to the edge of the bed.

"Logan!"

"Trust me, Kitten, I got you." He slid in another inch as his hands held her, keeping her from falling.

Her legs came around his waist and he eased into her even more. God, her pussy grabbed him with flaming heat. He stroked her long and slow, then quick and fast, feeling her fingers bite into his shoulders, liking how the muscles of her abdomen rippled as she held herself up. Like him, she considered her body an instrument to be wielded.

Sinking even deeper into her heat, Logan kissed her ear, her neck, and breathed in her scent as he pumped into her. A sheen of perspiration dotted her forehead, and he wanted her to come undone for him. With that goal in mind, he thrust harder, feeling her pussy contract, seeing her eyes close.

"Now, Harper," Logan said, with one more deep and fast stroke. White fiery flames licked at his spine, and he wanted her orgasm before he gave over to his.

"Yes, Sir!" Harper cried out the words. Her body rippled as the pleasure rolled through her. Nothing was more beautiful than this woman, right here, falling apart for him. She gripped his shoulders hard.

Still stroking her, Logan gritted his teeth, feeling the weight in his balls as he sank to his hilt. Pinpricks of heat danced behind his eyes as he let go and ejaculated in one hot stream, deep within her.

Easing her down to bed, he slid out of her, left her and disposed of the condom, then came back to her. He swept the hair off her shoulder, bent, and pressed a kiss to her soft mouth.

"You're so damn gorgeous," He wrapped an arm around her, bringing them against the pillows.

"So are you, Sir." Harper reached for him, her voice sultry with desire.

Logan kissed her forehead and curled her into his body.

"Sleep, now, Kitten," he said. He traced her hipbone, and nuzzled into her, knowing he was a lucky bastard.

The thump, thump, immediately sent hyperawareness through his veins. He reached over, flicking on the table sidelight. "Stay here Kitten, don't come out no matter what."

Harper, looking pale with fright, nodded. He kissed her mouth, driving reassurance into her. "It's nothing I can't handle."

Logan threw on a pair of shorts and a T-shirt and made his way to the pounding door. He opened it and cursed. Being a search and rescue tech, he had seen stuff that still gave him nightmares, and working for Axis Management a piece of his soul had been left in the Baskin Valley. But none of that carried the absolute purity of loathing for the short, balding man who was leaning against his doorframe.

"Ed, what do you want?" Logan crossed his arms over his chest and stepped into the doorway. The sight of this man always made his mouth taste like ash.

"What I want is for my company to increase a profit by twenty-five percent. You were right with the donation to the firefighter's charity. It brought a lot of publicity," Edwin slurred. "And now I need another publicity stunt. I want you at the board of directors' dinner in two weeks, Logan, to announce your permanent position."

"I told you I would be there." He glared at the pitiful man.

"I'm just checking." He leaned to the right, peering beyond Logan into the condo. "You got a girl back there?"

Logan wanted to wrap his hands around his uncle's throat and squeeze. Instead, he asked, "Do I need to call you a cab?"

"No, I got a driver. Remember, two weeks or Paige and Hana are cut off... for good." Edwin jabbed at his chest and every one of Logan's muscles tightened.

Sneering, he bent into his uncle's face. "Next time call."

"I wanted to surprise you." But Ed waved and stumbled down the hallway. Logan stepped out into the hall, making sure the man got on the elevator.

As soon as he was, he picked up his phone and called Hana, wanting to check in with her, despite the hour. "Hey, call me as soon as you're up."

Pumped up from that encounter, Logan knew he wasn't going to sleep. Back in his room, Harper was sitting with her legs tucked under her.

"Sorry about that." Logan kissed her cheek.

"Is everything okay?"

"Edwin showed up. He's worried I'll back down on my word to join the company."

"Logan, you always keep your word." Harper rubbed his shoulders and Logan caught her hand, kissing her fingers. Her belief in him made his heart swell. No other woman had ever given him the steadiness she had. She made him want to put up a white picket fence.

"Ed made me this offer right after the mission to rescue Mulberry. You know how that went. I couldn't leave the guys like that, and I didn't want to say goodbye to Axis Management. I needed another job to go well."

"Oh, Logan. Jordan's death affected everyone."

"Yeah. When Quinn's head was too fucked up to see straight, Xander put me on that archeologist job, remember?"

Harper nodded. Axis Management went where others didn't. They cleaned up messes and protected and rescued people. When Xander sent Logan, Gabe, and Nick to the Middle East to retrieve a renowned archaeologist, who wasn't there for legal purposes, it had been the mission he needed, the one that proved to him he could still do this and that he didn't want to leave the adrenaline charge that being an operative with Axis Management gave him.

"Yes, Ida Kavanagh. You guys were dark for three days. I was worried."

He stroked her jawline gently with his finger. "The day after I got back, Edwin started hounding me to go work for SolCan. I had hedged him off until then, but I knew it was a running clock. When I told Xander, he advised me that I was looking at this all wrong. I could go work for Ed and pretend to kiss his ass—while I'm there, eventually oust him and gain control of the finances. I was too angry with Edwin and the hell he made Hana's life, to see the solution." Logan shrugged. "Xander reads people. That's the magic sauce of Axis Management." He slung an arm around her, bringing her close. He had been unsure why he was telling her all this at first, but now he knew.

"It's going to be hard to leave Axis Management, for both of us, Kitten."

"I know," Harper whispered.

"I need to go do a workout to discharge some of the angst I feel after the knock on the door. Can I get you anything?"

Harper bit her lip. "No. I might go into the living room and watch a movie."

Logan stood up, grinned at her, and moved the two wall canvases of the mountains off the wall, revealing a massive TV.

"That works, yes," Harper said, snuggling into the blankets.

"Okay. I'll be back soon, Kitten." Logan kissed her pouty lips, wishing he could crawl into bed with her.

He hated Edwin but working full time for SolCan would give him the stability he'd never had before. It wouldn't make Harper worry if he was going to come home or not, and that one part of the equation helped ease his angst more than any cardio workout ever could.

16

CHAPTER SIXTEEN - XANDER

Xander hung up the phone, displeased. Another talent agency wanted to hire Axis Management for their bodyguard services. He rolled back his chair, stood, and paced in front of his large window.

From the Mulberry Stevens', they'd had many entertainment industry people interested in them. For years, Axis Management had been in the background, no matter the job. He preferred it that way. It was why he'd started the company, to have a group of highly skilled professionals who had the abilities required to get this high octane, often dangerous work done.

Xander smiled, thinking how ironic it was because his friend Ian owned a talent management firm and discussed gaining Axis Management's services when Harper crashed into his life.

He didn't want to be only a bodyguard firm, and it concerned him that if he kept taking on celebrity clients and became more visible, the other branches of Axis Management would fall.

He picked up a tray from a shelf that held pieces of glass and wiring that were spread out in a specific pattern. Taking a pair of tweezers, he tinkered with it for a few moments, trying to clear his thoughts.

Ever since he had ordered Harper out of his room, his head had been a jumbled mess. He couldn't get that night out of his mind, no matter how hard he tried. Her firm body under his hands, responding on cue to his commands as if she had been doing it for years, as if she was a submissive he had trained. More than once, he had replayed that night over in his head in the shower while jerking off to the memory. But Harper didn't need him as a lover. He was too old, his expectations too uncompromising. He would break her.

For the last two weeks, he had been incredibly lonely without the camaraderie he shared with Harper. He missed her. Ares thought he should apologize to Harper and see if she would consider dating him.

Xander scoffed. The idea was absurd.

Checking his watch, Xander strode out of his office, on his way to visit Team Tech, nearly crashing into Gardenia, her hands filled with files.

"Sorry, Mr. Montague."

"No, I was distracted and didn't see you. Are you all right?"

"Yes, I came up to give Harper a few more profiles on potential assistants. She's lying down with a migraine." Gardenia blushed.

"You are nothing but capable," Xander soothed, putting his hand on Gardenia. "I appreciate your attention to detail."

Gardenia nodded and hurried out of the office.

Xander scrolled through his calendar on his phone, frowning. Reaching into the top drawer of Harper's desk, he sorted through the jumbled pile of stuff until he found her bottle of medication.

"Angel?" He opened the door, stepping into her space.

The lights were off.

Harper had kicked off her shoes, lying with her feet up on her chaise, an arm on her forehead.

The sight of her in pain twisted his heart. Xander laid a hand on her shoulder, and she startled.

"Sorry. My head is pounding. I needed to lay down for a few minutes."

"I brought you this." Xander passed her a water bottle from the table and shook out two pills into his hand.

"Thanks." Harper winced as she sat up. "Couldn't find them in time, needed to cut the lights. I didn't sleep much last night. I think that's what brought it on."

"Marrock keeping you up all night?" The words were out before Xander could think about it. He turned away from her.

"Edwin came to visit in the middle of the night."

Xander bit his cheek, keeping his expression neutral. It annoyed him that Harper didn't deny being with Marrock, though he knew that's where she was. He wanted her to hide it? That was absurd. Maybe he wanted her to realize how much it sliced him, to know how many nights she was spending in Logan's bed. But the pure hatred he felt for Edwin pushed those thoughts to the side. He couldn't stand people who preyed on those weaker than themselves, and Edwin Greyson didn't know how else to be a human. "I guess that's something Logan and I have in common," Harper said. "Awful family members."

Xander picked up the two files on the table beside Harper and quickly flipped through them.

"Hire her."

"Jillian Levi? Why?"

"One of her jobs while in school was a part-time admin for a construction company. She can handle us."

Harper shook her head at him. "What would people do if they found out how talented you were?"

Xander laughed. "Run the other way."

Harper grinned at him, and it felt like nothing had changed for a moment.

A beeping sound alerted him to someone entering the office. "Rest as long as you need to, Angel."

Seeing her bordering on weakness only affirmed to him that keeping her at a distance was the right choice. Harper didn't need him to be anything more than her boss and protector.

"Good morning, Meg," Xander said. "Come on in."

"Is it? I thought it was still nighttime. Anyways, look what we picked up. I believe this is legit."

Meg bumped the corner of his desk, causing his tray of pieces to shake. "Sorry." He smiled, thinking someone out there was going to find her adorable.

"Here, look at this."

Xander took the iPad from her, looking at the censors that denoted the location of the technology they were trying to find.

"Mexico?"

"Yes, and if I combine with this"—Meg reached over and split the screens, showing a transcript of a phone call—"I think it's likely the sale is going down, and I think the sale originated here, in this part of the world."

His pulse raced, anger clouding his vision for a moment. If that was true, then the aircraft had definitely come from Dorian Martin.

"Time to get Team Stealth to the airport. Thanks, Meg."

After Meg left, he called the Bandit Brothers and told them to get to the airport, except for Erik.

"Xander, we've got a problem," Ares breezed into the office.

"We have several. What now?"

"After we had that meeting with Dorian, I put out my out feelers, seeing if anyone was searching for girls from Blakvasitakin. I thought it was a long shot, but Dorian's specific comment about a live-in whore made me want to cover the bases."Xander's mouth grew dry. Blakvasitakin was the country Harper and her family were from. "What did you find out?""Someone has been looking for a girl around Harper's age from Blakvasitakin."

Xander's mind whirled. It could be a coincidence. But he didn't believe in those.

"Is this the same ping as you got before, saying her family was looking for her?""I don't know yet," Ares said. "The first one searched for any girls her age on the Darknet. This one is searching for her by name."

"We have to find out." His heart hammered. Harper might think she was out of danger, but Xander knew better. He knew not to let his protection on her slip."I know. We're on it. We're doing everything we can." His brother was right.

Xander shrugged his shoulders, trying to release the tension in his body.

"You good?" Ares asked."I'm fine. You know you're always after me to invest in material things instead of people."

"Yes, I would like us not to work so hard."

"What do you think about this company?" Xander passed him a prospectus he'd been considering.

"You're a big softy; you know that?" Ares smiled.

Xander gave him the finger.

His brother whistled. "Really, eh?" "Might as well." Xander shrugged. If he could do anything to help Harper, he would.

***

"What's this about going to Mexico?"

Logan Marrock growled as he pushed open the closed door of Xander's office. Erik moved from the desk where he'd just showed Xander surveillance photos of Dorian Martin and Theo Densen, brother of Olivia Densen.

"Marrock, chill," Erik said. He glared at him, then flicked his eyes to Xander. "You got instructions. Why aren't you at the airport?"

"Why aren't you, Erik?"

Erik shrugged. "Those weren't my orders."

"Is this another fishing expedition to find a piece of technology that may or may not exist?"

"This is a job for Team Stealth. Finding and protecting objects is part of what you signed up for, Logan," interjected Xander. "I've explained why this is important. You're a smart man. You know why I want to trace this back to Dorian Martin."

"No, not really," Logan said. "Jordan's dead. Nothing is going to bring him back."

"Yes, but to prevent another situation like that, I want to know where the attack came from. Are you in or out, Logan?" Xander pressed. He felt sweat trickle down his back. He didn't love this confrontation.

Logan was the glue of Team Stealth. He didn't want to lose him, and he gritted his teeth. Maybe they should have implemented a no dating policy at Axis Management.

"It's bullshit," Logan said.

"You have your opinion all you want," Xander ground out. "But get on that plane or quit."

Logan got in his space.

Xander sighed. He thought they were over this.

"Are you sending me away, so you can take advantage of Harper again?"

Xander raised his eyebrows. "I did not take advantage of Harper."

Fury vibrated through him. So this cocky bastard thought he would take advantage of the woman he'd protected all these years? That was taking things too far.

"Didn't you? You could have said no, walked her out of there and the least you could have done is wrap your dick up!" he yelled.

Xander glared at him, trying not to show how Logan's words had just gutted him. He clenched his hands because he would not let Logan see the truth in his words. But the bastard was right. It had all happened so fast with Harper. That night was so intense, and he'd tried everything he could think of not to dwell on it.

Because he wanted more.

He had to talk to Harper. But it didn't matter from his point of view. If she ended up pregnant, he would take care of her.

With his lip curled into a snarl. "Get on the plane or leave Logan."

"I'm not going to let my teammates down, asshole." Logan's eyes flashed with fury. "But this is the last job I do for Axis Management. It's obvious you want Harper all to yourself!"

"Harper is free to decide for herself," Xander said.

"How could she, with your influence? You don't let the woman far from you, and then when she shows interest, you reject her!" Logan took a step toward him just as Harper walked into the office.

Xander moved forward and smiled at him. "And I thought you had that temper under control."

"You bring out the worst in me! You could give a woman anything, you emotionally stunted juvenile," Logan said, his fist drawing back.

Erik quickly stepped in and grabbed Logan's arm. "Don't, Logan."

"Enough! I can't take this," Harper said, distress threaded through her voice.

"Harper, you know how he gets before a job," Xander said.

"I didn't know you were there, Kitten," Logan said, taking a step towards her. She took a step back, shaking her head. "This is too much. You are arguing over me. I didn't want this."

"Wait, Angel, I'll send Carli to take you home."

"Come back to my place," Logan reached for her.

"No. I can't be fought over like this. You both mean the world to me. I can't do this," Harper said. She backed away, and Xander watched her as she grabbed her bag and ran out the door. Xander wanted to go after her but knew it was the wrong thing to do. She needed space.

"Harper!" Logan ran after her, coming back in a moment later.

"The elevator closed just before I got her.""She needs space."- "No, she needs reassurance." Logan paced in front of Xander's desk.

Xander ignored him and punched in Janette's number. "What do you need, Mr. Montague?""I need to know where Harper is at all times. Get a detail on her as quickly. She's just left Axis Management.""I'm free. I'll find her and take one of the new hires with me," Janette said.

Xander shook his head. He had good people, and he didn't deserve them half the time. "Thanks, Janette."

"Why do you even need a detail on her?"

"That's her story to tell, Logan. Maybe she doesn't trust you enough with it."

Logan glared at him. "Last job, Xander, and I'm out. Harper agreed to wear my collar."

"Did she? I didn't see it around her neck."

Logan flipped him off and stalked out of the office.

Xander shook his head and turned to Erik. "I know you would have preferred to be on that job."

Erik shrugged. "I go where you tell me to, boss. No matter what comes of your investigation, they will always blame me for Jordan's death."

"It's not your fault," Xander said.

"That's what I tell myself. What do you need?"

"I need you to follow Dorian Martin. I want to know if there is any link between him and Theo Densen," Xander said. "Theo would destroy me if he could."

"All right," Erik said. He gave him a salute and headed out.

Xander sighed. He and Theo used to be good friends until his sister Olivia was paralyzed in a car accident Xander had caused.

He sighed. They all had their battles. It was what they did with them that mattered.

17

CHAPTER SEVENTEEN - HARPER

It was ridiculous that she had nowhere to go.

Harper went through the possibilities of where she could escape to. She needed space to sort out her head and her heart, and with the migraine pounding at her temples, she needed to find somewhere quick.

When she was around the corner from Axis Management, she called Gardenia.

"Did you decide who to schedule an interview with?"

"Yes, Jillian. Hey, I don't know if you had plans after work tonight, but my migraine isn't any better, and I don't want to go all the way home. Can I crash at your place?"

Silence on the phone for a moment. "It must be bad if you're leaving work early," Gardenia said. "Sure. I didn't have any plans other than watching a movie with Kayleigh. Just head to my building, and I'll tell the front desk to give you a key."

"Thanks, Gardenia," Harper said.

"And help yourself to anything. My younger sister stayed with me last week, and she left a bunch of clothes in the guest bedroom that'll fit you. I'll see you later," her friend said.

Harper put her phone in her purse and sighed. She knew Gardenia came from a big family and had four sisters. A pang of jealousy niggled at her. *It must be nice to have people who care about you, people who you could rely on. It must be nice to have a family.*

Usually, she didn't think about it too much, other than on her birthday when she missed her parents and her one aunt. Whatever happened to her aunt? And she missed having family on the holidays. Okay, so maybe she did think about it a lot. With a past like hers, it was hard not to. But Ares and Xander were her family now, and she also had Josie, and her mom, Fleur and the Bandit Brothers felt like big brothers and through them, well, they all had Kayleigh, who was like everyone's tag-along sister.

Harper shook her head, stopped at the café next to Gardenia's building and got a tea. As she was waiting for the barista to brew it, a prickling sense came over her as she glanced out the windows to see a black-haired man walk by.

"Here you are," the barista said, handing over the tea.

"Thanks," Harper mumbled. She looked behind her, but no one was there. She shook off the feeling as she turned into Gardenia's building.

"Miss Blake, I was told to give you a key." The concierge said as she walked in. Harper startled, forgetting for a moment that she was the one being addressed. Her migraine was playing havoc with her head.

"Thank you."

She pressed the elevator button quickly. She longed to hear her father's name for a moment and knew that wasn't a possibility.

At Gardenia's door, she let herself in, putting her shoes on the rack. She hung up her purse on a hook, then knelt and scratched Snowflake, Gardenia's grey and white tabby. "Do you want a treat, kitty?"

Walking into the open concept kitchen, the view of the buildings downtown was memorizing, with a peekaboo view of the ocean. Gardenia's condo, though upscale, wasn't as big as Logan's, and the tiny living room had enough room for a love seat and a tv that stood on a wooden stand, piles of books, were in stacks all over the room, and a plush white carpet completed the look. But it was still Gardenia's own space. Family photographs lined the walls, and awards for equestrian riding stuck out here and there behind photos. An empty coffee cup rested in the sink.

She took down the cat treats from the cupboard above the sink, shaking the container. Snowflake came running at the sound. Harper smiled and offered the cat two treats in her palm. Snowflake wrapped herself around Harper's legs in thanks as Harper washed her hands and then finished her tea.

Harper went back to the small guest room, riffled through the closet, and found yoga pants and a UBC sweatshirt. She folded her work clothes neatly, leaving them on a shelf in the closet.

She lay down on the bed, staring at the ceiling, feeling the tears form in the corners of her eyes. She was selfish.

Not wanting to lose either man, she wanted to commit to both of them. But because Logan had asked her first, she guessed it was him. But losing Xander was too high of a price. She didn't want them fighting about her, yet they had done nothing but fight ever since she'd started seeing Logan.

Harper didn't know how she could love two men, but she did, and even after Xander was cold and awful to her, she couldn't help remembering how much passion and possession there was in the touch of his lips against her skin, how his eyes grew a shade lighter when they looked at her, his touch demanding.

But her loving both of them wasn't fair to either of them. She should do the mature thing and end it with Logan, then tell Xander her feelings were misplaced, that she wanted to go back to being friends and only his executive assistant.

Harper pulled the blanket up to her chin and snuggled down, shutting out the world.

***

"Can you believe they wanted me to answer the phones?" Kayleigh said, handing Harper a glass of wine. "I worked with them for two years, writing articles and interviewing people for their podcast. I am not a receptionist."

"So you quit?" Gardenia asked.

"Yes, I quit," Kayleigh said, taking off her oversized cat glasses and wiping them on her shirt. "It was the best thing for my mental health, you know?"

Harper smiled at her friend. "You'll find something soon. Or you could always go back to school."

"No, that's not for me. I don't know how you do it online and work full time."

"She has no life," Gardenia said, "outside of work."

"That's not true!" She knew she was blushing.

"Yeah, it is," Kayleigh insisted.

"Though both Xander and Logan look at her as if they could eat her," Gardenia said.

"I've been on a few dates with Logan," Harper blurted out. She usually kept to herself, but the look on her friend's face was worth it.

"Ew! Don't want to hear this," Kayleigh said, covering her ears.

"I do! Logan is yummy," Gardenia said.

"He is not! Ew," Kayleigh shook her head.

Gardenia's phone buzzed. "Food's here."

"I'll get it," Harper volunteered, wanting a moment away from them before answering any more of their questions. This, she told herself, is normal. This is what women my age do. Sit around and eat Chinese food and talk about men. Completely normal.

She opened the door, paid the delivery person, and took the food to the counter.

"Do you think you and Logan will get serious?"

"It must kill Xander to see you two together," Kayleigh said, grabbing plates.

"I don't know. Things have been a little tense between Xander and me. You're having lunch with him tomorrow, Kayleigh. Maybe you could bring it up?" Harper shook her head, wondering what was wrong with her. She didn't need Kayleigh to tell her that Xander's heart was crushed.

"Maybe I will," Kayleigh said. "Maybe I could bring up working at Axis Management."

"No!" Gardenia and Harper said in unison.

"It's very stressful," Gardenia added.

"You would hate it. Remember how much math there is?" Harper said.

Kayleigh's face crumpled for a moment, and then she shrugged. "You're right. I want to know what happened to Xander's former girlfriend. It's very hush-hush whatever went down with him and Olivia."

Harper bit her lip. She had just come into Xander's life as he'd broken off with Olivia, and it was like the cloud over him got darker when their relationship ended. Why Xander wouldn't pursue a relationship had a lot to do with his former one.

"Put your journalistic skills to the test, Kayleigh. See if you can get Xander to tell you something," Gardenia said.

"I will." Kayleigh's face set in a line of determination.

"What about you, Gardenia? Seeing anyone new?" Harper asked.

Gardenia shook her head. "My last date was so boring. He also didn't believe me when I said I worked for Axis Management. People expect us to be celebrities because some of our clients are."

"You'll find someone," Kayleigh said.

"What about you, Kayleigh?"

"Nope. I'm too busy working or not working now, I guess. I don't want to be with anyone."

"Anyone on Team Stealth that interests you?" Gardenia asked with a smirk.

"Hey! Those guys are practically my brothers, all of them, you know."

"Except for Erik," Harper said.

Kayleigh glared at her, and she raised her hands. "Hey, I'm just teasing."

"Erik is one wicked guy I wouldn't want anywhere near me."

"I would be happy if any of them looked at me as more than a background person," Gardenia said.

Harper patted her friend's shoulder and shook her head. "Those guys are a lot, anyway."

Her phone rang. She grabbed it, expecting it to be Xander or Logan.

"Hello?""Harper Blake?""Yes," a shiver of panic crawled over her. "Ivan Nowak calling from *Canada's Best Dancer*. We are calling you back for another audition tomorrow morning at ten."The breath went out of her lungs. In everything that had been going on, she had forgotten about it. How could she have forgotten about the show? She cleared her throat.

"Yes, that's fine. I'll be there."

"Great! See you tomorrow." Her mouth went dry. *I can't believe I told him I'd be there.*

"Would you ask Nick out?" Kayleigh said.Gardenia shook her head, blushing. "No way."

Dazed, she took the plates away, stacking them.

"Hey, I was still eating!" Kayleigh complained.

"Sorry," Harper mumbled. She dropped the dishes in the sink, turned on the taps, and scrubbed.

"I can do those," Gardenia said.

Harper barely heard her and kept running the water over the plate, running the sponge over it back and forth.

"Harper, you're freaking me out. Say something, please."

Harper dried her hands and turned to face her friends. Gardenia, her big brown eyes luminous behind her glasses, her long sandy hair magazine perfect and Kayleigh, with her purple hair, candy skull leggings, concern on both their faces.

She couldn't share her past with them, but there was no reason she couldn't let them in on what was going on with her. Well, not the sleeping with Xander part. Or the wanting to sleep with Xander part, but the rest of it, she could share.

"Okay, but you have to promise me not to mention a word about this to anyone at Axis Management, no matter what."

"Are you going to work somewhere else?" Kayleigh asked.

"No," Harper said.

"I promise," Gardenia said. "Spill."

"Kayleigh?"

"Promise," Kayleigh crossed her fingers.

"A couple of weeks ago, I went to the open audition for *Canada's Best Dancer*, and that was them calling me back for another audition."

"That's amazing!" Gardenia hugged her.

"Oh, my God! No way," Kayleigh screeched. "Wow. How can you even keep that a secret? They'll see it on TV eventually."

"Yes, eventually, but I want to keep it quiet for now," Harper said. "This is something I did just to see if I could."

"I didn't even know you danced," Kayleigh said.

"Yeah, I did when I was a kid," Harper's heart twisted at the words.

"I tried to take dance once, but then a wardrobe fell on me, and I couldn't follow the routines or stay in line, and it was awful," Kayleigh said.

Harper shook her head and patted Kayleigh's arm.

"One of my sisters took contemporary dance for the longest time," Gardenia said.

"What time is your audition tomorrow?"

"I have to be at the theatre at ten am. I have nothing here to wear for that," Harper said.

"Let's go get something!" Kayleigh said. "The stores are still open!"

Harper laughed as Kayleigh grabbed her arm, pulling her near the door.

"Yep, I'll drive," Gardenia said.

"It's okay. You guys don't have to." Harper suddenly felt nervous, shy about them making a fuss over her.

"Yeah, we do," Kayleigh said, putting her arm around Harper. "And when we get back, you can practice your audition!"

"We'll be your biggest fans!" Gardenia giggled. "Until Xander and Logan know about it!"

"Thanks," Harper murmured.

"Come on!" Kayleigh held open the door.

Harper grinned. An immense weight had just been lifted because she didn't have to hide everything from her friends. She felt like an ordinary girl hanging out with her regular friends, and it felt good.

18

CHAPTER EIGHTEEN - HARPER

Stepping backstage this time felt different. Fewer people were in the wings, just her and fifty other dancers. Harper's throat tightened. She took a deep breath, stretched, jumped on the spot to warm up, stretched again, and tried to tamp down her nerves.

While telling Gardenia and Kayleigh about the audition felt freeing, it also made her more aware and made her feel more pressure. And it brought to the surface how much she wanted to get through to the next round, the Top Twenty. They would begin filming in three weeks, and then there was no way around it. She would have to tell Logan and Xander if she made it that far. Her stomach dropped thinking about it. That almost felt as scary as going through with this two-minute audition in front of a panel of five judges.

She smoothed down her number across her waist, closed her eyes, and briefly visualized herself dancing across the stage. Opening them, she threw her shoulders back and waited. The woman in front of her got sent to a group dance-off.

"Break a leg." A firm squeeze took her hand, and Harper smiled at the curly-haired woman, waiting to go next to her.

"Thanks, you too," she said.

Two judges stood up for a moment, stretched. One checked his phone, and the others sipped from their coffee mugs. The assistant director gestured for Harper to go on stage. A camera followed her as she moved. When she reached centre stage, she stopped.

She looked right at the judges' table and gave a little wave.

"Harper Blake, nice to meet you," the man with long brown hair said. "How long have you been dancing?"

"I'm happy to be here," She locked eyes with the judge. "I've been dancing forever since I was a small child. My mother taught me."

"Your mother was a dancer?" the woman with the long blond hair asked.

"Yes, she was." Harper swallowed over a lump in her throat. Her beautiful mother had wanted her to dance on the stages throughout the world as she had in her youth.

"What kind of dance do you do?" a judge with big hair asked.

"Contemporary ballet," Harper said.

"Let's see what you have." The judge with the long hair waved at her, folding his arms over his chest.

Harper turned, took three steps back, extended her arms and smiled, the blood rushing in her ears, the beat of her heart reaching down through her toes. She remembered her mother's hands on her shoulders for a moment, telling her to be confident.

The soft notes of her music started, silencing all her thoughts. As the music floated in the cavernous space, there were only steps and beats, and Harper gave her all to every extension, every roll, every high spin. She leapt with her head back, her fingertips pointed, her arms soft but stead, and she danced.

Her thoughts only centred on the next step. Harper gave herself over to the dance and knew that she wanted freedom no matter what happened after here.

No more gates and bodyguards and maybe no more Axis Management, and, she realized with a start; the thought breaking into her concentration, no more hiding her feelings. She loved two men. A determination spread through her centre as she landed the last jump. Right after this audition, she would call them and tell them both. They deserved to know. Both Xander and Logan had asked for her to be honest, and she was going to do what they asked.

"Fierce!" The big-hair judge started clapping.

Harper glanced at the judges' table to see all of them on their feet.

"Well done," the lead judge said. "You're through to the next round. We'll see you in our Top Twenty. Congratulations."

"Oh, my God!" Harper gave a high kick in response and ran off the stage.

The adrenaline coursing through her system made her feel like she could float. In the theatre's lobby, she was directed to stand behind a screen.

"Now for some interview questions for the promotions," another director explained. Harper spelled her name, gave her age, and answered where she was from, all while looking right into the camera and imagining Logan on the other side of the lens.

"You said your mother used to dance. What does she do now?'

The question hit her in her solar plexus, and Harper put her hands on her knees. Someone passed her a water bottle, asked if she could continue, and Harper gave the okay.

"My mother, both my parents, were professional ballet dancers. When they came to Canada, they opened a studio on Vancouver Island. They died in a house fire when I was twelve years old."

Harper swallowed, wiped the tears with the back of her hand, and kept her gaze on the camera.

"That must have been very difficult."

"Yes," Harper said. "I lost my parents and my home, and I lost dance for a few years. Now I'm happy to have it back."

"Good luck in the Top Twenty."

"Thanks."

But she felt shaky. She hadn't shared that with Logan. She leaned against the changeroom doors, trying to get herself together. How could she have spat that out to the camera? *Because I'm tired of hiding it.*

Time to tell Logan about her past. The decision steadied her. She entered the frenzy of the change rooms, threw on her street clothes, unpinned her hair, and checked her phone.

Yeah, Xander was wondering where she was and getting a little more insistent as the day wore on, and she hadn't returned his calls.

Her stomach twisted in guilt for evading the security team Xander had assigned. Maybe she shouldn't have, but they were new to Axis Management, and Harper knew their chances of being cut were already pretty high. Xander wanted people who were all in and committed to the job, but no matter how much they screened and tried to get the best people in, sometimes it didn't work out. Harper had glanced at the pair of them on their cell phones when she got back from the shopping trip with Kayleigh and Gardenia and knew they weren't all in this gig. Not even close.

Dancing, Harper thought with a smile, was easier than working for the Montagues.

"Hey! You did great!" the curly-haired woman came over to Harper and hugged her.

"Thanks. How did you do?"

"I'm through too!" The woman smiled. "A few of us are going to get a smoothie in celebration. Want to join us?"

She didn't want this moment to end, even though she knew she should go back to real life.

Logan wasn't back yet, she justified. I'll tell them when we're all in the same place. "Sure," she said, slinging her bag over her shoulder. "I'm up for a smoothie."

The woman clapped her hands. "I'm Jade, by the way."

"Harper."

"Nice to meet you." Jade put her arm around Harper's shoulders, and together, the two women went out the stage door, joining other dancers who were waiting.

19

CHAPTER NINETEEN - XANDER

"Good morning, Gardenia. Have you seen Harper?"

Gardenia ducked her head and hurried by him without a word. Xander frowned. He knew the HR girl was nervous, but she'd never ignored him before.

"Gardenia?" Xander slid his hands into his pockets.

Gardenia turned back down the hall and looked at him briefly before focusing on the carpet.

"Is everything all right?"

"Yes, fine, just busy, you know, with the new teams of bodyguards. Is there something you need?"

Xander took two steps forward. Placing a hand on her shoulder, he raised an eyebrow. "Gardenia, do you know where Harper is?"

Gardenia sighed, darted a glance at Xander, and looked away. "She's fine. Just has some things to do this morning."

"She stayed by your place last night?"

"Yes."

"Thanks for letting me know," Xander said.

Gardenia bobbed her head again, and Xander checked his watch, taking the stairs to the lower level. As the doors swished open, he texted the team he had on Harper, asking them for another update.

Damn, I'm a dumbass. Briskly striding toward the R&D labs, he shook his head. He should have apologized to Harper. He should have chased after her. The hurt in her eyes had kept him tossing and turning all night.

She didn't go home last night, and the team on her wasn't returning his calls. He cursed himself for not putting a new tracker on her phone.

Some professional security operative I am.

"Hey, boss." Ryder Klassen, head of R&D, looked up from his table of parts and tools.

Xander clasped the man's outstretched hand. "Show me what you got."

The shaggy-haired man smiled.

Xander scanned the screens, noting progress on a government contract they had due for next month.

Ryder pulled a metal basket near him, dropped it on the counter, and placed a thin glass piece with a solar panel in it.

"As you can see, the casing is smaller. I've rigged one up, and using this method; it can be twice as powerful as the smallest panel currently on the market with more output." Ryder swiped his hands over the table's flat keyboard, and Xander smiled as the model appeared on the screen.

"Great job. When can we get this to the manufacturer?"

Ryder rubbed his face, pushing his glasses up his nose. "Another two months."

"If I get you more people?"

"Six months." Ryder grinned.

That was the problem with hiring the best in the fields. They didn't like to share space with others. Xander wanted to spend more time in R&D. He wanted to get back to tinkering with his inventions, but Axis Management had grown more expansive than he and Ares could have ever imagined, and he needed to play the role of the CEO. Unless he wanted to give up his control of Team Stealth. He couldn't do all the things, and it pissed him off.

He spent a few minutes greeting the other team members, examining what they were working on and then, at an empty worktable, he pulled up a tray of glass fragments and tweezers and examined them under the microscope.

"May I?"

Margot Phillips smiled at Xander.

"Of course," he said, passing his tray over to her.

"The goal is to mimic the seashell as much as possible," Margot said. "And if I blow up the image, you can see the hexagon patterns on the glass. We are working on making the bend just right so your phone screen doesn't bend to the touch." Margot smiled.

"Brilliant," Xander said. "You know this technology is a pet project of mine."

Margot flashed him a smile. "I know."

Xander's phone buzzed in his pocket. He frowned, not news of Harper but Ares asking him to come and meet him in the conference room.

"See you soon," Xander said to his R&D team.

Ares stood in front of the empty reception desk. Xander smiled. To his brother's annoyance, he was always a step ahead of him.

"Xander, come here. I got someone for you to see."

Xander shook his head. "Nope, I know that tone of voice. It's the same one you used to use when we were kids, and you dared me to do something, like steal Mrs. Grady's garden gnomes."

"You had fun, didn't you?" Ares slung his arm around Xander's shoulders, and he shook his brother's arm off.

"Listen, Xander, we're getting slammed with requests for personal security details, for bodyguards, and we don't have enough staff. You're right; that prospectus has potential. I want to acquire three more companies by the end of the year. I want to focus on more projects like that, not constantly running people. This Spring, we have new jobs for Team Stealth, and we know you want to keep those contracts. Something from Axis Management has to go."

"I know. I was just thinking I would like more time to tinker with technology up in the labs."

Xander's phone buzzed.

"What is it?" Ares said.

"The team on Harper only texted me with a thumbs up. They haven't given me an update, and I don't know where Harper is. She didn't come home last night."

"Maybe Harper told them to back off," Ares said.

"Yeah, I don't like this. I think we need to get rid of that team."

"How many times have you called them? Maybe they're finding you to be a distraction?"

"They need to communicate," Xander said bluntly.

"After you." Ares opened the door to the barely used conference room.

They were confronted by a stack of boxes that had been dragged up from storage, some old desks, and a kitchen table in the vast room.

"You got to be fuckin' kidding me," Xander said, glaring at his brother.

River Stone was straddling an old kitchen chair with his thick arms crossed in front of him. The first guy Xander had ever hired for Axis Management. They'd disagreed and parted ways, and it wasn't all that amicable on either side. River opened Stone Security.

"Consider his offer, Xander. It's a good one."

"Xander, good to see you." River extended his hand.

"I don't know if it's good to see you. I don't like things being done behind my back."

"If I told you, you wouldn't have agreed," Ares said.

Xander shook his head, pulled out the chair at the top of his table, and spread his arms. "So, how's business?"

"Great. Couldn't be better. What about you?"

"Fine," Xander said.

River returned Xander's stare unflinchingly. In the second year, Axis Management was in business; River Stone wanted to take on a job to help an old friend out of trouble. Said job involved ties to the mob.

Team Stealth walked the line. Axis Management paid good money for a host of lawyers but providing personal security to the niece of the head boss of the mob; Xander considered that too close for comfort.

River didn't like that Xander wouldn't okay the job, so he left and started Stone Security. He was the first employee to leave, and it stung. The people made Axis Management so successful and recruiting new people who had the skill, experience, and certain personalities to fit in was the most challenging part of the business. Also, as an ex-US Marine, River might have easily slid into Team Stealth.

"So, Ares said that you guys are being overrun with requests for personal security, and you might want to offload this part of the business?"

Xander glared at Ares, who was standing against the wall. Ares shrugged. "You know, it's true. We just talked about it."

Xander gritted his teeth. His brother managed to be a step ahead of him this one time. Ares was subtly giving him an ultimatum, and he didn't like it.

"So, you want to buy out the personal security branch of Axis Management. What's the offer?"

"I'll offer you one point three million." River crossed his arms over his chest.

"He insults us, Ares," Xander said.

"We have a contract from Ian McIomhair. His agency is set to bring us in, two-point-five million dollars' worth of business next quarter alone," Xander said.

River spread his hands. "I'm doing you guys a favour, and I know you will make more dough when this is off your hands. Tell me I'm wrong." River's steady green stare bore into Xander, and he returned it without flinching.

"I won't accept anything less than one point five," Xander said. "You know our contracts are solid, and our people are the best."

River stared at him for a moment. "I'll write the cheque right here and now if you can get me an updated assets list."

Xander rubbed his hand over his face. "The only person who can hand me that list hasn't come into work yet."

River shrugged. "I'll give you ten minutes."

Xander's phone buzzed in his pocket, and he swore.

"Xander, what is it?" Ares asked.

"The team on Harper has lost sight of her. I haven't heard from her all day, and this is the first update they give me." Xander pushed back from his chair.

"You have a security detail on your executive assistant? Wow, the working conditions here have sure gone downhill."

"It's a long story," Ares said.

"Want me to pick up their trail?"

"No." Xander glared at him. "Give us more time to get the list to you or withdraw your interest."

"You have until ten am tomorrow," River said.

"She'll call, Xander. Give her a chance to cool off." Ares's phone rang, and it was his time to curse.

"River, thanks for coming in. We'll get the information to you."

"Okay." River pushed the chair back in, clapped Ares on the shoulder and shook Xander's hand. "If you need help with whatever this is, call me."

Xander smiled tightly and made sure the door behind him was closed.

"Ares, what is it?"

"My contact at the police station. Someone just filed a formal missing person's report on Alina Volkov.""But you knew that," Xander stared at his brother, his mind blanking for a moment.

"This is a formal thing, Xander. Before, it wasn't."

Xander barely heard him. His heart pounded so hard that it felt like it would leap out of his chest and land on the floor.

The girl looked so scared out of her mind that Xander stayed as far back from her as possible, keeping by the windows. "What's your name, honey?" Nadia kneeled in front of her.

"My name is Alina Volkov."Despite the girl's terror, that voice grabbed Xander's heartstrings and twisted.

"We won't hurt you. I'm going to take care of you, I promise." He hadn't meant to say the words, but they flew from his mouth, and he wouldn't take them back. This girl was his, and he would take care of her, no matter what.

"Harper," he breathed.

"What does the report say? I know her aunt is still rotting in a Turkish prison," he spat out.

"Reported missing by her family," Ares said.

Xander thumped his fist on the table, calling the team on Harper. "Get Erik and Janette in here."

His worst fear was here, and Xander wanted to run out of the building, find Harper, and take her somewhere no one would find them.

He shouldn't have let her out of his sight for a moment.

His call went unanswered, so he tried Harper's cell again, and it clicked right over to voice mail. He texted her and shoved his phone back into his pocket, cold sweat breaking out across his shoulder blades. When Marrock started taking an interest in Harper, that's when he let down his guard. And he shouldn't have.

He knew she was feeling caged in, however, gilded the cage, but he should have done something, anything besides allowing the door to be opened.

Xander marched from the conference room, out the front doors of Axis Management, onto the streets as if he could tell where Harper was by breathing the outside air. Taking out his phone, he pressed redial so fast he knew he could break it.

"Come on, Angel," he said as it rang and clicked again to voice mail.

"Xander, wait!" Ares called behind him.

Striding back into the building, he jabbed at the elevator button, and Ares caught up to him. "Can't find Harper anywhere."

When the doors opened, he strode down the hall, right past Viv. He loomed over Gardenia's desk.

Her face paled.

"Tell me where Harper is," he demanded.

She swallowed hard, and her hands shook.

Taking a deep breath, he pulled out a chair and sat down. "She isn't answering her calls, Gardenia, and I'm worried about her. I have some urgent information I need to share with her."

Gardenia chewed on her lip.

"Tell me." Xander put as much dominance as he could in his tone.

"I know she was upset. You're a good friend, Gardenia. I'm glad she went to you." Xander tried to soften his words. "Where did she go today. Do you know?"

"She had an audition this morning." Gardenia's big eyes met his. "They called her back."

"Who called her back?" Ares asked.

"The TV people, from *Canada's Best Dancer*. She made it into the call-backs, which means she will probably be on the show. She's outstanding. Maybe she didn't tell you because she didn't want to ask for time off. Kayleigh and I told her she had to go for it because it's a once-in-a-lifetime thing, you know?"

Fury wound around Xander's heart, and he took a deep breath.

"This was her second audition?" Ares asked. He was scrolling on his phone.

"Yeah. She had the first one a few weeks ago."

"Xander, look." Ares showed Xander a clip on his phone for the show *Canada's Best Dancer*. It was a promotion clip. In a red leotard, with her head thrown back, was Harper, centre stage in a group.

"That's where that picture came from," Xander mumbled.

He turned away from Gardenia's desk, marching down the hall.

Fuck, Angel. You should have told me.

But of course, she hadn't because he would never have let her go to the audition. The more he tried to hold onto women, the more they escaped him and got in trouble. Xander cursed, punching in the security detail's number again. He called Carli, telling her to meet him at the front.

"Let me know what's happening," Ares called after him as Xander leaped into the car.

"Cali, get us to the theatre."

Xander's intuition screamed at him that something was wrong, and he didn't breathe until Carli stopped at the theatre.

He jumped out of the car, spotting the sign for *Canada's Best Dancer*. He looked down the street and saw a flash of shiny dark hair.

"Harper!" Xander shouted.

Harper, laughing at something the woman next to her said, her face washed in surprise when she looked up and met Xander's gaze. He waved at her, striding towards her. With a little goodbye wave to the people she was with, she walked toward Xander.

He smiled. She was safe.

A squeal of the brakes made Harper jump.

Xander's heart leapt into his throat at the grating sound of a van door being shoved open.

Harper screamed, dropping her smoothie cup. Two men jumped from the van and grabbed her, tossing her in the van.

Xander couldn't swallow, couldn't breathe, but a quick blast of a horn shook him out of it. Carli had pulled into traffic, chasing the blue van.

The world spun; Xander slumped against a light pole, dialling Ares.

20

CHAPTER TWENTY - LOGAN

The adrenaline rush of going on a job for Axis Management felt like reaching a summit, but sometimes, even better than the adrenaline rush was the relief after rescuing a person or guiding someone safely through a hostile environment or even delivering an object to save a country from going to war, even if the rest of the world didn't know.

That was what kept Logan invested in Team Stealth. Despite his parting words to Xander, he couldn't imagine leaving.

But this last job in Mexico left him feeling gutted. This time the intel was good. They crashed in on the sale. And if they didn't find the aircraft itself, they did find out where it would land after the guys who were doing the selling dropped their papers and ran. Not that they got far. Quinn had cursed as he picked up a paper that had fallen on the ground. "The Martin Group's stamp."They sent a report back to Axis Management, to Meg, and then a few phone calls later, Nick had the private aircraft intercepted at the airport. The Bandit Brothers hauled ass out of there for their pick-up.

"Why would Dorian Martin send this technology after us? I want to shoot the bastard myself." Logan broke the silence once they were back on home soil.

"It's not our job to figure it out." Gabe clapped him on the back.

"Does it bother you?" Logan asked Quinn.

"You know it does," Quinn replied. His friend's blue stare darkened. "But it's a job, and we all knew the risks signing up."

Logan had never factored in the risk of one of Xander's adversaries trying to kill them with invisible technology. His blood boiled. Until now, he hadn't confronted the senselessness of Jordan's death. But with it staring him in the face, there was no denying it.

"Better to know than to wonder whose fuck-up it was," Gabe said with a pointed stare at Quinn. "I plan to take on as many jobs as I can, and now I know it wasn't Erik's fault; it makes it easier for me."

"It was still his job to recon," Quinn said.

"Hard to recon when you can't see it," Gabe snapped.

Logan stared across the roof of the SUV at his friend's stony expression. Gabe was hurting over his betrayal by Ivy, and he was going to bury himself in work. "Seeing the physical proof of Xander's theory, I had a moment there. But the only thing we can do for Jordan is honour him."

The guys clasped each other's arms, then Quinn got into the SUV. "How are things with you and Harper?"

"I ran my mouth before leaving on the job. She walked out because she doesn't want to come between Xander and me." He smiled. "But she said she would wear my collar."

"Okay," Quinn said.

"What?" Logan shot his best friend a glance.

"I think Harper is looking for security, and Xander's been her security blanket for a long time. I don't think she knows what she wants, but she's made it clear she doesn't want you two fighting over her. Any thought of sharing her?"

"I always thought I would have no problem sharing a woman, but now that it's here, I don't know, man. Xander doesn't want to share, and he won't even tell her how he feels."

"You've got to figure it out before you break Harper's heart," Quinn said.

"Yeah." Logan pulled into Quinn's driveway in the suburbs.

"See you around eight at Club Bandit?"

"Yep. If you go now, you'll have a couple of hours of sleep."

"As if I sleep," Logan said. "See you."

He pulled out of the driveway, trying to loosen the tension in his shoulders. Quinn was right. If he didn't figure out if Harper was all in, her heart would get broken, and that was the last thing he wanted to happen.

His phone flashed. He saw it was Xander and left it unanswered. Sleep sounded like the exact thing he needed.

***

"Logan, what's your vote?"

Logan sent another text to Harper and flashed a grin at the men around the room. Zee leaned against the bar, his arms crossed over his chest. Gabe raised his eyebrows at him. Quinn wore the most impatient look on his face, probably wanting to get back to his wife. Logan snickered, and Nick cleaned his glasses. The other members had already cast their votes earlier in the day, and it was down to the Bandit Brothers.

"I don't know, Zee. I want to do what's best for you and keep his place going. We need it in the city. But I don't like having random people in here."

"And I like an occasional drink while I play," Gabe said. "If we opened it up, the bar would close."

"Ella suggested the bar serve energy drinks, water, and snacks like it's now for the friend nights," Zee said.

"Can you assholes vote already?" Quinn said.

"No, for opening Club Bandit to the public," Nick said.

"I would have thought you want new subs to torment," Logan said.

Nick shrugged. "It's not worth it."

"I'm for opening Club Bandit up to the public for two weekends a month and opening for member applications once a month. When we reach, let's say, two hundred members, close it to the public on weekends but still keep the workshops," Quinn said. "This is a great place, Zee, but I think your vision extended to more than twenty-four of us."

"Then we don't have to background everyone until they apply for membership," Gabe said.

"They do have to agree to the rules. And you'll need more Dungeon Monitors," Logan said.

"Yep, already accounted for," Zee said.

"Sounds good," Gabe said. "Everyone in?"

"Yep," they all chorused.

"We got an urgent call from Xander," Quinn said.

Logan snorted. "Are you going in?"

"Yes, because it's my fuckin' job. Like you told me months ago, stop being a pussy. Let's go."

Logan stared at his best friend and nodded. Sulking wasn't his personality, and it riled him that Quinn had called him out.

"Might be my last one," Logan said.

"You've said that before," Gabe said.

"I think we all say it," Nick said, putting his empty glass on the bar. "See you later, Zee."

They filed out into the parking lot. "See you there," Logan said.

Logan's phone buzzed against his pocket. A text from Xander was asking for his ETA. He didn't bother to answer.

He got on his bike and filed in behind his friends, driving the eight minutes over to Axis Management.

The conference room lights were on. Ares was leaning against the door. Xander stood behind a kitchen chair.

"Okay, you were right about the sale," Nick said. "Dorian tried to sell that helicopter, but we can't prove it was used on the attack. Are you happy?"

"We'll be happy about it later," Ares said.

"Xander, not to rush you, but I want to get back to my wife. What's up?"

Xander lifted his head and met Logan's stare, and something about his expression made Logan tense. He leaned across the table to Xander.

"What's wrong?"

"They took Harper."

"What are you talking about?" He leaned across the table, right in Xander's face. His steely stare didn't blink. Logan wanted to throw him against the wall.

"Logan, stand down." Quinn's voice was in his ear. "Take your hand off him."

He hadn't realized his fingers were around Xander's arm. Xander calmly held his stare, raising an eyebrow. His stillness made

Logan feel crazy but he forced his fingers to uncurl from Xander's arm.

"Start talking, Xander," Quinn said.

"I had a new team of bodyguards on her, but they didn't answer my texts or give me an update. I needed an asset list, and she's the only one who knows where it is." Xander's voice halted, and Logan watched him visibly swallow.

"Gardenia told me she went to an audition for the TV show *Canada's Best Dancer*. "*What*? And she didn't tell us?" Logan asked. "Why wouldn't she share that?" "Because she knows I would have sent her with more security. Or maybe she was afraid I would stand in her way, I don't know because she never fuckin told me," Xander said.

"What happened next?" Gabe asked.

"I got Carli to drive down that way, near the theatre, and I saw her with a group of people leaving a smoothie place. We'd just parked, and I was walking towards her when two men grabbed her and threw her in a blue panel van."

"Jesus fuck," Logan said. His mind whirled. He started pacing the floor, wondering why Harper had needed protection to begin with. Who the hell would take her?

Quinn said. "And why didn't you call us?"

"Carli peeled out after them, and she tracked them down to the city's edge before losing them." He glanced at Logan before looking to Quinn with his answer. "I called *all* of you, but your phones were off."

"Why do you even have a security detail riding, Harper?" Gabe asked.

"Yeah, I want to know that too," Logan said. His heart was galloping out of his chest, the same feeling he got when he started a climb or jumped out of a plane.

"There is a relative looking for her," Ares said. Xander shook his head at Ares. Logan couldn't stop bouncing on his feet. These details mattered, but he wanted to get out there to look for Harper. "You're keeping her away from her family?"

"Fuck off, Marrock," Xander glared at him.

Logan shrugged off Nick's hand on his arm.

"Eight years ago, Ian McIomhair and Nadia, his wife, met me for drinks at the Zetra, and Ian said he had an associate of his, a guy who owned a sports team, joining us. The guy walked in and said he had a way to make our night better, and the next thing I know, this girl was sitting down at our table. She wore a red strappy dress and high heels, and bright red lipstick. She looked like a girl playing dress-up in her mother's closet. She was skinny."

Beside him, his buddies swore. His mind whirled. Christ, is this what Harper was so intent on keeping from him?

"What did you do?" Logan choked out the words.

"Ian and I said he wanted to move the business up to our room. We rushed Harper upstairs while the restaurant filled. I called Ares, who was running late. Ares came in, occupied the owner of the sports team and asked for the name of the escort service under the pretence of wanting his own for the night while Ian and I got Harper into the room Ian had booked for the night luckily. He was going to surprise Nadia. Harper was drugged up and half-frozen," Xander said.

Logan's fingers curled into fists. Looking around the room, he knew every man in there felt the same as he did.

"Nadia gave Harper her sweater, sat with her on the bed, and offered her water. She barely spoke. Ares came in and told us that men were outside the hotel, probably keeping watch over the escort they sent in, so Ian and I brought her out through the kitchens, and I took her home that night, determined to protect her." Xander's voice was thick with raw emotion.

"So, she was an underage escort? Why?" Gabe asked.

"Because her aunt and uncle ran a human trafficking ring and were fed up with Harper's mother *not selling* the girls they brought over to her. So, they torched her dance studio on Vancouver Island, took Harper, kept her tied up for hours at a time and told her she was going to have to work in the family business. The first night they sent her out was in Zetra's."

The hard-closed expressions of every man in that room matched how he felt. "Thank Christ you were there," Logan said. His anger at Xander ebbed away. The man had done his best to keep Harper safe.

"Didn't her aunt and uncle come looking for her?" Nick asked.

"Yes," Xander said. "They looked, but we were on guard. Her aunt was dealt with shortly after that, and it's thought that other members of her crime family took out her uncle."

"Where's her family from?" Gabe asked.

"Blakvasitaikn. The Ralizphe mob."

Logan grabbed the nearest chair, suddenly feeling wobbly. He couldn't wrap his head around this. His beautiful, sweet Kitten came from a crime family that had terrorized the small country of Blakvasitaikn for decades and had started to make their way across to North America.

"Great, we have enough backstory. Now," Quinn said, "let's get to work. Nick, see if you can get footage from a nearby business. Everyone down that stretch has cameras. Gabe, get a canvass going and see if anyone reported a blue panel van speeding through the streets. Xander, I bet Carli got the plate number. Text her and ask her what it is."

"I'm going to find a number for the dance people and track down the group she was with last to see if they noticed anything about the men who took her," Logan said.

Quinn was already shaking his head. "Nope, you will sit here with Xander and Ares. You're going to get the tech people in and see if they can locate Harper's phone."

"Tech people are on their way," Ares said.

"Like hell, I'm sitting this out, Quinn," Logan snarled.

His best friend turned his icy blues on him. "Yes, you are. You are way too emotionally involved to think this through."

"We got this, Logan." Gabe clapped him on the back.

"Yep, we're good," Nick added.

Logan paced around the room, feeling like a caged tiger, but there was no way he would win this one, and he knew it.

He pointed his finger at Quinn. "Find her."

The Bandit Brothers filed out of the room, along with Ares and Xander. "How could you put a *new team* on her?" he bit out.

"I hire the best," Xander said. "I didn't think they were this green. You can point the finger at me, or we can be productive with our time."

Logan paced, heart-thumping into his ears. If anything happened to Harper that would be the end of him. "And you say you care about her."

"Fuck you, Marrock," Xander said. "Just because I don't wear my colourful emotions on my sleeve, just because I am not yelling and cursing about this, does not mean that my fuckin' heart isn't breaking. I love Harper."

"Yeah? Then why couldn't you tell her that?"

"Because me loving her isn't good for her," Xander snapped.

"Why not? You're a freakin' billionaire. You could give her everything," Logan pressed.

"And in the end, I couldn't keep her safe. And if she's with me, I'll destroy her," Xander said, his tone of voice so hollow it made Logan reel in his anger.

"You can't destroy someone, Xander."

"I destroyed Olivia," Xander said softly, staring at his hands.

Logan paced over to the wall of windows, turned, and faced his boss. "And how did you do that?"

"Let's focus on getting Harper back.""Yeah, I can't do that from here." He wanted to shake him. Logan wasn't made for sitting behind a desk. He needed to be doing something.

"Fuck this. They can't keep us in here. Let's go."

21

CHAPTER TWENTY-ONE - XANDER

"Owning the building has to count for something." His palms were sweating.

Luis and Asher stood, arms crossed in front of their chests, blocking the doors.

"Good evening, gentlemen. Let us through."

"Sorry, Mr. Montague, our orders are not to let you and Mr. Marrock leave the building."

"On whose authority?" Xander asked, but he already knew.

"Ares, Sir. You can follow Team Stealth through a video feed. A monitor has been set up in your office, and Meg Carlson is upstairs if you need any technical help."

"You got to be kidding me," Logan said, running his hand through his hair.

"Doing our job, Mr. Marrock," Luis said.

Xander cursed under his breath, turned on his heel and flung open the doorway to the stairs.

"Hey! I'm coming too," Logan said.

"I'm not stopping you," Xander said.

"If it weren't for you, she wouldn't be missing."

Xander stopped on the stair and turned to look at Logan. The man's eyes were wide, and a thin bead of sweat was on his forehead. As usual, before a job, Logan was looking for a fight.

"And maybe if you gave her the reassurances she needs, she would have told you about going to this audition."

"Maybe if you had given her what she wanted, she wouldn't be seeking it elsewhere," Logan scoffed.

"I have done everything to protect Harper, Logan. Not getting romantically involved with her is another way I protected her. How have you protected her?"

"I didn't know she *needed* protecting. You have the most highly trained staff on the planet, and you didn't tell us she was in danger!"

Xander continued on the steps, Logan's voice echoing off the walls. Xander knew he was right. He wanted to cocoon Harper and keep her safe, but he didn't want to share her. After Olivia, Harper became his redemption.

Throwing open the door, Xander marched into the executive branch, taking in the mess on Harper's desk.

"The more stressed she is, the messier she becomes," Xander murmured.

"Yeah, I've noticed," Logan said.

"When we had our date at the symphony, she asked if she could have one secret. She must have meant that audition. I should have pushed her harder, but she changed the subject."

"She's good at that." Logan nodded. "I've let her get away with distracting me more times than I should have. She hates talking about her feelings."

"She hates being vulnerable," Xander said.

"But I want to spank her ass for not telling you she was going to audition. For her not telling me."

"Forget the spanking. She needs a good caning, enough to crack through that tough shell of hers."

"Make her break down and cry," Logan agreed, nodding.

"This is pitiful," Xander said, picking up a pile of file folders, crumpling up granola wrappers, and revealing two electronic tablets that should have been in the safe. "I'll get her naked ass in here, organizing every piece of paper."

"I want her on a leash, never to leave my sight again," Logan said.

"She's in so much trouble," they said in unison.

Xander started at Logan's intense expression. "It doesn't bother you that I...?"

"Love her?" Logan asked.

Xander paused, moving another pile of paperwork to the side, meeting Logan's intense stare. "Yeah."

Damn, admitting it was easier than he'd thought it would be when it came to it. He should have done it before.

"You rescued her from a horrible fate, took care of her, protected her, and fell in love with her," Logan said softly. "I can't begrudge you that, but I love her, Xander. And denying that you love her isn't a way of showing *her* I love her. It would be me being a jealous prick."

"Some men would say the opposite."

"I'm not most men." Logan glared at him.

He'd hired Logan Marrock for his skills gained as a search and rescue tech and because he wore his heart on his sleeve.

Xander stuck his hand out. "I'm sorry, I was an asshole."

"I'm sorry I lost my shit on you." Logan returned the clasp. "Maybe we can work this out?"

Xander shook his head. "You taking care of Harper... I can live with that. I can't have another submissive."

"Why?" Logan asked.

"I once had a slave. I ruined her." Xander spat out the words.

"Sorry to interrupt the party, but I have things you need to see," Erik and Ares came out of Ares's office. Erik passed him an iPad.

"Show us."

"Pictures of Nadia and Theo Denson. If you flip to the fifth photo, it gets worse."

Looking at the pictures, seeing Nadia and Theo clink wine glasses, seeing him lock lips with her made his blood boil. Damn, that man was an awful human being.

"Who is Theo Densen?" Logan asked.

Xander turned him out as he scrolled to the next pictures. "Goddammit."

"Theo Densen is an investment banker with too much time and money on his hands. He's also the brother of Xander's ex-slave, Olivia."

"He hates my guts. I never thought he would come after me. I always thought he was too spineless. I was wrong." His voice shook.

"Here he is with Dorian Martin at some fundraising party and outside Dorian's manufacturing plant. If I guess, he invested in aircraft technology. Here's Nadia, Ian McIomhair's ex, locking lips with Theo in the doorway of his house."

"Yeah, they're pretty hot and heavy," Erik commented grimly.

"Nadia must have mentioned the poker game to Theo," Xander mused. Though Nadia was kind to Harper that first night, he had never liked her much and always thought Ian could do better.

"Why would Theo care?" Logan asked.

Suddenly, Xander's body felt heavy, as if there was a booted foot on his chest. He lowered himself into the club chair by the window and faced his friends. "He blames me for his sister's accident. For her becoming a paraplegic."

"His sister is a manipulative bitch who only wanted you for your money," Ares snarled.

Logan raised his eyebrows. "How long were you and her together?"

"Six years too long," Xander murmured. "I thought she was the slave I needed."

"She whined," Ares bit out. "Didn't communicate what she needed."

"I thought she was happy," Xander said. He ran his hands through the long strands of his hair and shook his head. "Until the night I came home with a prenup agreement. She shrieked at me that I didn't trust her. Ran out of the house in the rain."

"Xander went after her. She wasn't wearing a jacket or shoes," Ares said.

"And she crashed her car right into a pole, swerving to miss an oncoming vehicle."

"Theo showed up shortly after, accusing Xander of abuse," Ares shook his head. "Xander gave her that car the year before. She spent months in a private rehab, which Xander paid for."

"Theo was livid," Xander said. "But maybe he was right. I demanded a lot from Olivia."

"And she gave it. But there was little communication between you two," Ares said.

Xander glanced away from his brother. Ares had always tried to assuage his guilt about the accident.

"I brought Harper home just two months after Olivia's accident. And Ian and Nadia broke up that spring. I blamed myself for Olivia's accident. I still do. If I hadn't chased her out of the house..." His voice broke.

The past didn't matter. The only thing that mattered was finding Harper.

"You did not cause that accident, Xander. Olivia and her reckless driving did," Ares said.

"I haven't had a relationship since. Telling myself what I need in a slave is too much."

"But you never gave Harper a chance," Logan said.

"No, I didn't. As I had Harper to take care of, the pain Olivia caused faded. Logan, she's my redemption, and I will not risk her."

"But you're a different man now than you were then," Ares pointed out.

"What you've done to Harper isn't fair."

Xander's phone beeped, and he hit the speakerphone. "Quinn?"

"We tracked the van to the old Starlight Hotel's parking lot. Witnesses saw it enter the parking lot, but nobody saw the van come out of the parking lot. We figure they changed cars. We searched inside the hotel and asked the staff, but no sign of Harper. We're going to circle the area again to talk to anyone who has seen her." Quinn's voice was sure and steady.

"Good work, Quinn," Ares said. "We have full confidence in you."

"Going to send through a list of properties that I want you to search," Xander said.

"Yes, boss." Quinn clicked off.

"So, it's not Harper's family searching for her. It's Theo Densen?" Logan asked, pacing in front of Xander's desk.

"It's a big family. And it could be both."

"You're sure the aunt and uncle were dealt with, the one who set fire to her childhood house?" "Yes, her aunt was dealt with," Xander said, exchanging a look with his brother. He wasn't going to divulge how, but the Ambassador's daughter to Turkey was also a victim of hers. In exchange for Axis Management rescuing her, he had assumed she was either buried or in a Turkish prison somewhere. "But this operation is huge, reaching across many continents. She has more uncles and cousins all up to their necks in this business."

Xander reached over and hit the button for Meg.

"Yes, boss?"

"Run a search for all properties owned by Theo Densen and send it down to us."

"You got it," Meg said.

Damn, his heart was about to explode. He needed to find Harper. He needed to hold her, if only for a moment.

Ares's phone buzzed in his hand. "Ah, finally, here's the photo from the contact at the police station."

"It's just a kid," Logan said, looking over his shoulder. "A brother?"

The shape of the eyes bore a resemblance to Harper. "She doesn't have a brother. Is it possible he's the one who took Harper?

I don't know. Erik, have you seen him hanging about?""No. I would have remembered the resemblance."

Xander's tablet flashed at him, Meg sending him through a 3D blueprint of the hotel.

"This shows the entire parking lot."

"What if they dropped Harper off at the hotel? What if people were waiting there for her?" His stomach hit the floor as he pointed to a door beside the elevator block. "Look, this door here has to go somewhere."

Logan leaned over Xander's shoulder with a grunt.

"Call Quinn back to get them to check it out," said Xander, confident someone would do as instructed.

"Let's go meet them, Xander," Logan urged softly.

"You are staying here," Ares said.

"Look, Ares, we have a plan now. And I am feeling fine. I'll stand back, but I need to see her with my own eyes, okay? You do too." Logan slapped his hand on Xander's shoulder.

A lump formed in Xander's throat. "No, I can't."

"You have your best men at your back. Come on, let's go."

His palms were sweaty at the thought of leaving his office. After a few moments, he looked at Logan's steady glare and Erik's quiet presence and knew he would be in expert hands.

"Okay. Let's go do this," he said.

"I'm going to stay here, command centre it all," Ares said.

Xander nodded. His brother always had his back.

Logan clapped him on the back, and Xander tried to breathe. He could do this. For Harper, he could confront his fears and battle through his anxiety. She was more than worth it.

22

CHAPTER TWENTY-TWO - HARPER

Harper's pulse jumped, coming out of her skin. She wiggled her shoulders, trying to twist out of the duct tape her hands were bound with behind her back. Her body hurt.

Her mind kept replaying when two men had thrown her in the blue panel van, and her smoothie flew through the air like a strawberry ribbon. A knot of fear had lodged deep in her stomach. She froze. After all those years of being on high alert, she had failed when it came time to try out those hard-won self-defence skills. She hadn't had a chance to escape; the men had clasped her arms hard as they sat in the van with her, one on either side.

She tried to focus on the time and count off how many moments it was between her being thrown in the van and the van stopping, but as the man's fingers dug into her arm, it took all her focus not to cry.

It had taken her years to believe she wasn't in danger, that her family would not track her down and drag her back into their prostitute ring, into their crime. She had fought so hard to finish high school, get her degree, to make a life.

And as time went on, the memories of her aunt calling her names and telling her that her mother was ungrateful, bringing shame to the family, the memory of the fire at her mother's beautiful dance studio, their house, all of it had faded.

It had faded as Xander made her go to counselling. As he gave her a job as his assistant. She had never stopped missing her parents, especially her beautiful mother, who believed that dance could heal any broken heart.

Her mother's oval face, with her bright eyes, swam in Harper's mind for a moment, abruptly replaced by her aunt's pinched countenance, tying Harper to the rail in the basement, keeping her that way, night after night, until the night it was Harper's turn to be sent out.

And then, as if in a scene from a movie, she found herself whisked into the hotel room, huddled over by two big strong men, protected by them. It took her a long time to realize they weren't mad at her; they were angry at the people who had placed her in this situation.

God, Xander. She owed him so much, no matter what he said. She wouldn't have this busy, hectic, wonderful life if it weren't for him. She wished she had pushed him harder. She knew he liked taking his time with decisions. His read on people was so precise because he didn't rush into action. It was one of the things she loved about him.

Harper sobbed, her thoughts crowding her head. Xander had done so much for her. But it didn't matter. They would come and take her to... wherever they were operating these days, maybe back in Blakvasitaikn.

Her decision to keep the secret of who she was from Logan haunted her. He had shown her love and care, and attention. He might have supported her if she had been honest with him and told him about the dance audition. Not only honest, brave. If she had been brave enough to tell them both that she loved them, she wouldn't have felt it necessary to storm out of Xander's office, needing space, her heart aching. Maybe she would have seen a sign of this happening. Maybe she would have noticed someone following her. Perhaps she shouldn't have discounted the times she had felt like someone was watching her. She should have told them. She had ditched her security team. Sobs racked her chest, full out, messy crying.

In all the years since she had lost her family, it had never felt like she didn't have one. She had the Bandit Brothers. Quinn, who was like a big brother to her, she could have easily spilled her secrets to him, and once or twice she had thought about it. Gabe, a month ago, asked her if she was all right, with that crystal gaze of his that missed nothing. Nick always brought her favourite coffee just for her, even though it was on the opposite side of where he lived. She had Claudia, her assistant, Gardenia, her friend, and Kayleigh. Pure frustration ran like fire pinpricks through her system. She screamed, the heartache choking her.

A clanking sound from outside rattled her. Here they were. They were going to take her. She'd wrecked her life. She bit hard down on her lip, and the pain crystalized her thoughts.

Recalling her self-defence training, she took deep breaths and focused. The dark space smelled musty. Her knees felt the floor's hardness, and her shoulders ached from her hands being secured behind her.

The clanking sound echoed throughout the room, and Harper's heart thumped like a pair of Congo drums. Tightening her core muscles, she arched her back and brought her hands down just above her hip bones. It hurt, but she felt the tape give a little.

She took another deep breath and tried it again, picturing exactly how Janette Jennings taught her in her women's self-defence course.

For a moment, she stood still, shocked that it worked. But then she shook out her wrists and felt the tape give. She pulled the tape off her wrists as she ran to the door.

As she reached for the handle, the door was flung open, and a man with a silver mustache glowered at her.

"Where were you going?" He smirked. "I've waited years for this." He stalked towards Harper, and she gulped in the air, trying to stay calm.

God, to be so close and not make it. No, she wouldn't let desperation cloud her thoughts. She ran by the man, and he grabbed her around the waist.

Harper kicked at him and screamed. He tightened his hold. "No, you don't. Xander destroyed something precious to me. It's time for me to do the same to him."

Harper leaned all her weight against the man's arm and kicked back at him. He let go, and she dropped to the ground, scrambling up as he grabbed her ankle.

Not a chance, Harper thought as she kicked and twisted out of his grasp. The man caught her by the arm, jerking her off the floor. He threw her to the ground, his body over hers. His eyes blazed with hatred.

She screamed.

With a shriek of rage, Harper formed a point with her fingers together and jabbed the right one into the man's eye.

"You fuckin whore!" Holding his left eye, he stumbled to his knees but snatched her by the arm in a bruising hold.

From behind her came a *BOOM*!

"Don't think so, buddy." The twangy Québécois accent of Nick Laurent felt like a breath of hope.

Her rescuer heaved the guy to his feet, and Gabe gripped his other arm.

"Hey, Harper. You hardly needed us at all," Quinn said.

The instant she put her hand in Quinn's, tears clouded her eyes. The air rushed out of her as she slumped against Quinn's chest.

"What the fuck, Theo?" Logan marched into the room. And behind him, not even sparing a glance for Theo, Xander.

"We're here, Kitten."

She fell into those muscular arms with a sob, catching the familiar scent of woodsy mixed with leather. "We have you, Angel."

Without letting go of Logan, Harper reached for Xander, his solidness, and the familiarity and comfort of the two men she loved.

23

CHAPTER TWENTY-THREE - LOGAN

Logan held her tighter as she trembled in his arms.

"Here, Angel, let's get you outside," Xander said.

"Xander, we called the police. We'll keep an eye on him until they get here," Gabe said.

"Guess we had to," Xander muttered. "Come on, Angel."

They got her out of the concrete storeroom. On her right, Xander on her left, Logan guided her out of the building. She took two steps and stopped. A shudder wracked her body. She fell forward to her knees. Logan wrapped an arm around her side. Thank fuck they found her. Xander rubbed her back.

"We got you, Kitten."

"I was so scared," Harper said. She rubbed her wrists, which had duct tape on them. Xander held her hand between his and removed the tape from her without saying anything. Logan rubbed her wrist, taking it in his hands.

"I hate they had their hands on you. Did they hurt you?" Logan said.

The pain on Xander's face made his stomach lurch. It was precisely how he was feeling.

"No. Janette's self-defence training came into play."

"I'm so proud of you, Angel."

A police car pulled up next to the curb, and two officers climbed out, making their way over to them.

Xander rubbed Harper's back, whispered in her ear, "Let me take care of this," and then stretched out a hand to the first officer.

"Hello, officers," Xander said.

"We were told we'd find you here. We're going to take Mr. Densen into custody, but we need a statement."

Xander levelled a glare at them. "You can direct all questions regarding Miss Blake to my lawyer. She's expecting your call," Xander said, holding out a business card.

The police officers exchanged a look, and Logan could feel their annoyance. Xander stared them down, not budging.

"As you can see, Miss. Blake is fine. Tell them, Harper."

"Yes, I had a scare, but I am fine. I just want to go home."

Logan stared, shaking his head. *What would it be like to have that kind of power*? He pulled Harper tight against him. "Let's get going, Kitten."

"Okay, Mr. Montague. Your lawyer will hear from us."

Xander turned to Logan as the police car drove into the garage.

"My lawyer can hold them off, at least for tonight. They'll want to talk to her eventually, though." "Its fine, Xander. I feel okay, and Theo can't get away with what he did tonight, whatever his plan was. Thank god you guys came."

"I've arranged for Dr. Redden to meet us at the house, and Fleur will drop by tonight."

"No its okay, you don't have to—" Harper broke off as Xander glared at her.

"Oh, Kitten, you have no idea what we must do. We figured it would be easier for you not to go to the hospital, but you need to be checked over, and Xander's right. You need to talk to someone about this."

Harper shook her head. Logan sighed. Stubborn woman.

"Yes, you do, Angel," Xander said, holding her hands. "This might bring back unpleasant memories, and I want you to touch base with support right away. You have a show to get ready for, I heard."

She dipped her head, hiding her face.

"Oh yes, Kitten, we'll talk about that, too."

Erik pulled up in an SUV and jumped out. "Hey. I can drive you home if you want."

"Thanks, Erik, we're okay," Xander said.

"Yeah. We got it."

Erik saluted. "Harper, take care of yourself, or let these two do it."

Logan drove while Xander sat with her in the back, holding her hand. Logan met Xander's eyes in the mirror.

We need to take care of her.

Logan glanced at the GPS before turning onto the bridge.

"We're so happy you're all right, Angel."

"I didn't know who had taken me. I thought it was my family," Harper whispered.

"And we were out of our minds with worry," Xander said gently.

"I'm sorry." Xander wrapped an arm around her. "What matters is you are safe with us." "*Where you belong*," Logan said. He said it for Xander. Logan hoped Xander knew Harper belonged with both of them because the three of them worked. He loved Harper. He liked having Xander around. He was more than a friend, more than a brother. He was the other half of Harper's heart.

He drummed his fingers on the steering wheel as he drove into the neighbourhood brimming with stately mansions. Did all this wealth make him uncomfortable?

Yeah, a little bit.

"This is your house?" The gates swung open onto the vast estate. Logan whistled.

"Yeah," Xander said.

Logan rolled onto the stone driveway, past a small house, Harper's apartment, he guessed, past a fountain in the courtyard.

"Go around the back. The doctor is waiting for us," Xander said.

He couldn't give Harper this. He could keep a roof over her head and take her on vacation or two, but this was so outlandish that Logan couldn't believe what he was seeing. He didn't compare to Xander. Why would Harper want him?

A small-frame woman with short hair was leaning against her car. "Dr. Redden, thank you for coming," Xander said.

"Not a problem. Harper, let's get you inside and checked out. How are you feeling?"

"I'm okay. I'm just tired and shaky."

Xander took her arm. Logan took it all in, the beautiful landscaping, the stone patio under a pergola, and an entire outdoor kitchen. "Wow. Why do you ever leave here?"

Xander smiled slightly but didn't answer.

Inside, the doors opened to the chef's kitchen, high ceilings, and sleek modern finishes in black and white and gold palettes. Logan followed down a sprawling hallway, right to a bedroom door.

"Harper, why don't you change into something comfortable, and I'll be in when you call me?" the doctor suggested.

"I'll help you," Logan said.

"Anything you need, Harper, you let me know," Xander said.

"I can manage." Harper gave them both a small smile.

"You guys sit tight. I'll talk to you soon." The doctor gave them a look.

Logan followed Xander back to the kitchen.

"Drink?" Xander offered, going to a cabinet at the side of the counter.

"Whatever you're having."

Xander poured him a deep amber scotch. They clinked glasses, and Logan tossed it back, revelling in the buttery feel as it glided down his throat.

"That's marginally better," Xander said.

"Agreed." Logan sighed. "So that girl needs boundaries."

"Oh yes. She needs that caning."

"And to be pushed past her comfort zones. She needs to know we're here for her," Logan said. He stared at Xander. "You're in?"

Xander huffed out a breath. "For now. I need to make sure she's on her feet. I'll stay as long as I can."

It wasn't the most optimal news, but Logan would take it for now. He needed Harper to know Xander loved her. And he loved her, and she was completely safe with them, both of them.

Xander's phone beeped. "Fleur is here." He hit a panel on the wall.

A tall, slim woman entered the kitchen with a halo of curly dark hair. "Hello everyone! I hear Harper's had an adventure."

"Yes. I just want to make sure she's okay. I'd appreciate it if you could talk to her until we get her to the psychiatrist?"

"You know I won't divulge her confidence, Xander."

"I wouldn't dream of it. She's with Dr. Redden now," Xander said.

"I'll just pop down the hall. Here, Josie sent you all dinner." Fleur put a paper bag down on the counter.

"You're the best, Fleur. Thank you."

The woman nodded and brushed his hands away. Xander's phone rang again.

"Got to take this," he said.

Logan sighed, watching Xander pace back and forth in front of the patio doors.

What would it be like, Logan wondered, to have all these people at his beck and call? It would make life easier. He thought of Hana and how money didn't make her life easier. And Quinn's wife Simone had grown up with every privilege and found it suffocating.

No, money only helped when it was wielded so that it didn't cut off those closest to the wielder, and Xander, Logan realized, did that very well. Both the Montagues were quick to write a cheque and paid their employees generously. It was why he had been able to buy his condo.

It wasn't just the money, Logan realized. It was the personal connections and the relationships.

"So that was Ares calling to say he would stay at Axis Management tonight."

"How many bedrooms do you have here?"

"Ten, I think?"

Logan whistled. "Good of him to give us privacy, I guess."

Xander smiled thinly.

Dr. Redden entered the kitchen, nodding at them.

"Is she all right?" asked Logan.

"Not a scratch on her. I left her a script for a sleeping pill if she needs it and anxiety meds if this experience brings back memories. Monitor her, Xander and call me for anything.""Thank you."

"Of course."

"Is that the all-clear to beat some sense into that girl?" Logan growled.

"Absolutely," Xander said.

"Good." Logan couldn't wait to get her hands on her. Now that she was safe, he allowed his emotions to roll through him. She could have been seriously hurt or worse because she had lied to them about the audition.

"Xander, call me if you need anything. Harper says she's fine." Fleur put her hand on Xander's chest as she passed. "Go easy on her."

Xander leaned down and kissed the woman's cheek.

"You're the best, Fleur. Thanks for coming so quickly."-"Anything for Harper," Fleur waved goodbye and left.

"Let's go," Xander said.

It was a race to the bedroom. Xander knocked softly on the door, opened it and stepped through. Logan right on his heels.

Her light floral scent surrounded him. Light cream walls, a white iron Queen bed, and photos of a younger Harper with Ares and Xander decorated the wall, with lots of artwork of the ocean and beach.

"Hey, guys."

"*Hey, guys*? Darling, is that how you greet your Doms?" He took her hand in his, kissing her wrist, his tension easing by touching her.

"I'd hope she had better manners than that," Xander said mildly. He strode forward and took her chin in his hands. "Or did you forget?"Her eyes closed, her face scrunched up. "I'm so sorry."

"We don't want an apology," Logan rubbed her back. "We are happy you are okay, Kitten. But we are very..." Logan trailed off. He didn't want to say "angry" because he could never be angry with her.

"*Annoyed* by your behaviour," Xander finished for him.

"Why didn't you tell us about the audition?"

"I don't think that new team is going to work out for us," Harper said, winding a piece of her hair around her finger.

She did not just try to change the subject on us. He exchanged glances with Xander, knew he noticed that, too.

"Harper." Xander ran two fingers along her jawline. "Your Dom asked you a direct question. Answer it now or present your ass where you will feel both our belts across it." Xander nodded at Logan. Logan cupped the back of her neck.

She flushed, looked down, sighed, and glanced at him.

"I'm waiting, Harper" He pressed his thumb into the hollow at the base of her slender neck, noticing her body soften under their attentions. "If I told you, I would have to tell you about my past, or it felt that way. If I told you,"—Harper gestured to Xander—"You would have told me no. Or sent me with so much security I wouldn't have a chance."

"Do you believe that?" Xander asked.

"Yes." She flushed her gaze on their shoes.

His eyes met Xander's. He nodded, smiling slightly. This had been a long time coming, and their submissive needed it.

"You need to know we are here for you, no matter what, Kitten," Logan's hands slid down to Harper's waist.

"Hey!" she cried out as he flipped her on her stomach.

Xander gathered her abundant hair in his hand. "Pretty words Angel. Some of them are true."

"But not the whole truth," Logan said. His palm came down with a thud across her ass cheeks. Harper yipped in surprise.

"You left out how you felt. Remember? I told you to never hide from me. I want to know what you are feeling, what you are thinking."

Xander's hand came down hard again, causing Harper to twist away, and Logan held her in place.

"Oh, we're just getting started. Our belts need to meet your ass. Five sounds about right. You will count them, won't you, Angel?" He whispered in her ear. She shuddered, her eyes closing briefly. "Yes, Sir."

Together, they took off her pants and moved her arms, so they were stretched out in front of her. Logan rubbed his palm over her smooth ass. Xander stood up and ran his hands along with her calves. Logan joined in, rubbing her shoulders, warming their submissive up.

With a flourish, Xander took off his leather belt and wrapped the belt buckle in his palm. He flicked the belt between his hands. Harper jumped at the leathery whistling sound. Xander struck her ass.

"Ouch. One, Sir."

Logan heard the inhalation of her breath. God, she was so responsive, so eager to take this as if the three of them had done this before. He found Xander's dark gaze and saw how he felt reflected in his eyes.

He did the same thing with his belt, flicking his wrist so the very triangle tip of the strip of leather landed between her ass cheeks.

"Two Sirs," Harper said.

His cock stirred at hearing "sirs" from her mouth. Xander must have felt the same because, without a pause, his belt landed hard.

"Three, Sirs."

Harper yelped as Logan's belt snapped across the top of her thighs, her stomach lifting off the bed.

"Harper?" Xander reached over and pushed her down on the bed.

"Four Sirs." Logan placed his hand on her back, so damn proud of her.

Xander rubbed her ass, bringing his hand to the back of her neck. "Your ass is so rosy."

Logan snapped his belt, landing on the lower swell of her ass cheeks.

"Five thank you, Sir," Harper said. Her voice caught on the end.

"And one more for being out of position," Xander threw his belt across her ass before the words were out of his mouth.

Harper's shoulders tensed, but she stayed in position.

"Six, thank you, Sir."

Her body arched off the bed, her hand going to her ass. Xander caught it in his, threading his fingers through hers, tugged her in his lap.

"You will never leave this house without our permission again," he sat down next to them on the bed, tossing the belt on the floor. His palm caressed her cheek. She closed her eyes against his touch.

"You won't eat, sleep, or breathe without our permission," Xander said, cradling her.

Logan held her face in his hands, kissing her luscious lips so hard they swelled. He let her go and turned her to Xander, who seized her mouth like a starved man. The sight of their dark hair, the care Xander took with Harper as he kissed her, was damn sexy.

Logan put a hand on her neck as Xander deepened the kiss. Then he turned her to him, and, as his lips slanted over hers, he tasted the faint scotch breath. Harper moaned, and the sweet sound flooded his brain, hardening his cock. Xander ran his hands along her ribcage, over her breasts, kissing her neck.

"Yes, Angel, show us how much you regret not letting us in. Kiss him with all the passion you have."

And she did. Her tongue searched out his, Logan slung his arm between her and Xander's chest, and it felt so damn right. The three of them here, together.

He brought her forward on Xander's slap, his hands to her shirt. Together they pulled it off and slipped her baby blue lacy bra down.

Logan's hands moved over her smooth back, around her waist, over her hair. She was so good; it made him want to be better. Xander played with her breasts as Logan kissed her lips. It was so damn sexy he couldn't stand it.

"Do you like having both of us touch you?" Logan asked, breaking the kiss.

He felt Xander stiffen and saw him carefully study Harper's flushed face. Her eyes met his, then Xander's.

"Yes." Harper's words were breathless. "Please."

Logan nibbled her ear and pinched her nipple. Xander captured her lips and pinched and squeezed her other nipple. Harper's breathy squeals urged them on. Their hands roamed over her body. Logan caught her hair in his hand and pulled it.

"Then we will ravage you, and you're going to take all we give you, Kitten." Logan wanted her begging. He wanted to watch Xander's calm, calculated dominance make her beg.

"Yes," Harper said.

And it was his turn to kiss that mouth as he tugged her hair. His mouth fell on hers, demanding that she open to him. His tongue swirled with hers, and her taste went right to his cock.

Xander's hands cupped her breasts. "Offer your Dom your sweet nipples, Angel."

Her eyes dilated, the scent of her arousal heavy in the room—God, how their girl loved that kind of order.

She cupped her breasts, turning to him. Logan slid to the floor on his knees. His mouth came over her nipple. His tongue swirled around the hard point. Her squeal of pleasure sent shivers down Logan's spine. Logan sucked, lapped and nipped to the sounds of her sweet pants and mewls.

"Does his mouth on your nipple make you wet?" Xander pinched her other nipple in his hand. "Are you wet for us?"

"Yes!" Harper cried.

Logan took her other nipple in his mouth, sucking at it, biting it slightly as Xander squeezed the other one. She cried out, and a wave of desire coursed through Logan's body.

"Xander. Taste this nipple. It's so sweet," Logan said. He held her breast, angled up to the other man.

Harper whimpered as Xander took her nipple into his mouth. Harper's nails dug into his biceps.

"Please," Harper said.

Xander released her nipple, sliding her off his lap. "You are so sweet, Angel. You could fill me up forever."

Logan lifted her, sliding her on the bed.

"She's so beautiful," Logan said, tracing his hands on her leg.

"Naked and open, exactly how she should be," Xander said. "Spread, Angel."

She opened her legs, bringing her knees back.

Logan's fingers explored her swollen pussy.

"Xander, she's already soaked," Logan said.

"Let's see" Xander held her pussy lips apart and pressed on her clit.

"Xander!" Harper cried out as his fingers moved over her clit. Harper closed her eyes, her hips rising off the bed.

Xander removed his hand, took her head in his hands, and kissed her. Logan dipped his fingers into her folds. Logan drank in every sound, every expression that crossed her face. Feeling her clamp around his fingers as Xander took a nipple back in his mouth was a bolt of ardent desire to his cock. So damn hot. Harper's eyes closed, and her body arched forward. Xander moved his hand to her clit while Logan trailed his wet fingers over her hip, kissing her neck.

"Her clit is hard," Xander said. "She likes that."

"Good."

"I need to..." Harper moaned.

"Oh, I don't think you've earned it yet, Xander?"

Xander withdrew his fingers.

"Not at all. This is punishment, my sweet sub."

Xander's fingers dove into her again as Logan held her leg further apart. With a hiss, Logan felt her tremble beside him, kissing her mouth and sliding his arm around her body.

"She is so soaked. I could fit my fist in here."

Harper jerked at the words. Logan laughed, kissing her neck. "We'll have to try that someday, won't we?"

She moaned. Logan couldn't get enough of her. His mouth slid to her breasts. He took her hardened nipple into his mouth.

"Clean these fingers for me, Angel," Xander came on the other side, holding out his glistening fingers to her mouth.

Logan felt her vibrate with need, he let go of her nipple and stretching out beside her.

Harper's eyes widened, and her cheeks hollowed. Logan grabbed her hair, nibbling her ear. Her flush was so hot.

"I can't wait to feel her around my cock."

Damn, he couldn't hold out much longer, but he wanted to.

Harper bit her lip.

"Please."

Xander raised an eyebrow at him.

Yep, he agreed with a nod.

Harper's eyes closed again as he traced her jawline.

Yeah, the three of them needed this. This comingling was how they were going to reassure themselves that every inch of her body was okay. Logan needed to imprint her with his touch, and he knew by how deeply Xander's lips locked with hers. The same compulsion guided him.

24

CHAPTER TWENTY-FOUR - HARPER

Harper moaned as Logan pulled her nipple into his mouth, her legs closing, tension humming low in her pelvic floor. Xander's fingers circled her breast on the other side. His hand wrapped around her hair, and he tugged.

"Not yet. You won't like the consequences if you come before we allow you, Angel." Xander's dark eyes were glossy, full of wanting, and Harper's heart raced. She couldn't believe these two men were here with her. Both of them giving her pleasure, sharing her.

Urging them on, Harper spread her legs wide in an invitation, mewling. Logan's lip glided along her belly, around her mound.

"God, Xander, she smells so good. Taste her sweet cunt." Logan's heated glance sent pinpricks of desire all over her body.

Xander let go of her hair, switched spots with Logan, and Harper cried out as his tongue circled her clit, his fingers parting her labia.

Logan kissed her mouth, swallowing her cries, running his hands through her hair, his hot palm over her nipple. He squeezed and pulled. Her hips arched off the bed.

Xander slapped the inside of her thigh and flicked her clit.

"Wait, Angel," he said.

She nearly wept as his fingers left her throbbing clit. He wrapped his hand in her hair as Logan kissed her. Harper moaned low in her throat.

She touched their flat planes of muscles. She loved being sandwiched between them.

"I can't."The intense pleasure rolled through her, needing to explode.

"Yes, you can," Xander said in her ear as his hand squeezed her breast, his tongue gliding down her neck.

Logan's tongue swirled over her breast driving her to pleasure.

"I need..."

"Oh, we know what you need, Angel. But you denied us your needs, didn't you? So now we'll deny you and make you take what we give you. You will not come," Xander flicked her nipple.

Harper cried out. "Ow!" she covered it with her palm, desire flaring deep in her pelvic floor.

"Do you think she's good and sorry yet?" Logan said.

"I don't know. I think she should show you," Xander said.

"I think that's a great idea."

Xander pulled her hair around his fist. "On your knees," he said. He tugged her off the bed, and she followed his pull. Shaking and hollow, her pussy dripping with desire, she settled herself between Logan's feet. Her heart hammered. Xander stroked her hair, his hand cupping her chin. The slightest touch and she was his to command.

Her hands immediately went to Logan's waistband, and her trembling fingers unzipped his jeans. "I can't wait to see how you suck him," Xander said, his hand on her shoulder. Her skin grew heated from his words.

"I can't wait to feel your hot mouth on my cock, Kitten," Logan said, his hands on her cheeks, brushing her arms. Harper glided her hand around his long, thick cock, the skin soft, and her fingers could barely circle it.

"What are you waiting for, Angel?" Xander asked from behind her.

Harper needed no more encouragement. His cock slid right into her mouth. His male musk assaulted her, making her moan low in her throat. Logan played with her hair as she licked and sucked, drawing his length into her mouth as much as she could.

"Take all of him, Angel. See how he likes that? You look so beautiful sucking his cock," Xander said, his hand on her back. God, this made her feel so desirable, somehow. Logan's fingers danced along her throat, under her jaw.

"That's it, Kitten. Your hot mouth feels like heaven." Logan's low tone made her whimper.

"Don't forget his balls, Angel. Reach out and caress them. Give them a lick after you're done dragging that pretty tongue of yours from his tip to his root." Xander's instructions urged her as if she was a matchstick he had lit. She was wet and needy again, longing for cock to fill her as she licked and lapped Logan's full heavy testicles. Her mouth covered the tip of his glistening penis, and Logan threw his head back.

"See how his muscles bunch for you as you lick? He wants you. He's restraining himself." Xander's warm hand on the small of her back kept her grounded to him as she floated away, a heady mix of longing, desire and power coursing through her. She hummed around his cock, trying to take him deeper and deeper, so deep he bumped the back of her throat.

Xander rubbed his hand along her ass, around her tailbone, his touch sending all kinds of sensations racing along her body. She jumped as his hand landed on her sit spot.

"Don't think you're in charge, Angel," Xander said. God, how this man could read her.

"You so aren't, Kitten," Logan said, his hand fisting in her hair.

Xander knew what made people tick, and he knew what turned her on, which emotional string to pull to get her to play the tune he wanted. Logan loved sending her in a tizzy of scorching physical need. He loved pushing the physical boundaries and then getting into her mind. Between the two, she had everything she always wanted.

"Enough!" Logan roared, pulling out of Harper's mouth. He exchanged a look with Xander, and Harper cried out as Logan's hands came around her. "Now, you will take care of Xander. Convince him you are very sorry, Kitten."

Harper glanced over her shoulder and saw the set line of Xander's mouth and, for a moment, felt like he was going to reject her and send her away again.

"I can't promise you always, Angel," he said, his voice thick and hoarse.

She shook her head. "I'll take what you can give."

"Show me," Xander gritted out.

Harper sucked in a breath, met him on the floor, on her knees, and eased his pants off his feet. Then, reaching behind her, she twisted her hair into a bun and glided her hands up his leg. His cock stood erect, precum glistening.

Taking his hard cock in her hands, she licked the precum off, taking his cock slowly into her mouth.

"Suck it, Kitten," Logan said from behind her, his hands brushing over her nipples. She glanced up at Xander as she swallowed hard on him, hollowing her cheeks. His head was thrown back, his long black hair around him like a proud cape.

Behind her, Logan squeezed her nipples, pulling them up so hard that tears sprang to her eyes. She arched back against his muscular chest. Yes, she wanted this so much.

"Does sucking him make you as wet as when you did me?" Logan whispered, releasing her nipples.

God, their every touch was making her come apart. Logan's fingers dove into her pussy, his thumb pressing hard on her clit. She lapped Xander, cupped his testicles, saw his dark eyes held hers, and felt adored, as she was exactly where she wanted to be, between these two men.

"If you don't stop, I will explode, Angel." Xander wrenched her hair up as Logan pinched her clit, making her cry out in the exquisite pain they wrought.

Xander lifted her from the floor and took her back to the bed.

"Flat on your back, Kitten now," Logan said. He took off his shirt, placing it on her dresser.

"I want to feel your walls around me nice and deep, Angel," Xander removed his shirt.

He climbed on the bed, settling between her legs. Logan positioned himself beside her, kissing her neck, the swell of her breasts. Her entire being hummed with need.

"Are you ready for us, Kitten?" Logan asked his hot breath on her ear. "Yes!"

She felt the heat from Xander's eyes as he settled between her legs. She licked her lips, seeing his hand around his hard cock.

"Please, Xander." She wanted him to know how much she needed him.

"You can do better than that, Kitten. Beg him."

Xander took his cock in his hand, touching it ever so slightly to her pussy.

Ach! It made her crazy. "Please, Sir, fuck me with your cock" Xander closed his eyes, his pushing her thigh open. He pressed his cocks head against her pussy lips, and Harper cried out as his thick cock entered her.

He slid it in and out, slowly dragging it along every nerve ending she had, lighting her up with firey desire, making her need too big to ignore.

"Beautiful. Look how your hips come to meet his thrusts," Logan whispered, his hot breath against her ear making her shudder as his fingers took her nipple between them.

"God!" Harper moaned, unable to hold it in.

"Does that feel good, Kitten? Do you need his cock?"

"Yes!" Her body folded forward. She grabbed the sheets as Logan devoured her lips. Xander hammered her. His power, his innate masculinity, blanketed her. Harper cried.

Too intense. The relief loomed just out of reach, and she arched, frustrated.

"No, not even," Logan said, his hands under her head.

"Angel, you feel so good."

Harper closed her eyes, her hips arching to meet his pounding thrust when he suddenly pulled out. Harper cried, twisting away at the absence.

"Please, Logan. Please, Xander," she said.

"Please, what?" Logan moved down the bed, positioning himself at her entrance. "Please, sirs, may I have an orgasm?"

Harper gasped. Logan's cock was deep in her, long strokes that she felt right by the entrance of her womb. And then Xander's mouth covered her, his hand on her breast, his leg over hers. God, it was everything. Everything she had wanted and longed for and dreamed about.

She wanted to crawl out of her skin, the wicked sensations making her gasp. Then it was Xander's cock, quickly pumping in and out. Logan's hands on her nipples, pulling them, twisting them, made her scream. Xander withdrew. He slapped her breasts so hard the sound echoed in the room. "God, yes!"

Logan lifted her hips and plunged into her.

She felt so stretched, so aching. Her pussy walls clamped around his cock, sending her higher and higher. Logan drilled into her, her whole body aflame, in pleasure or torture, she couldn't tell. Her head spun.

"Look how red your breasts are, Angel. Look how you are nothing more than pure need. Need for us to take." His hands came under her breasts, and he pulled her sensitive nipples. "Come for us, now." A burst of pleasure rolled over her, tears running down her face, her vision blurred.

"Harper!" Logan yelled her name. His hot release gushed in her. He leaned forward, keeping his weight off her, and kissed her, searing their joining.

She collapsed against Xander's chest and reached for his cock with her fingers.

"I want you too," she said.

"Being greedy, are we?" Xander said.

"Asking for what I need."

He gave her a small smile and shook his head. "What are we going to do with her, Logan?"

"Give her so many orgasms she can't think."

Again, as if they had always shared her, they switched places, Logan stroking her hair as Xander settled himself on his biceps.

"You are so gorgeous, Angel. You mean the world to us." Xander eased in his cock, right to his balls and stayed there for a moment.

Harper grabbed at thick, muscular arms. Xander's. Logan's. Both.

"He's a very patient man, Kitten," Logan said, trailing his fingers along her jaw. "You're going to take it."

Xander closed his eyes. "She's gushing, swamping with juice."

His powerful body started to shift above her. Slowly he thrust deep into her. He increased his speed until he was pounding her. Logan grabbed her ass and propped her up, so her arms were on Xander's shoulders.

This orgasm hit her like a tornado. She screamed, tears leaking down her face as the starburst of pleasure consumed all her thoughts. She opened her eyes a little and saw Xander's face go slack. His head lifted as she felt his hot semen in her.

Logan reached down and kissed her softly. Xander rolled beside her.

She lay with her head on Logan's shoulder, breathing hard.

Harper laid between them as her heart rate decreased, a hand on both of their chests, and she couldn't feel any more content. After a while, she shifted from between them.

"Where do you think you're going?" Logan said.

"To the bathroom."

"It's like she doesn't listen," Logan said.

"Sometimes she's so stubborn," Xander said.

"Ow!"

The next thing Harper knew, she was flat on her stomach across Xander's lap, and his hand came down hard on her ass.

"Remember when you agreed you wouldn't do anything without our permission? We meant it." Logan's growly voice sent a tremor of fear through her, and Harper moaned.

"Absolutely." Xander spanked her hard, tears leaked from the corner of her eyes. "What do you say now, Angel?"

"May I go to the bathroom, Sirs?"

"Yes, you may." Logan kissed her forehead. "All you had to do was ask. I think a shower's a great idea, don't you, Xander?"

"You have five minutes of privacy before we join you," Xander said.

"What are you waiting for, Kitten? Go!" Logan swatted her ass playfully, and Harper ran into the bathroom of her old bedroom. Washing her hands, she glanced at herself in the mirror. Her eyes were bright. Her lips were swollen. Her breasts were still flushed from their administrations. A few hours ago, she had thought of not being back with Logan and Xander, and she had longed for them. It was surreal that she was here with them now. Harper took her time to the very last minute and tried to shut her thoughts away. She was here, with the men she loved, and she was safe.

A knock on the door had her drying her hands on the towel and smiling as Xander and Logan crowded the doorway.

"Get in that shower, Kitten," Logan said.

"Yes, Sir."

From the panel beside the shower stall, Xander set the temperature, and the full-body jets flared to life. Harper closed her eyes, lifting her face to the gentle spray. She moaned as Logan kissed her neck, brought her close to his body, and mewled as Xander climbed in behind her. Between the two men, desire spiked through her. Xander's hands roamed her back. Logan captured her mouth in a demanding kiss.

Xander nudged her legs apart as the kiss went on, arched her bottom against Xander's erection as Logan circled his arms around her. Xander kissed her, waking up new waves of need as Logan plunged his fingers into her.

"You drive me wild, Kitten."

"I want more of you. What do you think?" Xander said in her ear.

"I... that won't get me clean," Harper said. As Xander nibbled on her ear, her words felt slurred as his hands came around to knead and squeeze her breasts.

"We said to get in the shower. We said nothing about clean, did we, Logan?"

"No, I don't believe we did."

God, it was too much. The warm spray of water flowing over her head, two sets of hands running over her, fingers strumming her clit. Harper gasped as Xander sank his thumb in her anal whorl and stood on her tiptoes as Logan pressed on her clit.

Logan's lips slanted against hers. Then Xander's mouth was on hers, kissing her, squeezing her flesh, heating her skin. The heat in her simmered, and with one more touch, two more touches, fingers filling her, tongues dancing with hers, she shrieked as the growing inferno of pleasure couldn't be contained, she screamed, falling against them.

A strong, muscled arm came around her. "Angel, you are so beautiful."

Logan opened the shower door, water dripping off his toned skin. He held a big fluffy towel out for her, and Xander backed her into it. Together, the men dried her off from head to toe. She watched as Xander dried his long black hair, as Logan quickly dried off. She tried to form words. How could she express how grateful she was for both these men?

After Xander hung up all the towels, they brought her into the bedroom. Logan lifted her off the floor and into bed and wrapped an arm around her. Xander stood by; Harper watched the tense expression on his face and stiffened.

"Come to bed, please, Sir," she said.

He flinched for a moment.

"Come on, Xander, let's make sure she's safe and warm tonight," Logan said.

Xander nodded. "For tonight."

Sliding in next to Harper, he took her chin in his fingers. "Few things I wouldn't do for you, Angel," he said, kissing her deeply, and when he broke off the kiss that made desire bloom again, Logan was there, his tongue dominating her, making sure she knew he was there for her.

"Sleep, Kitten," he said. Bringing her against his chest, Harper snuggled against him, Xander slipped his leg between hers, and Harper drifted to sleep, snuggly sandwiched between the two hearts she loved.

25

CHAPTER TWENTY-FIVE - XANDER

A trilling from somewhere startled Xander awake. He carefully eased out from under Harper, her hair spilling across the pillow as he tucked the sheet around her chin. She sighed her sleep and snuggled closer to Logan.

Damn. Last night had blown his mind apart. He had never thought about sharing Harper, never considered he could have anything with her and Logan's ease with sharing her; inviting Xander in felt like a gift. One he would treasure always.

He grabbed the phone from his pocket. "Yes?"

"You promised you would leave me alone! What did my brother ever do to you! You can't ruin his life like you ruined mine!"

Xander moved quickly. Closing the door, he went through the glass doors to the balcony at the end of the hall.

"Olivia?" he said.

"Yes, you asshole. Who else would call you? Did you ruin anyone else's life lately? You promised to leave me alone."

Xander shut his eyes against the memory. The last time he visited her at the rehab facility, he had gone to make sure she was getting everything she needed. That was when she had told him she didn't love him and had been pretending for three years.

He had been crushed. As someone who felt he was great at reading people, Olivia's deception had cut him deep.

"Your brother made his own choices. Choices have consequences," Xander said through gritted teeth.

"Fuck you, you asshole." Oliva slammed the phone on him. He probably deserved that because if he had caught on that being a slave wasn't really in Olivia's soul; he would have released her. Not plan to put a ring on her finger. She felt because she let him be kinky with her, he owed her. He shook his head.

He didn't want to chance it with Harper. He couldn't.

As extraordinary and out of this world as the night had been, that's all it was, one night. He was damn lucky to get that. The wind whipped his hair around, and Xander went back inside, grabbed a shower, and quickly dressed.

"Morning." Logan met him in the kitchen, looking clean, his shirt undone and his pants on.

"Coffee?" Xander offered.

"No, got anything else? How did you sleep?"

"Dreamlessly. You?" Xander tossed him a sports drink.

"Same. I'm just so relieved to have Harper safe with us, where she belongs."

Xander filled the coffeemaker, pressed start, and turned and faced his friend.

"Logan, last night was incredible, but it's not realistic. You know I can't give Harper everything she needs."

"What are you talking about? I thought we covered this. You can give her way more than I ever could. She trusts you."

Xander shook his head. "And I can't risk breaking that trust. Last night was a one-time thing. I'm too old for her. I've done my best."

"That's bullshit, Xander. You're scared. You read her so well. You know when she needs a firmer hand when she needs discipline, and I'm still working on that. You give the boundaries that she craves."

"You'll figure it out, Marrock. You're a smart guy."

Logan crossed his arms over his chest and shook his head. "So, what was your plan? To leave us in the middle of the morning? Without saying goodbye?"

"I had hoped to be out before you two had woken up. I was going to send a text or an email or something."

"Fuckin coward."

"Never said I wasn't," Xander replied evenly. "Now that Harper is safe—"

"Are you sure? We haven't tracked down who was looking for her yet."

"Erik's on it. I'll find out who from her family is after her and keep her safe."

"How, if you're going to leave? You know I can't be a part of Axis Management, right? You can't just expect us all to go back to normal. If you care for her, Xander, you got to give it a chance, us a chance."

Xander's throat muscles clenched, and he stared at Logan. "If you want to walk away from Axis Management and leave Team Stealth, I get it. I'll make sure there is a security detail on her until her family is caught."

"What do you mean, my family?" Harper came around the corner of the kitchen, leaning on the wall. "They're looking for me?"

Her face was ashen, and Xander mentally kicked himself. Logan ran to her and held her. "Kitten, we'll figure this out."

"Xander, you knew someone was looking for me and didn't tell me? How could you?"

"Angel, I was keeping you safe. I thought someone from your past was looking for you before we realized it was Theo Densen, getting back at me through you, and I am so sorry for that. I've kept you safe for years, Harper, and I will never stop looking out for you."

Harper hid her face in Logan's chest and shook her head. "You were just going to leave me to wake up to find you gone? And then what, expect me to answer your phones on Monday? You say I mean the world to you, but here you are treating me as if I am only your assistant."

He stalked towards her and peered into those eyes. "You have always been more to me than an assistant, and you know it. I am sorry I can't be what you want me to be."

She gasped. He flinched, seeing the hurt in her eyes.

"Xander, you told me I was strong."

"Harper, you are the strongest I know."

"But I believed that because I saw how strong you are, even though your anxiety gets the best of you, and you had your past and Olivia. You care so much about the people you surround yourself with, but now, Xander, you are being something! I don't know! You're choosing to ignore what happened last night. It was the best night of my life because both of you were with me." Harper slipped her hand in Logan's. Reached out for his. "Stay and work it out with us."

Goddess knew he wanted to.

But he couldn't.

He had to go and do what he could to take care of them both.

He strode out of the kitchen, his heart trying to beat its way out of his chest. It was better if he locked himself away and gave them time to decompress. Give him time, too, because his heart couldn't take being around the two people he loved most.

In his bedroom, he paced, trying to calm himself. He clicked open his laptop, lost himself in the updates from Team Tech and before he knew it, an hour had passed. Knowing the coast was clear and hating himself for being the coward Logan had called him, he called Carli to pick him up. He couldn't be with the girl he wanted to be with, but he could help make sure her future was bright, and she was taken care of.

***

"So, it's going to take longer than you like." Alicia Doyle adjusted her glasses and peered over her iPad screen.

"How long?" Xander asked their top lawyer.

"Four months at a minimum. You'll have control of SolCan and Martin Industries by the spring."

"Axis Management will need a new department just for these hostile takeovers," Ares said.

Xander glared at his brother. "Then we'll make another department. We are losing the Personal Threat Assessment and Division department."

"Yes, the bodyguard assets. I have that final bid right here. Just sign." Alicia held out a pen and passed the document to Ares.

"Are you sure?" Ares asked.

Xander pushed his chair back and walked the length of the room. When he'd first started Axis Management, he wanted to help people. He wanted to provide top-notch security services across all different areas and hire the best people he could find. The bodyguards kept them afloat for their first years in business. The Mulberry Stevens case had brought so much business that it had helped pay for this building. But he didn't want just to guard celebrities. He wanted to rescue people who needed rescuing; he wanted to know the people who needed a highly trained team of former military personnel and needed those services could count on him, not to have his name highlighted in the press each time they took on a high-profile client.

Damn, he was going to miss the people. "Yeah, I'm sure." Standing next to his brother, he scrawled his name and passed the paperwork to Alicia.

"God help anyone who messes with you two," Alicia said, pushing her chair up. "Anything else?"

"No."

"See you later." Alicia grinned and waved at them as she strode out of the conference room.

"This doesn't bring back Jordan," Ares said.

"No, but I won't have people fuck with us, Ares. I will destroy Dorian Martin. I will take everything his great grandfather built and make it as if that company never existed. He could have told Theo to fuck off; instead, he handed over his technology, either knowing what Theo was doing or not bothering to find out," Xander said.

"The story about Theo being abusive to his paraplegic sister has been leaked. What did Harper say in her statement?"

"I don't know," Xander said.

"She's such a strong woman. I don't know how she has the strength to keep going."

"I don't know either, but I got to figure out who from her family is looking for her. I am not resting easy about that. So far, Erik hasn't turned up any leads about who that man is who filed the report."

"What's happening with the show she auditioned for? Is she going to go through with it?"

Xander shook his head. "I don't know."

"Didn't she come home with you last night? There's a lot you don't know about the woman you've looked after for all these years."

Xander brought his fist down on the table. "Got a point here, Ares?"

"Yeah. Why did you walk out on Harper?"

"Because it was time. Because I am too old for her. I'm too Dom for her. Because I don't want to break another woman to have her brother come at me years later, okay?"

Ares held his hands out. "Okay. I was only asking."

Xander shook his head at him.

"We still haven't figured out how Theo knew Team Stealth was there that day." "Working on it," Xander said.

"Is this your new office, then? Should I have tech people bring down all your equipment? I'm sure it's going to be hard not to see Harper every day."

Nobody goaded him like his little brother. "I'm going to check on R&D. Want to come with me?"

"No. I trust that we are going to make a mint with SolCan. Thanks for letting me acquire."

Xander shrugged. "It's a good idea. We can't always just rely on people."

"You would know," Ares said. "See you later."

His brother gave him a mock salute, and Xander sighed. He knew this was the best path forward, but his heart screamed at him that it would be a lonely one.

26

CHAPTER TWENTY-SIX - HARPER

"Thanks for helping me!" Ella said. "I have to get these orders shipped today. I've been working non-stop on them, and they're finally done."

"They're so pretty," Harper said, fingering the silky fabric of a corset laid out on the table. "I'm happy to help. I've been a little bored lately."

She carefully wrapped the corset, boxed it up, taped the box, applied the shipping label, and went on to the next one. Outside, they had a panoramic view of the rainy grey skies, but inside Ella's cavernous living room, with the fire in the fireplace and the lights dimmed just right, it was warm and cozy. Though it was hard not to feel friendly and happy being around Ella.

Ella used half of the great big space, with its wooden beams and sloped walls, as her workspace, where she handmade custom kink wear and corsets and donated the entire proceeds to charity.

After a little consideration, Harper had told Ella about the show and that she and Logan were living together. It felt good to be living in the open.

"I thought you would be busy rehearsing. *Canada's Best Dancer*. That's so exciting!" Ella said.

Harper flushed. It was weird to be open about things. But even with all the activity surrounding her preparation for the show, Harper had felt unsettled.

"I rehearse tomorrow. It's a tight schedule, so it's nice to have a break," Harper said, moving over to the next order to be wrapped.

"What does Logan think about this?" Ella asked.

Harper frowned as she wrapped. Logan hadn't said much. He had been helping a friend of his out at the indoor rock-climbing place, working out a lot. They had dinner together every night, and the sex in the bedroom was great, but Logan didn't seem to care when she left her dishes on the counter or didn't pick up her clothes. She forgot to study for the test she had with her course and got a low grade on it, and Logan had just smiled at her and said she would do better next time.

"He wants me to do what I want."

"Well, it's nice to have his support," Ella said, fixing a skirt on her dummy so it fell just right.

"Yeah. And I love being with him." Harper sighed. After everything she'd been through, she really couldn't complain. But she missed Xander horribly and hadn't thought life with Logan would be so predictable. She wanted more. But she knew he was under stress from Ed and SolCan and getting prepared to work there full time.

"It's always been clear how he feels about you, Harper," Ella said. "Living D/s twenty-four seven is a big change. Is it what you expected?"

"No." Harper closed the box and stacked it on the other one, moving to the next piece to ship out. "I wanted more... structure? I don't know."

"Then you have to ask for it," Ella said.

Harper sighed. Logan liked big gestures and exhibitions at the club, but Harper wondered if he wanted the day-to-day intimacies she was craving.

"I thought I had," Harper said. "I'll try again."

Ella smiled. "Communication or bust, as Zee says."

Harper returned the smile. She wished she could have what Ella and Zee had, both of them in sync with each other, meeting and being fulfilled by each other's needs.

"This one will be ready in a moment; we're down to five more to box up. I couldn't have done this without you, Harper."

"Yes, you could have, but you're a good friend for inviting me over."

"You seemed so sad on Tuesday. But give it time, Harper, and trust the people you love to make it right." Ella squeezed her arm, and Harper smiled gratefully.

"It's a change." Harper felt the tears start at the corners of her eyes.

Ella hummed as she worked around her skirt, sewing quickly, and Harper focused on packing up the beautiful garments. She didn't know how she would get through the days without Xander. Working for Axis Management gave her a purpose. It gave her drive and focus, and Xander's demands kept her brain in the moment.

Since living with Logan, she'd begun having nightmares again. Logan held her, stroked her hair until she calmed down, and she'd had two sessions with her psychiatrist, but that wasn't how Xander would have handled it. Xander would have told her to write it out in her journal, so she was ready for her appointment. The following day, he would have given her a list of tasks, and though he would have made sure she was okay, he wouldn't have mentioned what had happened in the middle of the night. Logan had told her to take it easy the next day at breakfast and then left her in the empty apartment to take a meeting for SolCan.

She loved Logan. His attitude toward life was intoxicating, he loved having fun, and she felt safe with him. But with Xander, it was a different sort of safety she felt.

"I can use a coffee," Ella said as she carefully took the skirt and garment off the dummy and laid it on the table. She smiled. "That's good work, and I'm not up until midnight."

Ella floated over to the kitchen, and Harper finished packing up the garment.

"I can make our coffee."

"Sure. I keep my favourite kind in the freezer." Ella pulled out a stool at the island.

Who'd have thought Harper would miss making coffee for Xander? But Logan didn't have a morning routine. He usually grabbed an energy drink out of the fridge or made a protein shake. He liked to cook dinner, and they ate out often because he wanted to be around people who weren't wearing suits. Harper sighed, pressing the button on Ella's machine.

"I miss working at Axis Management," Harper said.

Ella tilted her head. "Yes, I imagine you would. Maybe when your rehearsal schedule picks up, you'll feel busy enough."

Harper shrugged, grabbed cups from the mug tree on the counter and poured coffee for her and Ella.

"Creamer in the fridge. I like the hazelnut one," Ella said with a chuckle. "Though Zee tells me it's a good way to ruin a cup of coffee."

Harper poured, stirred, and passed Ella her mug, sitting down across from her.

"But he doesn't mind if you have it?"

"Not at all. He likes me happy, and creamer in my coffee is a little thing." Ella smiled as she sipped.

"I miss Xander," Harper said. She stared at the wooden beams above her, not wanting to cry. "I love Logan, Ella, but Xander demands more of me. He doesn't think I can handle his needs, and his past relationship was terrible, but I've loved him for a while. And living with Logan is just making me miss Xander more."

"Have you told Logan?" Ella asked, the gentleness in her voice somehow making Harper cry more. She wiped furiously at her cheeks.

Harper bit her lip, wondering how much to tell Ella. She didn't want to burden her friend with her past, but Ella was one of the few people who knew Logan and the Bandit Brothers worked for Axis Management.

"Xander and Logan and I, we... a couple of weeks ago..." Heat flooded her cheeks. She looked up from her cup, meeting Ella's warm expression.

"I love them both. I don't know how or why. I just do, and a couple of weeks ago, the three of us had an amazing night and then Xander left because he can't handle it or thinks he's too old or that I can't handle it. And then Logan left Axis Management. I think he's been feeling anchorless ever since."

Ella's warm hands closed around hers. "Harper, you love who you love."

"I miss him so much." She wiped at the tears falling down her face.

"Then you have to tell them, both of them, and it sounds like Xander needs reassurance."

"Xander? That big powerful, always in control man needs reassurance?"

"In my experience, all Doms do," Ella said, smiling at her.

Harper bit her lip. He was a big powerful, always in control man whose anxiety often got the best of him. Maybe he did need her reassurance.

"Ask Logan. If he's as aimless as you make him out to be, he's looking for a similar thing you are. Xander might be it. Now let's get back to work, and you can help me carry these packages into the post office if you don't mind."

"No, I'm happy to."

"I can see that." Ella laughed as Harper cleared the mugs, rinsed them, and put them in the dishwasher.

Harper smiled. "I didn't think I was a service sub before this, but yes, I miss doing the tiny thousands of things Xander had me doing every day. Logan is more self-sufficient and doesn't think to ask me."

"It takes all kinds." Ella smiled. "And maybe to meet your needs, it takes two."

Harper smiled, relieved that Ella understood. Now she had to make Logan realize what she needed and tell Xander.

***

"Come to Submissive Night next week," Ella said as she dropped Harper back home. "If you can."

She had already thought about going. Last week, going stir crazy, she had begged Logan to let her attend a Submissive Night, and he'd agreed.

"I'll check the rehearsal schedule and let you know. Thanks for the company," Harper said.

"Anytime."

She waved at Ella, turned and walked through the doors of Logan's condo. Her phone buzzed. A neighbour's yappy dog jumped on her as she took her phone out of her purse. The woman smiled in apology. Harper pressed the elevator button as she said held the phone to her ear, and said, "Hello?"

"Hi, Harper, sorry to bother you. But I need to know the password to the scheduling program," Gardenia said.

Harper's stomach dropped. "Why?"

"I'm trying out an office temp today, and we need to get into the scheduling software. Not on your machine or anything, just this piece of it."

Harper walked away from the elevators, trying to breathe. It seemed like a punch to her stomach, but Axis Management still needed to run without her. Her scheduling system was a point of pride for her. Every person in each team had their own colour, and the system tracked all the hours everyone put in. With one glance, she could tell who needed time off. She was worried about Erik Knight because he was racking up the hours, and Gabe Arthur hadn't taken downtime in months.

"Gardenia, I can't remember it. I have to check my electronic safe," Harper said.

"Okay, if you can get back to me by the end of the day with it, that'd be great," her friend said.

As she dropped her phone back into her bag, Harper tried to shake off the wave of sadness. Her friend was just doing her job. They couldn't operate without that schedule. Just because Harper had created it didn't mean that she owned it. She knew this, yet, she felt broken-hearted about a place she had given so much to operating without her being there.

A gloved hand came around her biceps and yanked her out as she stepped into the elevator.

Harper screamed and kicked out furiously, but a firm hand clamped over her mouth and another arm around her waist.

"I've come to rescue you." The accented voice made her shudder.

The man pulled her to the front doors. Using all her weight, Harper made herself as heavy as possible, so the man had to drag her. Her heart slammed furiously against her ribs.

"It's all right, you're going to be all right," the man said, loosening the hand over her mouth. That accent sent fear rolling down her spine. She thought she had escaped her family.

Harper bit the man's hand, and when it fell away, she screamed.

Suddenly, the man flew to the floor, and another arm was around Harper's waist.

"Harper, it's Janette. I got you. Just stay with me over here."

Harper looked into the familiar face of Janette Jennings and wanted to cry. Janette led her to a bench while Janette's partner, Finn, had the man on the floor and was on his phone.

"How come you're here?" Harper managed to squeeze out.

"Xander's orders." Janette took her hand in hers. "Long slow breaths. You don't have to do anything right now, Harper. We'll take of you."

Harper believed her. "I want to call Logan."

She fumbled in her bag and finally found her phone, but her hands were shaking too much when she tried to press the call button. Janette took the phone from her and made the call. Across from them, Finn had the man upright, holding his arm. They didn't want to attract too much attention.

Ten minutes later, two police officers took her statement and hauled the man away. Janette and Finn walked Harper up to Logan's condo.

"Can you stay for a while?"

"Of course. I can make you tea," Janette smiled.

"No, I'll do it." Harper flipped the kettle on and grabbed two mugs. "Why were you there, anyway? I thought you worked for River Stone, now."

"Not till the end of the month. Xander's had detail on you for the last few weeks. We were driving past, and I saw that man trying to drag you outside. And I saw you fight back. Good job, Harper."

"He got me, though," Harper said. Tears wouldn't stop streaming down her face.

"Harper, you fought. You should be proud of yourself," Janette said in her no-nonsense way.

Harper shook her head. It didn't matter how much Xander tried to protect her. She couldn't escape who she was. Being related to criminals would never go away. She glanced up as Logan entered the kitchen.

"Hey, Finn. Thanks for holding the place down, Janette." His gaze settled on Harper. "Come here, darling."

And Logan's powerful arms were around her, and the plane of his hard chest against her cheek. Harper wept, uncontrollable big gulping sobs.

"I'm here, Harper. I'm here." Logan stroked her hair and held her close.

It felt so good to be in his arms, breathe in his outdoorsy scent, and feel the warmth of his body against hers.

Logan said goodbye to the bodyguards and locked the door. “Come on, let’s go to bed.”

27

CHAPTER TWENTY-SEVEN - LOGAN

"You don't have to look after me. I can go."

"Go where, Kitten? You belong here with me." Logan stroked her hair and felt her tremble against him.

"It's never going to end. You can't look after me. My family will find me wherever I go, no matter how much security I have. You don't want this life, Logan," Harper said.

"And what life is that?" He softly kissed her lips.

"A life of looking over your shoulder, of having to run because they found me again. I can't ask you to live like some criminal on the run."

Logan wiped away a tear with his thumb.

"You don't get to tell me the life I want, Harper. You can trust me to keep you safe. We'll figure this out. Right now, we know nothing about the man who attacked you. We don't know who he is, how he found you, or what he wants."

Shaking her head, harper sat upright, swinging her legs to the floor, and paced. "I know. That accent is the one of my childhood. That means they have found me! And I care about you too much to risk you. I know you're skilled, but you have never faced this before."

"Harper, you listen to me." Logan put his hands on her shoulders and stilled her movement. "I'm not scared of your family. I don't care how mean they are or how far-reaching they are. I can keep you safe, and I don't care what life throws at us. As long as you're in my life, I have everything I need." Logan captured her lips, breathing in her exhale, feeling the tension leave her body. He kissed her until her he felt her sag against him.

"But what if they come back? What if they never give up looking for me? What if they take me? I can't go back, Logan. I can't." Harper trembled against him.

He nibbled her ear gently; he traced her eyebrows with his fingertips. "Shush. I said I would take care of you, and I will. There is no more discussion of you leaving or telling me I can't be part of your life. No more words about what-ifs, Kitten." Logan kissed her hard, sealing his dominant intent. Her arms came around his neck, and she urged him on.

"Is that how it is?" Logan asked.

"You made me stop thinking for a moment," Harper said.

"Let's see if we can make it two." Logan kissed her hard, trying to drown out her thoughts, wanting to take all her fears, wanting to absorb them into himself. He could handle this, and he wanted to show her he could. God, how soft she was under his rough hands. He breathed in her sweet scent between her shoulder blade and neck, trailing kisses down her collarbone. Deftly, he lifted her top and kissed her collarbone, trailing soft kisses over her lilac-clad breasts.

"Free these for me, Kitten," Logan said, his thumbs caressing her nipples through the lacy fabric. He loved how sweetly she moaned as he applied more pressure. He removed his touch and sat against the headboard. Harper unclasped her bra with a small smile, and Logan flicked a lush nipple.

"Cup them for me," he said, leaning forward.

She did, sliding onto her knees. He leaned down, his hands encircling her waist, and sucked her nipple. Harper's hands moved to his shoulders, and her moans urged him to keep pace.

He didn't let go until her sweet nipple was swollen red. And then he took the other one hard into his mouth as Harper moaned. He could feel her anticipation, her eagerness to let him have his way.

She wanted to be dominated. It was how her body swayed towards him, how she yipped as he bit down, and how the pressure of her fingertips dug into his shoulders firmly as she felt him lift off.

"Stay right there," Logan said.

"I could undress you?" Harper said.

Logan grinned. His slacks hit the floor, and his T-shirt was over his head instantly. "You got to be quicker."

Logan kissed her softly and noticed her eyes flicked away. "Kitten, what is it?"

She shook her head and pressed herself to him. Her breasts on his chest felt so good. Her soft lips on him made him lose his resolve.

"Please, Sir, I need this," Harper said.

And in her eyes, he saw her naked fear, and it clutched his heart. "I got you, Kitten." Logan brought her legs apart, guiding her knees, so they were bent, so she was opened. He parted her labia. "You won't come until I tell you to."

"Yes, Sir." Harper's breathy tone was like an electric current.

Ah, her tangy scent dispatched all the remaining blood to his cock, and as he sucked her salty cunt, Logan didn't think this could be any better. Her legs closed around him, and he pushed them back, demanding she stay open. He swirled his tongue around her clit, his fingers in her pussy. Above him, Harper cried out. "Yes!"

"I'm going to give you what you need, Kitten."

He kissed her flat stomach, working his way up to those bountiful breasts, sucking them only before finding her soft lips.

"I'm going to take you so hard, to make you forget everything, except that I love you and I got you, Harper. I will do whatever it takes to protect you," Logan said, then kissed her deeply. As her body opened to him, her murmur of pleasure raced through him.

God, how beautiful she looked, with her face flushed with rapture. Pride stirred in his chest that he made her feel that way.

He slid his hands to her waist and brought her onto him. "Ride me, Harper."

A quick look of surprise crossed her face, and Logan grinned. "Show me how much you want that orgasm."

Harper moved her hips.

He thrust into her hot cunt, feeling his balls tighten. He could stay buried in her forever and be a happy man.

Her eyes closed, and she bit her lower lip.

She was so damn sexy. Logan slid in and out, teasing her, revelling in her wetness on his cock as she writhed against his hips.

He smiled, admiring her strength as he let his hands float up and over her breasts, playing with her nipples.

"Give me more, Kitten."

Her eyes flared open, and she circled her hips, moving in slowly and damn if he didn't lose his control right there. He grabbed her hips, holding her down, and glided right to the hilt into her core.

The heat of her pussy sizzled. He held that position for a moment. As she gyrated her hips, a fine sheen of sweat covered her body.

Damn, he almost didn't want to make her wait. She tilted her hips; he held her in place. She tried to circle, and he clamped down.

"Please, Sir."

There was nothing he wouldn't give her.

"Hold on, my love."

His hands moved to her back and as he seated himself deeper. He nibbled her ear and started to thrust. Her breathy little sounds urged him to drive out her worries.

"Logan, I can't hold... please," she said.

He bit down hard on her shoulder, and she screamed. Holding her hips, he hammered into her, letting his determination roar in full, primal force. Sweat formed along his spine and rolled off his back. His balls tightened, his orgasm threatening to tow him under, and he wanted her to follow.

"Now, Harper, come with me," Logan said.

She screamed his name, but he didn't stop his relentless pace, pumping in and out as if he could drive out every doubt ever to cross her mind, and as he felt the reverberations from her orgasm, he let go buried deep in her core.

They both panted, covered in sweat. Her mouth met his, and he devoured her, not wanting this to end.

"Come with me," he said, disentangling them. The absence of her fire made him bite back a groan.

Taking her hand in his, he led her into the bathroom, turned on the water, made sure it wasn't too hot, held the shower door open for her, and followed her in.

He helped steady her on the wet tiles.

"Can I wash you, Sir?" Harper said, picking up a sponge.

"Yes, Kitten."

God, the care she took, washing his chest and his arms, made him want to hug her. Instead, he stood still, noticing the pleasure on her face as she sponged between his legs and ran the sponge over his cock, washing away all traces of their sex.

He brought her around him, and she got the sponge along his back, over his ass, with full attention and care. Logan groaned in pleasure.

Taking the sponge from her, he kissed her. "Thank you, Kitten."

She glowed.

His stomach sunk, the feeling he had tried to ignore for the past couple of weeks threading through his body. She needed more than what he could give her.

Holding up her hair, he ran the sponge over her neck, between her breasts, over her ass.

He tossed the sponge, and his fingers slid into her depths. He brought her back against his chest.

"Can you give me one more of your orgasms?" he asked.

"Yes!" Harper cried. He flicked her clit, his fingers deep in her pussy, and he felt her go on her toes as he mercilessly finger fucked her.

"God, Logan!" Harper cried. He caught her in his arms, turned the water, and helped her out of the shower.

"Can you stay on your feet for one moment?"

From half-lidded eyes, she nodded.

He grabbed a towel, drying her from head to toe. He quickly dried himself off and scooped her up in his arms because he could.

He tucked her in bed, pulling the sheet under her chin.

"Tomorrow, Kitten, we need to talk. Nothing is wrong. I just need to figure out how best to care for you," he said, kissing away the frown on her forehead.

His cell blasted, and he found it in the pants pocket on the floor. Damn it.

"What is it, Ed?"

"Logan, you need to get your ass down here right away! No more fooling around. I need to see you tonight."

Logan sighed. He didn't want to go. "Can this wait till tomorrow?"

"No, it fuckin can't," Ed snapped.

"Okay, I'll be there in thirty," he closed his cell.

"I understand," Harper said.

"Thank you. You walked away from your whole life, Harper. I can stop playing hero and go work for the bastard. It'll give me enough money to take care of you the way you should be."

"Logan, you don't have to take care of me."

He pressed a finger on her lips. "I told you, not another word about it. We'll talk tomorrow. I don't want to leave you here by yourself."

"I'm okay," Harper said.

"I didn't say you weren't. I'm calling one of the Bandit Brothers. Say another word, and I'll paddle your ass. Who would you rather have if you get to pick one?"

"Gabe," Harper said without hesitation. "He needs the distraction, and he's unobtrusive and won't want to install crazy software on my phone."

"Nick's a bastard like that." Logan smiled. He gave her another kiss, stepped out of the room, and called Gabe.

Gabe agreed to come over to keep Harper company. "I'll be there in ten."

Logan paused, thinking he might call someone else, but shook his head. She hadn't mentioned his name, and he wouldn't until she did. But it was clear Harper was missing something, and he knew exactly what it was and who could give it to her.

He spent a few minutes reading the latest report from SolCan, refreshing his memory on all the details, and wondered what was so crucial that Ed had to see him at ten o'clock at night. But Logan had promised he would do everything he could for Hana, and he knew Harper had distracted him from that goal a little. Ed might be an awful person, but Logan had given his word.

When he finished reading the file, he returned to see Harper had changed into yoga pants and a long-sleeve T-shirt.

"I'm going to bake something while you're gone," Harper said.

"I can't wait to come home and eat it and then eat you again," Logan said.

Harper laughed as he spun her around and kissed her. The doorbell's ring interrupted them.

"Be good. I'll be back soon," Logan said. Opening the door, he clapped Gabe on the shoulder.

"Thanks for coming."

"No problem, I heard what happened earlier. Harper, I heard you kicked ass. Good job." Gabe held his hand up for a high five, and Harper returned it.

"Still feeling a little nervy."

"Understandable. I got this, Logan," Gabe said.

"All right. Don't eat all the cookies."

"We won't." Harper flashed him the brightest grin, and his heart swelled.

He would do anything and everything he could do to make things good for her. Logan gave them a wave and waited until he heard the click of the deadbolt. Outside he got on his motorcycle and left to see a man who, though he hated him, held the keys to his future.

28

CHAPTER TWENTY-EIGHT – XANDER

Xander rubbed his face and placed the bitter bad coffee he made on the old kitchen table in the conference room. Damn, he missed Harper and her coffee-making skills. He missed how she emailed him his itinerary for the day each morning, and they would have a back and forth about how much was too much to cram into the hours. He missed how she reassured the staff, always making them feel valued and treasured and—he just missed her.

Not seeing her was torture. He hardly slept, hardly ate, and couldn't get her face, scent, and laugh out of his mind.

There weren't many people on this earth he could let down all his carefully curated guards. But he could with Harper. She was that rare someone who he could show his complete self to. And now that he didn't have her, he had retreated. Xander clicked the video forward a few seconds, leaned in and watched, adjusting his headphones.

He had been at this for hours, checking the security feeds from when Axis Management had been hired to find Mulberry Stevens. Someone had leaked their location, and someone had told Theo, who'd told Dorian.

And then Dorian had unleashed his technology, and it had cost Xander one of the best men he knew. He paused the video, watching Jordan laugh at something Harper said. Xander's heart clenched. If only he had acted sooner.

The day after the attack on Team Stealth, he'd had all the doors rewired, struck the reception area downstairs, and installed biometric locks on all the entrances. No one came into the building unless they worked here or were invited, and even then, guests were met at the front door and escorted to the offices.

Deliveries were met downstairs in the parking garage. But the measures had been too little, too late, and Xander had lived with that every day.

He played the video, watching as Jordan left the office and Harper took a phone call. She made notes on her iPad as she talked. Harper knew not to say anything pertinent out loud.

She clicked off, grabbed her purse, said something to her assistant Claudia and left. Xander traced her image on the screen, shaking his head. He could mull over what was gone, but this wasn't getting him anywhere.

This wasn't the first time he had gone through his video feeds, trying to figure out who had leaked that Axis Management was hired to rescue Mulberry Stevens to the press. In the days after the incident, he had sat through hundreds of hours of video, going through the same motions as he did now, looking for anything or anyone out of place, trying to make sense of what happened and how.

But now he was going back further, the week before the attack, searching for something new, something he had missed, looking for anything that stood out.

Theo Densen had acquired his information somehow.

After another hour of watching, Xander rubbed his eyes, stood up, and stretched. He paced the conference room. His phone trilled, and he snatched it, waiting for the other person to speak first.

"Guess I bet on the wrong horse, eh?" Dorian Martin said.

Xander's hand fisted, and he ground his teeth.

"Should have taken our offer when we made it, Dorian."

"So you just take it? My whole world, my great grandfather's legacy, all destroyed by you?"

"You're the one who destroyed it when you engaged that aircraft on Theo Densen's orders. I don't think your grandfathers would play rogue soldier the way you did, would they?"

Dorian swore. "No matter how many companies you take over, no matter how you try to destroy me, you'll never be me, Xander. You'll still be a rich guy who got here by being lucky. You want to talk about playing soldier? Isn't that what your whole company does?"

"Dorian, I have nothing further to say to you. Speak to my lawyer from now on."

"I didn't know, Xander. For what it's worth, I didn't know there were people out there when Theo asked me to try out the stealth helicopter. I thought that stretch of dessert was empty, and he just wanted to see how it flew because he had investors interested in the system. I wasn't out to kill or hurt anyone."

"You're responsible for your toys, Dorian. Where did you get this info from?"

"Is there anything I can do to stop the destruction you have aimed at me?" Dorian's high pitch hurt Xander's ears.

"I had men out there trying to rescue a terrified woman, Dorian. Good men, trained men, all former soldiers who served their country and after all that, one man lost his life in a stretch of the desert because you didn't think to ask enough questions before you hit launch." His usual control slipped, and his voice rang off the walls. "And who told you that I had my own? What was it? 'Modern courtesan'?"

"Theo. Xander, it was a poor quarter. Theo came to me last summer, telling me he had investors for our new technology. I felt hope for the first time in months. One night we had drinks, and there was a picture of Ares in the paper for donating to the hospital, and Theo said a lot of stuff about you. But that's when he said that you had a personal whore because you were too agoraphobic to leave the house."

"You believed him."

"Xander, it was just talk. What does this have to do with Theo wanting me to test out the stealth technology months later?"

"Everything," Xander said. "Don't call me again."

He tossed the phone on the table, shaking his head. Good people make bad decisions. He'd known the Martin Group had had a lousy quarter. That was why it was easy to pull off the hostile takeover; their shareholders were eager for a new direction.

And he could see how Dorian got emotionally manipulated by the more assertive personality of Theo. Xander pressed play again on the video feed.

He sat forward, pausing as a group of men entered the executive floor. Gardenia gestured at them with her shy smile, and they put down several boxes. Xander frowned. He hadn't remembered a delivery that sizeable before.

He had paused the video to try and see a name on their shirts when his phone rang. His mouth went dry, seeing the number flash on his screen.

"Angel."

"Xander, I…" her voice was breathless, and her tone scared, and Xander strode out of the conference room to the front doors, glancing out the window at the dark street.

"What is it?"

"I know I shouldn't call you."

He closed his eyes against a fresh wave of pain. "You can always call me. No matter what. What's happening?"

"Logan has been gone for hours. He got a call from Edwin around ten."

"You've been there alone the whole time?" He thought Marrock was smarter than that.

"No, Gabe is here to babysit me. I'm fine, Xander. A little shook up, but fine," she said.

His heart swelled. There she was, offering reassurance and comfort to him. Going through each member of her family he knew about to match to the guy who made the missing police report was going to be his next task.

"So, Ed called at ten, and Logan's still not back yet?" Xander checked his watch. Ten to one.

"I can't explain it, Xander, but I heard Edwin through the phone. He sounded unhinged. I can't get Logan on his cell. It's silly of me to worry about him and call you about it, but…"

"No, it isn't. Where's Gabe?"

A pause. "I know you probably have a pair of bodyguards watching the perimeter of the condo. The man looked so worn out. I made him soup, dimmed the lights, and he fell asleep. He's been on the couch for about an hour."

Xander sighed. He knew that Gabe would be up and ready for action at the slightest sound. He was glad the man was having a few moments of peace. He seemed intent on burning himself out.

"Harper, I'll check out what's going on with Logan. Go to bed or try to read. Even take the sleeping pills the doc left for you. I got this."

"Thank you, Xander," Harper said, ending the call.

Xander sent Ares a text, giving a heads-up, and paused.

He could call Carli and get her to drive him to SolCan's headquarters. Or he could be as brave as his Angel and get behind the wheel himself—for the first time since Oliva's accident.

His stomach twisted in knots as he rode to his office, his sanctuary, the black forest. Stopping at Harper's chaotic disarray, he shook his head. For her, he would do it. Inside his office, he grabbed keys to the spare SUV, and a moment later, as his hand closed around cold metal, he closed his safe, armed to go see what trouble Marrock had landed himself. He slipped on the holster. At least there was a use for the suit jacket, Xander thought, taking it out of the closet and throwing it on.

The headquarters of SolCan was at the edge of the business district, in a nondescript office on the third floor. The front doors opened to his touch, and Xander frowned, wondering about Edwin's lack of security. He had expected to call Logan to see if he was here, not walk right through the front doors. If he hadn't wanted to stop a developer from another overpriced condo, Axis Management would probably still be in that house they'd started from, and he wouldn't have daily calls from the press, so to a point, Xander got the rather unattractive office choice.

Silently, he took the stairs and paused outside a door, noticing a glow beneath it. The knot in his stomach tightened, and his palms grew sweaty. He listened and only heard footsteps.

And then, a few moments later, a raised shrill voice.

"You knew about it! Do you think I'm stupid? Look, there's a photo of you and Montague in the fuckin' paper from the Firefighters Fundraiser! There's no way you could afford that condo on an army pension, Logan. I've long thought you were one of their bodyguards."

"Edwin, even if that was true, I know nothing about this takeover. Business is not my thing. I climb rocks and teach other people how to climb. The only business experience I have is shaking people's hands for SolCan and convincing them solar panels will save them money on their year-end."

"I don't believe you!" Ed shouted.

Xander touched the door, cracking it open a little. Across from a reception area, he saw the door to Edwin's office open wide. The man was red-faced and sweating as he pointed a finger at Logan. He held up a bundle of papers and threw them across the room.

"You wanted to take SolCan for yourself! That's why you told your boss to attempt this hostile takeover!"

"Edwin, all I want to do is make sure Hana has a good life that she doesn't have to struggle or join the army to get an education. You give her the money to cover school, sign whatever you need to sign to make sure she has her inheritance from her grandfather, and you and I are good. I committed to a year. That was the deal, and I'm ready to do that full time."

Xander eased himself inside the outer office, keeping out of the light. He heard the determination in Logan's voice, and he loved the man so much in that moment.

He hated doing the marketing stuff for SolCan, but for his half-sister, he would do anything. And that was the main reason Xander had hired him. They shared the tenet of loyalty.

"I don't believe you! If this goes through, I have nothing left!"

"Edwin, we can talk about this tomorrow," Logan said.

"There's nothing to talk about. You've cost me hundreds of thousands in legal fees to fight this. You asshole!"

Ed lunged across at Marrock, silver in his hand. Xander cursed as he saw the knife, the blade aimed right at his stomach. It happened so fast. Xander watched, stunned, as his giant of a friend stumbled back. Edwin came around from his desk, holding the knife with two hands over his head.

Logan groaned in pain.

Xander didn't hesitate. From his holster, he pulled out his gun and fired centre mass. Edwin flew backwards, his face frozen in anger, and fell to the floor.

"Logan!" Xander reached an arm under his friend's upper body to keep him upright.

"Fuck, I didn't expect this," Logan said. His face paled before Xander's eyes. Xander took off his suit jacket, curled it around the knife, and pressed hard.

"The rumour about you once being a spy is true?" Logan's voice croaked out.

"Here, put pressure on it as much as possible," Xander instructed.

"Yeah, good idea."

Logan's skin seemed to be growing paler by the second. Xander took his friend's fingers, squeezing them. "Keep putting pressure on that."

Xander closed his eyes, briefly running through the options. There was only one person he could call in this situation.

"Xander?"

"Edwin stabbed Marrock. We are at SolCan. I need your guys here, now."

"Activating them now," Ares said. "And I'll be there as soon as I can."

Xander clicked off.

"We make a good team, Xander." Logan coughed and wheezed.

"You know what you're doing, Logan."

"Come home with us. She misses you."

"We can talk about it later."

"She does that too. Change the subject. It's annoying. Is Edwin dead?"

Xander glanced over his shoulder. He didn't want to leave Logan to check on Edwin, who was on the other side of the room. "I don't know, but yes, I think he is."

"What am I going to tell Hana?"

"Logan, press harder." Xander took over, holding down the suit jacket with as much force as he could.

"We'll take care of it. You'll tell her that there was a break-in at his house, okay? That's the story."

"This sucks."

"Yeah. It's not how I wanted to spend my night either."

He watched his friend's eyes roll to the back of his head.

"Logan!"

He heard footsteps from the hall and released a pent-up breath.

Six guys, dressed in black from head to toe. The one wearing a headset signalled to Xander checked Edwin, and shook his head. Then three of the guys took Ed away.

Dr. Redden rushed over to Logan, checking his pupils. "He needs blood, IV saline, and the hospital," she said.

"Dammit," Xander said.

Logan opened his eyes again, his breathing laboured. "Sorry for the trouble." His mouth twisted into what might have been a grin before he closed his eyes.

"Logan, listen."

Logan's eyes fluttered open. Xander could tell he couldn't focus, but he had to make the next step clear to his friend.

"Dr. Redden is going to take you to the hospital. You don't remember anything. You tried to help someone, gave them money, and that person had a knife. They ran away, and you don't remember much. Got it?"

"Yeah," Logan said, his voice fading away. Xander could only hope he'd understood the instructions.

"I'll drop you right at the emergency," Dr. Redden said.

"Thanks, Doctor."

"Don't mention it." Dr. Redden signalled to two team members, and they helped lift Logan, carrying him out of the room.

"Well, this is a mess," Ares said from the doorway.

"Good thing I have you to clean it up," Xander said.

"Yep. You know what to do," Ares said to the guy in the headset. "Full clean-up. Check for security videos here and across the street. Make sure there isn't even a fingerprint. Random robbery at Edwin's house."

"It'll be done," the guy with the headset said.

Ares gestured outside, and Xander followed his brother out of the room.

"So, you drove?" Ares asked.

Xander laughed at the ridiculousness of it all. "Yes."

"Make it a habit."

"I will," Xander agreed.

"You're going to go tell Harper?"

"I was going to call Quinn."

"I'll call Walsh. You go tell Harper."

"Ares, I don't want to...."

"She needs to hear this from you, Xander. She needs to be read in on what happened here tonight."

Xander stared at his younger brother. Ares's expression was stoic.

"Okay, you're right. I'll go over there now."

"Get that driving practice in."

"Yeah. See you later. And thanks."

"Hey, it's what we do." Ares clapped him on the shoulder.

Xander swallowed a lump as he pushed open the door, the cool night breeze clearing his head. He had to go see his girl.

29

CHAPTER TWENTY-NINE - XANDER

"I'm on my way up to Logan's door," Xander told Gabe.

"Okay, boss. Everything good?""No," Xander said, stepping onto the elevator. "Quinn will fill you in. I'm around the corner."

"Okay," Gabe said.

He hated that he would hurt Harper with the news, but he couldn't help it.

"Hey, everything's been quiet here," Gabe said. "I heard you took a nap."

Gabe's face scrunched up, and Xander waved a hand. "Don't worry about it. You would have been on your feet in a second if you needed to be.""Boss, you have blood on your shirt."

"I didn't notice." Gabe held the door open for him, and his phone buzzed. "That's Quinn. Harper, I'm taking off. You're in good hands. Thanks for the soup."

Harper appeared from the hallway. His breath hitched seeing her, her hair in a messy bun, her breasts free under her cream-coloured t-shirt, the yoga pants hugging her ass.

"No worries." Harper smiled.

Gabe waved bye, and Xander closed the door.

"Hi, Angel." He wanted to go to her, sweep her up in his arms.

She took a few steps toward him. "Hi." Xander tore his eyes from her, trying to stop his racing thoughts, his galloping heartbeat.

He turned, taking in the living room. "What the hell is with the stripper pole?"

"It was here before I came."

"It figures. He has a whole wall of..." Xander felt the corners of his mouth upturn. Damn Logan and his unabashed ego

"Yeah." Harper couldn't help smiling. "I call it his wall of self-love."

"If only we could all love ourselves so blazingly."

Harper glanced away from him. "Xander..."

"So you're all moved in then?"

"I have a few things back at the house. Ares brought some stuff over for me."

"You'll always have a home with us, Angel. You know that."

Harper looked down, biting her lip. Xander took a step towards her and reached out a hand to her.

"Is that blood on your shirt?" Her voice trembled. "What happened?"

"Angel, let me get this shirt off. Would you mind finding me one of Logan's?"He took off the black diamond cufflinks, put them on the coffee table and unbuttoned his shirt. Harper stared at him for a moment, her eyes roaming over him and then she shook herself.

"I'll be right back."

The way her body moved, with her usual fluid grace, grounded him. He was going to take care of her. Logan was going to be okay. It would be all right.

He followed her down the hall, watched as she opened the closet, and took a pale blue dress shirt down. "It might be a little big."-

Xander snorted. He was six-two, but Marrock had height and breadth on him.

"Thank you." He put on the shirt and rolled up the sleeves.

"Xander, say something, please." She stepped in front of him, and he took her hands in his.

"Sorry. Seeing you took all my words. I've missed you."

She closed her eyes.

"Tell me." She put a hand on his chest.

He grabbed her hand, pulling it off his chest. He kissed her hand, holding it for a long moment. Turning her around, he put his palm on her back, leading her to the living room. Still holding her hand, he brought her over to the couch, sitting her down.

Then slowly, he kneeled in front of her, putting his hands on the top of her legs. She gasped.

He rubbed her arms gently. "You were right to call me. Whatever instinct sparked that phone call, Logan can thank you for, later, when he recovers."

"What happened?" her voice trembled.

"He's going to be fine, Angel. The man is strong and healthy and has a lot of muscle to protect his stomach." Xander put a finger on her lip as she bit it. Tears fell from her eyes, and he wanted to kiss them away. "Did you hear me?"

"He's going to be fine."

"Yes, keep that in mind, okay?" Xander brushed his fingers along her lips.

"Okay."

"Edwin stabbed Logan. The blade sunk into his stomach. There was a lot of blood. Logan is at the hospital."

She sucked in a breath. "God, Logan. He thought Ed was becoming more scrambled. Hana, what am I going to tell her?"

"There's more, Angel. Edwin was going to keep stabbing him. Before I left, I took a gun out of my safe."

"You? You never..."

"I did, Angel. And I used it. I stopped Ed from hurting Logan further, then called in Ares's clean-up team. They will make it look like a robbery at Edwin's house."

"The best-kept secret in all of Avis Management, it's the Archangel with the clean-up crew," Harper said, glancing away from him.

"We're not going to tell Hana anything until Edwin is discovered at his home."

"We should get to Logan. I should get to Logan." Harper went to stand up.

"Angel, stop." At his cool tone, she slid back onto the couch again. "I told you, he's going to recover. Ares called Quinn. You know Quinn will call everyone."

"Logan will hate it."

"He'll like some of it, the attention whore."

Harper laughed and shook her head at him. "Bad, Mr. Montague. Can you take me to him, please?"

"They won't let any more visitors in until the morning. Quinn swore he was his brother, so they let him in. The last update I got was that he was trying to refuse the anesthesia for being sewed up. "

"That poor staff. I'm going to call Quinn."

Xander nodded, took her hand and guided her from the couch. She grabbed her phone from the counter.

Her brow furrowed as she said, "Yes," to Quinn, and Xander paced around the kitchen. Damn, he felt so useless. He hated that he had to come to her door tonight and hurt her. His job was to protect her.

"Logan," Harper said, her voice breathless.

Xander strode over to her. He rubbed small circles on her back as she nodded against the phone.

"Okay. I'm good. Xander is here."Xander's hand went to the nape of her neck, and he tried to massage the tension out of her tight muscles.

"Okay. Get some rest, Logan. I love you too." Her eyes were wide as she passed her phone to him. "He wants to talk to you." Xander took the phone, his fingertips brushing hers. "Marrock?"

"What a night, man. What if you hadn't shown up?""But I did. You can thank your submissive for that.""She's yours too, Xander. You know that." Logan's voice sounded groggy.

"We've been over this," Xander gritted out the words as he took his hand away from touching Harper.

"Yeah, and you're so stubborn. You know she needs you. What are you going to do? Leave her tonight? Call someone else because you're a scaredy-cat? Take care of our girl tonight."

Xander closed his eyes. "Are you giving me orders?"

"Xander, her submission belongs to both of us. I'm just telling you." Logan's voice slurred with grogginess.

Sometimes the giant was wiser than he seemed.

"For tonight. You get some rest to get back here." His voice caught at the words. "They're forcing me to. Come as soon as you can to spring me tomorrow?""Deal," Xander said. He closed the phone and met that cool green gaze that had factored in many of his dreams. "Angel." He hugged her, bringing her to his chest. He closed his eyes, inhaling her light floral scent.

"Xander, can you..."

"What is it, Angel? Tell me.""I want to feel your hands on me." She reached up, putting her hands on either side of his face.

"It would just be another night, Angel. And it hurts us both." "You belong with us, Xander."

He closed his eyes, barely touching her lips with his. If only that were true. There was nothing in this world he couldn't buy for her. She was asking what he couldn't pay for because the cost to her would be too high.

"It's worth the hurt, Xander." Damn, her soft voice had her unquenchable determination behind it and once again, he couldn't deny her. Gently, he took her hands off his face, bringing her arms around him, and kissing her.

Her mouth opened for him, and softly his tongue danced with hers. She groaned under him and tipped her head to him.

"Angel, I don't even know how I can stay away.""Then don't." She grabbed his hand and pulled him to follow her.

And he let her take the lead, following her to the bedroom.

She gave him a small smile as she lifted her shirt over her braless breasts, and slowly, her hands went to unbutton his borrowed shirt. Her hands ran over his abs and stomach, and he closed his eyes, savouring her touch. She was like a blaze of heat and the gentlest rain all at once.

She whimpered as he made slow circles with his palms over her breasts, she leaned towards him, and he fused her lips to hers, needing to kiss her again.

Her hands slid down to his belt buckle, so expertly she slid it out of its loops and tossed it on the floor. Another day, he would wield it against her bare ass, but he wanted to make love to her tonight.

And then her hands paused on his waistband, a look of worry flashing across her face.

Xander grabbed her chin. "Stop, Angel. He's fine, and by tomorrow, all of the Bandit Brothers won't be able to keep him down. Got it?"

She let out a shaky breath, "Okay."

He groaned as her fingers returned to his waistband, and she slid his slacks off him. He stepped out and grabbed the drawstring of her pants, bringing her close to him She laughed as he untied the knot. He held her hips as she stepped out of the loose pants

"Let's go to bed, Angel." He gently placed a hand on her back as they walked towards the brightly geometric covered king bed.

Harper pulled the comforter off, pausing to fold it. Damn, she was so beautiful. He could watch her fold things naked all day. She tucked it away in the closet and smiled at him.

"Better?""I only have eyes for you, Angel." He pulled her against him on the bed, and her body moved in time to his gentle tongue strokes.

Her hands danced over his broad shoulders, over his chest, down to his hips.

Her light feather touch fluttered down his back, her eyes bright as she slid her hands over his hard cock.

He hissed as she circled it. How could he live without this woman?

"You are so beautiful."

His eyes held hers as he lapped the inside of her thigh, as his tongue moved over to her folds and slowly licked the softest, most intimate parts of her.

The sweet-salty taste of her short fired his brain. It was an effort to stay slow and gentle. “God, Xander.” She grabbed his shoulders, her hips rising off the bed.

He reached for her fingers, and she shivered as his tongue found her clit, and he sucked gently.

She spread her legs wider, urging him to where she wanted him. His hands caressed the length of her, and he responded to her request as he moved to position himself at her entrance, her legs wrapped around him.

He slowly sunk into her with his renowned control, inch by inch. He took his time, watching every emotion cross her face, watching as her lips parted in an o, her eyes closed, her head tipped back. She cried out as he entered her, finally allowing himself to be deep in her, and he groaned at the divine heat that gloved his cock.

“Angel, you’re all I need.” He dropped soft, light kisses on her neck as he rocked inside her. She gripped him harder with her legs, her hands pressing on his shoulders. She whimpered, and he nibbled her ear.

He held himself back, stroking deep and slow in her hot core, her scent all around him.

She was like a blazing furnace made for his cock. He went even deeper, her body opening to him, accommodating his want, his need.

Damn, how soft and sexy she looked, with those little pants escaping her lips, her flushed body under his.

He rocked so damn deep in her and watched her eyes close tight, felt her muscle contract around him as the wave of pleasure erupted over her. He stayed with her, rocking deep in her until her legs started to shake.

"Angel." Burning desire licked his spine, and his balls drew tight. He exploded, his release hard and fast in her pussy. He collapsed forward onto her and stroked her brow.

She cried out his name as the wave of pleasure erupted over her; he stayed with her. He kissed her, long and tenderly, still embracing her; he shifted them so she was spooned against him.

"I love you," she said.He couldn't breathe for a moment. He held her, feeling her tense in his arms. "Angel, you are my heart."

He kissed her until she softened against him again. As her eyelids closed, he tucked the sheet around her and held her close to him, surprised to feel tears on his face.

30

CHAPTER THIRTY-LOGAN

"There's no use holding you, so you're fine to go home. But rest for the next week. Take it easy, no weight lifting or anything." The doctor levelled him with a glare. Logan wanted to reply but felt himself wincing as he sat up.

It felt like his insides had been sliced open and rearranged. It hurt to breathe and to laugh.

"We'll make sure he doesn't lift heavy things," Xander grumbled.

"Even if we have to tie him down." Harper giggled.

Xander took her hand, and if he weren't so annoyed by the white-hot pain flaring through his insides, he would have high-fived them.

He raised an eyebrow at her; the doctor threw her hands up and left with a smile.

"I called your mom. And Fiona," Quinn said from the doorframe.

"Wish you hadn't. I don't want to worry them."

"Because she can check in on you, even from Boston. And your mother's anger is fun", his best friend grinned.

God, his mom would be so mad.

"We'll keep an eye on him," Harper said. "He won't need his mom or Fiona."

"Impossible, all of you," Quinn said. "Need a hand there?"

"Fuck off," Logan said. He lifted himself up, but his friends didn't listen. Quinn came over, taking his arm and Xander grabbed his other one.

"They suggest a wheelchair for a reason, you know, it's their policy. You could just use it," Harper said.

"Feeling mouthy today, are we?" Logan leaned against the wall, his fingertips reaching for her waist.

Harper blushed, and Xander raised an eyebrow.

"The relief she feels at seeing you in one piece is making her forget her place."

"We'll remind her," Logan grunted as he took a few more steps. Damn, it felt like a workout.

Xander glanced away from him, and Logan bit the inside of his lip. Why did the man have to be stubborn? They made a perfect trio, and Xander belonged with them.

Slowly and with much cursing, they got outside of the hospital. Logan tilted his face to the sun. It felt so good.

"Want to sit down over on the picnic table? You need to catch your breath," Xander said.

"Just for a moment," Logan mumbled. He and Quinn eased him down to the bench. Logan felt sweat on his forehead and wiped it away.

"How are you?" Harper asked. Her eyes were filled with worry, and he took her hands in his.

"It hurts, but I'll be fine."

"You can take the pain meds they gave you," Xander said.

"You know I won't."

Xander shook his head. "Stubborn mofo."

"You're one to talk."

"Can we make him take the pain meds?" Harper asked.

Xander smiled. "Yeah, I think we can find a way. I'll blast goth punk until he agrees."

Harper giggled. "I'll make him watch reruns of Swan Lake."

They grinned at each other like loons, and Logan shook his head. They fit so well together, the three of them.

"You guys can team up on me all you want, but I will be fine in four weeks, and payback is a bitch."

"Four to six," Xander and Harper said in unison.

Harper giggled, the sound high and sweet, and Logan exchanged a look with Xander, a smile that said this is how they wanted their girl.

"Tell me, how much damage control do we have to do from last night?"That was Quinn for you, always analytical.

Logan winced as Harper's expression changed from light to intense.

"We need to check with Ares and follow up," Xander said.

"Excuse me! Alina, Alina!"

Harper's face became a white sheet. Quinn was on his feet, moving to stand at the head of the picnic table. Xander slung his arm around her, holding her tight.

Quinn stood in the man's way, blocking him from the table.

"Please, I just want to talk to her."

"It's the relative who's been looking for her," Xander's face was stone.

"Kitten, you're safe." Logan reached across and grabbed her hands. "The three of us aren't going to let anything happen to you. I want to hear what the guy has to say."

Xander nodded in agreement.

Quinn clapped a hand to the guy's shirt. "Stay away from her, say what you came to say and leave her alone. Are you following her?"

"Yes. I'm sorry, but I needed to tell her. I was trying to save you."

"Trying to save me?" Harper exclaimed. Then her expression changed, a flash of recognition in her eyes. "Nico?"

"Yes!" He moved to reach out to her, and Quinn blocked him.

"Stay here," Quinn warned.

"He's my cousin," Harper said. "I haven't seen him since I was tiny."

"Why did you try to grab her from the apartment building?"

"I wasn't trying to take her. I was trying to save you. For weeks I saw you, surrounded by these guys. You go in and out of the building, but nobody can enter. I couldn't reach you. I thought you were in a prostitution ring, the one our aunt ran for years."

Harper wrapped her arms around herself and started to rock on the bench. Xander brought her close to him, whispering in her ear.

"How did you even find me?" She reached across, squeezing Logan's hand.

"We knew your parents were in Canada. Your mother wanted to keep dancing, but the family said no. We heard she came here and made a dance school anyway. So when I came here for school last year, I started asking about your mother and then searched for you on the web."

"The dark web," Xander spat out.

"Yes, I wasn't sure if your mother was underground." Nico looked at Logan. "Someone from the web told me if I was looking for a dancer, they were filming *Canada's Best Dancer* here soon. So, I watched the theatre. But I couldn't get through the line to you, and I wasn't sure it was you at first. And then I saw the first commercial and saw your face."

"Why come find me now?" Harper asked.

"A lot of time has passed. The family isn't what it used to be," Nico said.

"Are they still looking for Harper?" Logan asked.

"No. Nobody is left who remembers her, except my mother and me. My father died in a raid. My mother lives in Oregon. We moved when I was eleven. I'm not sure where our other aunt is, but most of the cousins are in prison back home. The government shut down the family business about seven years ago."

Harper trembled, unsure how to take this news and wondering if she could believe Nico. But an image of her Aunt Sophia laughing over tea with her mother swam through her mind.

"The police just let you go?" Logan asked.

"Yes, they didn't have enough to charge me," Nico said.

"There is no more Relizphe mob?" Harper asked.

Nico shrugged. "After your father's brother and wife disappeared... it fizzled. What happened to your parents?"

"They died," Harper said. "In a fire."

She closed her eyes, shivering.

"I'm here, Angel," Logan stood, biting against the pain. He walked behind her, placing his hands on her shoulders.

"I didn't want to upset you. I just wanted to see you again. Don't you remember when we were children and stood at the sea's edge, skipping stones?"

"Yes," Harper said. "How did your mother stay out of it?"

"My father took a mistress," Nico said. "Our grandfather was still alive at the time and recognized the mistress, cast out my mother and me. We had nothing, but we got lucky."

"You did," Harper said bitterly. "Nico, I'm glad to hear Aunt Sophia and you are okay, but I don't know if I can have you in my life. I've worked hard to put all that behind me. You've brought up unpleasant memories for me."

"I understand, Alina."

Harper flinched at hearing the name. Logan glared at Nico.

"I don't think *Harper* wants anything to do with you right now."

"Get lost, and if you come near her again, we'll make sure the charges stick," Quinn said.

"Angel?" Xander asked.

Harper stared at her cousin. "I've worked so hard to put the past behind me. I wish you had never come."

"I'm sorry. But you are family. Can I give you my phone number and my mother's email if you change your mind?"

"No, but I'll give you my phone number. You can call in a month and see if *Harper* is feeling differently," Logan said.

Harper buried her face in Xander's arm, the relief evident in her face. Logan understood that if she had her aunt's email address, she would feel pressured to use it.

"Where do you live here?" Quinn asked.

"I'm a student at UBC. I live near campus. Third-year, mechanical engineering," Nico said.

"If I change my mind, I know where to find you," Harper said.

"Okay. I'll go now, and I promise I won't bother you again," Nico said, his hands raised to Quinn. He backed away.

Logan sat next to Harper. She reached for Xander, and they sandwiched their girl, pouring their strength into her.

"That was hard," she said.

"I'm so proud of you, Kitten." Logan hugged her.

"Looks like we both got rid of horrible family members," she said.

Logan laughed and coughed and cursed because it hurt so much. "Yeah."

"This guy has to get home," Quinn said. "Coming with me, or is Xander taking you?"

"Don't you have a rehearsal today?" Logan asked Harper. He wanted to stall, to see if Xander would come to his senses.

"It's okay. If I have to miss it."

"Kitten."

"Angel."

Logan exchanged a look with Xander and shook his head at him.

"You are not going to miss your rehearsal. I'll go home, Quinn will nursemaid me for a bit, and then I'll come get you after your rehearsal."

"No, you can't."

"I can send someone," Xander said.

Right, but he wouldn't come himself. He was already distancing himself from them, and it made Logan angry.

"I said I would be there, Kitten."

"Okay. Thanks." Harper squeezed his hand.

"Are you coming?" Logan asked.

"I got to check in with Ares. I'll give you a call later." Xander glanced away.

"Fine." Logan threaded his hand through Harper's.

"Xander, can you come with us?"

"Angel, I can't." His voice almost broke on the word, and Logan felt sorry for the bastard. He was throwing away something good and pure because he was a big scaredy-cat.

"Okay," she nodded.

"Let's get out of here," Logan grunted, taking a step and another between Harper and Quinn, leaving Xander behind.

31

CHAPTER-THIRTY ONE - HARPER

"Thanks for the cookies, Harper. I'll eat them while studying."

"Let me know how your exams go," Harper said, hugging Hana. "Come and visit us more."

"I will. You're sure it's okay not to feel too sad about Uncle Edwin?" Hana frowned, biting her lip, looking so young.

Harper put an arm around her. "It's okay to feel that way."

"Yeah, and If you're sad, you can always call me, right?" Logan said.

"I'll text you" Hana smiled at her big brother.

"And I'll text back."

Logan hugged his sister, and Harper smiled; they loved each other so much.

Logan opened the door at the knock.

"Hi, Mom! Thanks for getting me."

"No problem, I'm looking forward to dinner. Hi Logan, Harper."

"Hey, Paige. How you're holding up?"

Paige smiled slightly. "Fine. The press keeps asking for a comment, the board wants to meet, I have a lot to figure out, but I'm okay."

"Good to hear."

"Harper, we watch you on *Canada's Best Dancer*. Are you in the top five?"

"We'll have to find out."

"We'll be cheering for you," Page said.

"My dorm mates didn't believe me when I said you're my brother's girlfriend," Hana said.

Harper felt herself flush.

"Hana!"

"It's fine," Harper said. "You can tell them that if you want. It's true."

"Absolutely," Logan grinned, kissing her on the lips.

Paige grinned. "Come on, Hana. We'll be late for our dinner reservations."

"Bye, Logan. See you, Harper!"

Harper waved, Logan fisted bumped, and then he closed the door.

"I love her, but her energy is too much for me today."

Harper grinned. "I wonder where she gets it from."

He shook his head, winced and grabbed his stomach.

"Do you need a painkiller?"

"Kitten, it's been a week since I took them. I'm going to sit down."

Harper frowned, watching as he made his way over to the couch. She poured him a glass of water from the fridge, then grabbed a salad.

"Do you want me to warm up some of Josie's vegetarian chilli?"

"No, I'll get something later. How late do you think your rehearsal is going to be?"

"I can take a cab."

"Kitten, you can put down your fork, grab a paddle, and present to me."

Her breath caught in her throat. It's like Logan had learned from Xander that swift was best.

"Yes, Sir." She set her fork down, and from the closet, took out a wood paddle.

She stood in front of him and offered it.

"Rest your hands on the top of the couch." Logan lifted himself wincing.

"Logan..."

"Kitten." His hand came in her hair, and she hissed out a breath. "Sorry, Sir."

She breathed as she stretched out her arms. These past couple of weeks had been so hard on him. She knew he had struggled with not being able to do his usual routine.

Logan pulled down her panties and skirt.

She bit the inside of her cheek as the paddle swung through the air and landed across her cheeks.

"When I ask you a question, you answer. Correct?" Logan tapped the paddle hard against her ass.

"Correct, Sir."

She closed her eyes as the smooth wood touched her ass. The last couple of weeks had been hard on her, too though she wouldn't admit it.

"Yes, Sir."

As the paddle landed on her ass, she yelped. Logan brought it down, again and again, until the pain of it spread throughout her body, the tension leaving her shoulders. The smooth wood landed on her ass, hard and soft, hard again and again and her skin felt raised and warm. She could no longer feel the coolness of the wood.

"Good girl." Logan brushed his fingers over her heated flesh, and Harper shook her head, trying to stop the tears.

Logan threw the paddle down on the couch and brought her into his arms, pulling her on his lap.

"What is it?" Logan's expression of concern seared into her heart.

"Hana reminded me of my paper. The last paper I turned in wasn't as great as I thought it was. I got a C on it," she said.

"Hey, that's no big deal." Logan took her hand in his. "You're so busy with the show and full-time dance training. It's amazing you can study at all."

Harper shook her head, hot tears falling down her face. What she had with Logan was everything and she was selfish to ask for more. But this was the second time he'd comforted her over her poor grade, and she didn't want comfort.

She missed Xander. Xander would push her to be better, to give more to maintain a higher standard. Xander would tell her to email the professor and ask about a retake or what she could do for extra credit.

Xander, she knew, wouldn't accept it as her best because she hadn't made it a priority. He wouldn't accept it because he would understand that Harper didn't.

And in the depths of her submissive heart, she hoped, wanted Xander to punish her for not maintaining that high expectation.

"Kitten, talk to me," Logan said.

She wiped her face with the back of her hand. Logan sat forward, peering into her eyes. She sighed, knowing she owed him the truth.

"I love you, Logan. But I miss him. You can give me so much, you *do* give me so much, but there are things that Xander can give me that I crave, that I want. I love him too."

"Shush now, Kitten. I know your heart has been hurting in this last little while. I know you miss him every day. It's the service part, isn't it?" Logan held up a hand. "I know it's not just that. I know you love the moody bastard for more than what he can give you in a D/s relationship, but if you compare us, that's what he can give you in the kink department that I can't."

"Yes," Harper whispered. "I like the thrill you give me with D/s. I want to be shown off, and I want you to test my limits. But I crave submission with service, and you're not wired for that."

"I like it when you cook and do things for me," Logan said. "But it's more than that, isn't it?"

"Logan, no you don't. You like what I make when I cook or bake something, but you won't let me do things for you even with you injured. It's a mindset. Yes, it's a mindset, and Xander has always walked that line with me. Because we weren't D/s, obviously, but I miss anticipating his needs and doing things for him because of the attention he gives, intensity, and expectations."

"His expectations are high," Logan said.

"Impossibly so," Harper agreed.

"We're just going to have to show Xander that you need him and reassure him he will not break if he lets himself love you."

"Ella said the same thing."

"I should have done something about it sooner. But these past weeks, I've been selfish, taking up all the time and attention you can give me." His palm caressed her cheek, and Harper leaned into his touch.

"I'll make one-on-one time for you. We'll figure it out," Harper said.

"Yes, we will. You've been a little mopey this past month. I was going to flog it out of you before I got stabbed. But I think this is a more long-term solution."

"I wouldn't mind the flogging," Harper admitted.

"Good, because you're going to get it. Now go dance your heart out, Kitten." Logan kissed her, and Harper's heart felt like it would burst.

She slid off his lap and kissed his forehead. She loved this man so much.

"And you'll pick me up after."

"Yes, I can't wait," Logan grabbed her waist, brought her in the circle of his legs and kissed her as if he didn't ever want to let her go.

32

CHAPTER THIRTY-TWO - XANDER

Xander hunched over the microscope, ignoring his cellphone buzzing beside him on the counter. The quiet of the tech lab soothed him. He studied the newest tweak to the bendable glass. Damn, he loved his team. They were so close in a shorter time than expected.

He checked the text message from Ares. He sighed. His brother asked him to go to his office and bring home the most updated drawings of their building. Of course, Ares wanted the physical copies.

Xander had avoided the executive floor for as long as he could, and because he had made it a habit to float, checking in with each department, making himself available to staff, nobody thought it was odd. Or at least nobody mentioned it.

In the elevator's privacy, he closed his eyes. Today he had said goodbye to their bodyguards, offering generous severance pay for anyone who chose not to go to Stone Security. Shaking hands with his trusted employees spewed unexpected emotion. Still, the Threat Assessment and Personal Security Division had been a cornerstone of what they did from day one at Axis Management. He wished Harper was here with him. He wonders if he would have gone through with the assets sale if things were normal with her. He missed her so much that it physically hurt.

He wasn't eating. He was barely sleeping. He caught the promos for *Canada's Best Dancer* and watched the first episode, feeling absurdly proud of her.

For years, being her protector and provider had given him a clear purpose and as she bravely healed from her past. And as he was those things to her, he gained his own confidence, battling his anxiety. For her, he wanted to do better.

Without her, his world reeled. He went through the motions during the day and sought refuge in the tech lab at night, but it felt robotic. He lost his drive.

He paused by a vase of flowers at the reception desk, wondering who had replaced them. He never noticed before she left how many minute details Harper took care of, like the flowers on each floor, the delivery of his preferred bottled water, and he missed his daily calendar briefings from her. They were going to need a new assistant if they wanted to stay in business.

Xander frowned at the open office door. Maybe Ares was in a rush, and he forgot to lock up.

"Marrock." Logan leaned against the wall that went to Harper's sanctuary. Xander's eyes roamed over him. He looked a lot healthier than he did the last time he saw him. His muscles bulged as he crossed his arms over his chest, his leather jacket rippling.

"Xander."

"What are you doing here?"

"We have unfinished business," Logan said. "You saved my ass."-

"Don't mention it," Xander said.

Logan shook his head slowly. "Not how we operate. I'll forever be grateful that you showed up with impeccable timing. I thought I would return the favour."

"How so?" Xander asked.

He frowned, trying to parcel out the cadence in Logan's tone. He wasn't his usual arrogant, confident self. There was a whisper of worry? Or hopefulness? Xander's eyes landed on Harper's desk, and he startled.

"I've heard you haven't been doing so well these past couple of weeks. It seems like you might be missing someone."

"I am. But there's nothing to be done about it. We've been over this," Xander ran his hand over the spotless desk

"And I'm here to tell you, you're wrong, Xander. You're not too much for her. You're not too old for her. That girl has handled you and your business for years. She can handle you, the dominant. She *needs* the kind of dominating you do. You give her structure and boundaries. I give her the thrills. Together, we are her safe place to let go."

"Did she come and do this?" Xander said.

"Took her two hours to organize and sort everything. She also updated the calendar and the staffing schedule, pulling Gabe off rotation."

"Yeah, I owe him a phone call," Xander said.

"For years, you've demanded her real self. That she breaks out of that shell, she had buried herself in, that she be the best she could for you, Xander. Don't you owe her the same?"

"How would it work out?" Xander asked. Damn, he hated the catch in his voice. His palms grew sweaty.

"We'll figure it out. We've cared for her together, in different ways, these past couple of years and that one night we had together. It just felt right. I never thought I would want to share my collared submissive, but here we are."

"You collared her?""Not yet," Logan said.

"Okay." He felt at a loss for words. A part of him was happy Harper didn't wear another man's collar. Another part was sad that she didn't have that touchstone she so desperately needed.

"Don't suppose you ever bought a collar for her?"

"No. I thought you had?"

"We discussed it. But I didn't put it on her neck. She loves you, Xander. She loves you too."

"What are you saying, Logan?" Xander sighed.

"That we can share her and the signs we use to show that she is ours can be different. I bought her a ring. Unless you want to do the ring."

"No. I said I couldn't do this."

"But you can," Logan peeled off the wall and strode towards him. He put a hand on Xander's shoulder. "You are *exactly* what she needs, and you know it. How has your alternative been without her?"

Xander shook his head. "Damn you."

"And you will say that often to me, but we got to take care of her. She needs us both, Xander. She's waiting for you," the sly giant tilted his head towards Xander's office door.

"You have no doubts?"

"Doubt, no. Xander, you saved my life, and you saved Harper's. You give people purpose, Xander. Let us give you this. All you have to do is claim it."

Xander swallowed a lump in his throat. "You're good for her, Logan."

"Yes, but I am better with you," Logan clapped him on the shoulder and turned on his heel.

"Where are you going?" "Home. Ares told me you had an extra bedroom or seven I could use. We'll see you there tonight for dinner."

Xander shook his head, let himself into his office, and quietly closed the door behind him. His breath caught in his throat.

Damn.

Harper knelt, with her arms crossed over in front of her, her forehead touching the floor, with her back straight, in front of his desk.

Xander slowly walked around her, wanting to take in each detail. From her perfectly manicured nails to the golden circlet in her hair.

Xander rested his hand on her head. "Angel. This is a most lovely surprise."

Her breathing hitched. "A good one, I hope, Sir."

"The best one I could have asked for. Stand."

Flawlessly she did, her arms at her side, her feet slightly apart. He held her chin with his thumb and index finger, and that one touch seared his fingertips.

"To what do I owe this visit?" Xander asked. He stepped back, watching her. She licked her lip and met his eyes.

"I needed... I couldn't..." a slight blush spread across her cheeks. Xander crossed his arms in front of his chest and raised his eyebrow at her. He watched as she swallowed. She met his eyes.

"I needed to come and ask you to punish me, Sir."

"For what?" Xander asked.

He wanted to see how much she would suffer for him. He found the way she held together her composure while searching for the words exquisite.

"For leaving my work area so messy," the slightest smile appeared on her lips.

"Yeah, that has been a problem. One I've repeatedly mentioned," Xander said.

"Yes. I think I wanted you to do something about it."

"Like what?" Xander said.

"Make me clean it. Hold me to your expectations," Harper said.

Nothing on the planet was sexier than Harper, asking for what she wanted right here and now. Exposing her vulnerability, putting it out there. Trusting he would catch it.

"I'm going to undress you," he said.

She nodded.

He took the blazer off her shoulders, hanging it on the back of his door. Next, he slowly unbuttoned her red blouse, revealing a black lacy bra.

"Pretty," Xander commented. He trailed a finger around the bra's lace that cupped her breasts. Ever so slightly, she shivered under his touch.

His hands slid down to her waist, and he unbuttoned her skirt. Giving himself a moment, he folded it over the hanger and turned to her. Her long muscular legs were enclosed in black nylons. Matching black panties. And red high heels.

"I could keep you like this," Xander said.

"Yes, Sir," Harper said.

"But I want to see all of you." With his hands on her trim waist, he brushed his fingers along the nylons until they rolled down her legs. He nudged her heels off with his foot.

She stood there, naked and beautiful, except for the panties.

"These have to go too." Slowly, he pulled the silky fabric down, taking them off her.

His mouth went dry. She almost hurt to look at, standing here naked, in front of his black desk, as he had thought about so many times. Her breathing deepened.

"Turn around. Place your arms on the desk and spread your legs wide. Wider, there you go," Xander said. He placed a hand on the small of her back. "Is it cold?"

"Yes," Harper said.

He smiled. Her breasts were pressed against his glass desktop.

His hands ran over her ass, feeling her skin underneath his hands felt so right. "I'm going to use my belt on you, Angel. How many do you think with the belt?"

She gasped. "Whatever Sir thinks."

Xander smiled. With his hands on both her ass cheeks, he dragged his thumbs into the centre and pressed down. Then he grabbed them in his palms and vigorously shook her. He wanted plenty of blood to flow to the area. He wasn't planning on going easy with her.

He dropped his cufflinks on the desk beside her ear, each one tinkling as it hit the glass. Walking around the front of the desk, he rolled up his sleeves. Making sure she saw his every move, he undid his belt buckle and took it off with a flourish. He spread out its length between his hands, and then, wrapping the belt buckle in his palm, he put two ends of the belt together, making one strappy piece.

He walked around behind her, slapping the belt against his thigh. She didn't even flinch.

"How many days has it been since I've seen you last?"

"Twenty-two," Harper's thick, desire-laced voice floated around him. He breathed it in with his hand on her backside.

"Twenty-two sounds like a good number, doesn't Angel?" Xander asked.

"Yes, Sir," Harper said.

Before the words left her lips, Xander swung his finely made leather through the air, landing it perfectly across Harper's ass cheeks.

The stripe of red glowed against her creamy skin. He admired it for a moment, from a distance, and then, in quick succession, laid down five more stripes right on top of it.

Harper hissed at the last one. His palm felt the heat of her ass, ran up her back, around her neck, over her cheeks. He wiped away a tear.

"Shall we continue, Angel?" Xander said, the belt in his hand.

"Yes, Sir."

"Ask for it, Angel.""Sir, would you please give me seventeen more lashes with your belt?"

"Of course," Xander said. The belt swung through the air. Harper yelped as the next strike landed slightly above the light red line. As he rained down four more, her legs came together, and her back bowed off the desk. "Ow."

"You're doing so well," Xander said, his hand on her neck. "Back into position."

Harper sucked in a breath, spread her legs wide, and settled on the desk.

"Last seven, Angel," Xander said.

He pulled back his wrist, so the next too landed softly on the underside of her buttocks.

"Count these last five," Xander instructed.

He struck her fleshy ass repeatedly, her soft voice keeping count perfectly.

She yelped on the last one. He placed his at the base of her spine, giving her a moment.

"Five, Sir," she said after Xander landed the last one. "Thank you, Sir."

Xander tossed his belt away, and his hands rubbed her ass, feeling the searing heat. Gathering her in his arms, his lips crashed into hers. He kissed her as if he owned her.

"A million times, I have dreamed about you on my desk. I have thought about you kneeling under it a thousand times, waiting for my touch," he stroked her cheek and took her to the club chair in front of his desk. "And Angel, I've wanted to tell you I love you a hundred times a day."

Her beautiful eyes widened in surprise. Her hands ran along the cable of his hair. He tilted her face, kissing her mouth, possessing her tongue. He wrapped his arms around her, put her head on his shoulder and held her.

"You're mine, Angel. And his and we're going to make this work," Xander said.

She fluttered in his arms, burrowing into his neck. "Thank you."

"It's me who owes you the thanks, Angel. For putting up with me." He cupped the back of her neck. "For giving me your submission. And your love. Let's go home. He's waiting for us."

33

CHAPTER THIRTY-THREE – HARPER

She loved being with these two men, and her heart wanted to explode into happy pieces. She wasn't sure Xander would accept their gesture. She was afraid while kneeling, waiting for him in his office, that he wouldn't take their reassurance.

But his bravery warmed her heart. She loved Xander. He had Carli drive them home from the office, and the whole trip across the bridge, he held her. It felt so good to be nestled in his arms.

In the Montague's home, where she felt safest after the dishes had been cleared from the Thai takeout, Xander grabbed her arm, exchanging a glance with Logan.

"Think it's time to show her she belongs to both of us," Xander said.

"Right here with you." Logan took her other hand, and as Xander led them upstairs to his sanctuary, Harper's breath caught in her throat, reminding her of the last time she was in this room. Xander let go of her hand, flipped a switch, and the windows appeared with hanging lights in the shape of icicles. Harper grinned, they looked like tiny daggers, but she loved it.

"That softens it up a bit," Logan said drolly.

She didn't care where they were, as long as they were together.

Her pussy throbbed, and her ass smarted as Logan set her down on the king-sized bed.

"How should we show her who she belongs to?" Logan asked.

Xander grinned. The expression lit up his grey eyes. Harper grabbed the soft white blanket, resisting the urge to cover herself, but under their matching intense glazes.

"I think we should fill her up and fuck her until there is no doubt in that pretty head of hers," Xander said. "What do you say, Angel?"

Her body vibrated with want as she looked at her men. Her two Doms united over her. It made her heart swell with love. "Yes."

They exchanged another mysterious glance. Swiftly, Logan pinched her right nipple while Xander pinched her left. Harper yipped.

"Did you forget your manners? Yes, what?" Xander said.

"Yes, Sirs. Please fuck me."

"Good girl," Logan said. Both released her nipples.

"Spread your legs wide and finger yourself. Get ready for us," Logan instructed.

"Yes, Sir," Harper said. As she spread her legs wide open, the pressure on her ass reminded her how much it still stung from Xander's belt. Slowly, she made circles around her clit, her eyes drifting close. She felt a wall of heat from behind her and drifted up to awareness.

"Open your eyes," Xander said. His mouth slanted against hers, and she moaned low. Her eyes opened, taking in the sight of Xander's naked body, his hair falling around his back. He was beautiful.

"We'll take care of you, Kitten," Logan said. He dropped kisses along her collarbone, along her neck. Xander's hard, well-toned chest came across her, and Logan's muscled wall pressed on her back behind her.

They kissed and nibbled her like she was the feast they had been starved for, and never had Harper felt so secure, so desirable, and so wanting.

Her lips were sore by the time they stopped kissing her. Her clit begged for attention. Xander read her thoughts and pressed his thumb right on her hard clit.

"Patience," he said.

Harper sighed, and Logan's hands palmed her breasts, squeezing them. She leaned against him as Xander kissed her thighs, going so close to her pussy but not there. Not right there, where she wanted them. Harper moaned.

"Lean forward, Kitten and show Xander exactly how much you want his cock in your pussy," Logan whispered in her ear.

Her hands glided up and down around Xander's cock. He stared at her with the blaze of a forge. "Please, Sir, may I suck your cock?"

"Yes, you may, Angel," Xander said.

Harper murmured as she licked the head of Xander's thick cock. She moaned in pleasure as it glided in her mouth. She ran her tongue around the underside and heard Xander hiss. A thrill went through her as she made him lose a second of control. And then she squirmed as she felt Logan's finger on her anus. Xander's hands held her cheeks, positioning her exactly where he wanted her, and Logan's finger sank in, past her tight ring of muscles.

God. She closed her eyes against the tortured ecstasy.

Logan's strong touch sent her nerves buzzing, and Xander's fast pace brought tears to her eyes. Harper felt like she was going to explode from their sizzling touches.

She wanted more. She wiggled her bottom, swallowed down on Xander's cock, and felt them pull back, ever so slightly.

"Think you're in charge here?" Xander asked, petting her cheek with the back of his hand. Harper shook her head and gasped as she felt Logan's knuckle. It was too much and not enough.

The darting heat from Xander's eyes scorched her and saw right through her. She squirmed on Logan's touch as Xander didn't move an inch.

They held her like that, just by the strength of their touch, for an eternity, and finally, when Harper thought she couldn't hold Xander's cock in her mouth any longer, he thrust deeper, slamming quick and fast as Logan's fingers plunged in and out of her anus.

Her head swam, her eyes closed, lips and hands swept her up into dizzying sensations. So much pressure. So good.

Harper squealed as Logan's fingers reached around her to her throbbing clit. "She's gushing here, Xander."

"Good. See how she comes apart for us as we hold her," Xander said.

So full. Between her mouth and Logan's fingers pinning her, she felt so full. Like a slow roaring blaze, the orgasm blasted through her. Xander released her mouth, and she screamed their names as the heat of both of them sandwiched her.

Xander's fingers were on her clit, trying to wrench another one out of her.

"No, I can't!"

"Oh yes, you can, Angel," Xander said. His determined fingers hooked her G-Spot, and Harper didn't have anything else in her body. The pleasure rolled through her, but not enough to saturate.

Logan kissed her, and his hands were on her hips as he glided her back onto his cock.

So confident, these men were, with what to do to her.

Harper laid back on Logan as he positioned his cock in her back entrance. It fit just right. She almost wept from the fullness of it. She rested her head against his body, his hands guiding her hips.

Xander kissed her fast, sucking her lips, biting gently down on her bottom lip as he pulled away, his knees straddling over them.

"Ready, Angel?"

"Yes, please, Sir. Please fuck my pussy," she said.

Xander smiled, and the warmth of his approval sent hot waves of pleasure through her. He sank slowly into her, inch by inch, until he was seated.

Her mind blanked. In a red-hot ribbon of sensations, Logan lifted her hips to match each one of Xander's thrusts.

Harper whimpered, helpless between the two of them.

A mess of nerves and sensations as they coursed through her body at lighting fast speed, her skin aflame from their bodies, fucking her.

She couldn't tell whose hands were whose. She just knew, with every thrust, she belonged to them.

To both of them.

And they belonged to her. This trio was theirs alone.

Hard, thick, ridged cocks, in her pussy. In her sensitive ass. God, her head spun. She never felt so complete, so satisfied.

How could her body take both? She didn't know and didn't care; she just felt so delighted.

She leaned forward for Xander, her hands on his arms.

"Was there something you need, Angel?" He gritted out as he thrust deep into her pussy.

"Kiss me," she cried out. "Please, Sir."

His lips met hers, and Logan's landed on the back of her neck as they rode her, hard and deep, and she cried out repeatedly at the intense sensations flaming through every inch of her body.

Her body was nothing more than a receptacle for their hungry need and hot pleasure.

Logan slammed her hips on his cock, and Harper cried out.

Xander reached between them, fingering her cunt and found her clit. He drove into her, showing her that she was his, and he claimed her with one hard thrust that was so deep a shriek ripped from Harper's throat. Bombed with pleasure, she couldn't move. She was a boneless mess.

She closed her eyes. She felt Xander's withdrawal and wanted to cry, and then she felt Logan slide out of her, and her relief turned to emptiness.

And then, Logan wrapped his arms around her waist, snuggled up next to her back, and Xander wrapped his arms, snuggling her breasts against his chest. Harper had never felt so completely safe.

"We got you, Kitten," Logan said.

34

CHAPTER THIRTY-FOUR – XANDER

"Angel?" Xander called.

The sheets were rumpled, but he was alone in his bedroom. Throwing on a pair of soft cotton pants, he strolled out of his room. "Harper?"

She turned to him against the doorframe of one of the guest rooms, smiling.

"I guess he left us in the middle of the night."

She reached for his hands, and he put his arm around her waist, laughing softly against the column of her throat.

Logan slept like a starfish because, of course, he did.

"I think we should let him sleep" Xander pressed his lips to hers and she kissed him back, his heart so light at being here with her the morning after.

"Breakfast?"

"Great idea." Harper stepped in front of him, and he pulled the sash of her dressing gown, sliding it off her shoulders.-Curious what she would do, he waited, raising his eyebrow. His perfect submissive smiled at him over her shoulder as she walked downstairs.

He loved watching her walk naked through the hallway into the kitchen. She was so damn gorgeous.

"Coffee?""You know how I like it" He reached out and cupped the back of her neck, pressing her against the cabinets and kissing her hard. Damn, it pleased him so much, having her here with him.

"Your rehearsal is at four o'clock?" He took out his plain yogurt. Poured his granola mix and almonds into another bowl. Wondered who bought the box of chia muffins. Taking one out of the box and put it on a plate.

"Very nice," Xander murmured as she fixed his coffee and handed it to him. "Take the bowl of yogurt and the spoon." He carried over the coffee, the bowls of granola and nuts and the muffin.

At the table, Harper smiled shyly at him. "Yes, Angel?"

"You said something about kneeling at your feet every morning."

"Delighted you remembered. It might be impractical every morning, but it's just the thing this morning. Kneel."

She kneeled beside his chair. He set the things out on the table, grabbed his phone and tablet from the counter and sat. As he started to read his emails, he ate his yogurt. Stroking Harper's hair, occasionally.

After a moment, he cut the muffin in quarters. Put a piece in his hand and extended his hand to Harper. "Eat."

Her gasp of ... surprise? ...her glassy eyes and flushed face told him it was a gasp of pleasure, and it warmed his tortured heart. He focused on responding to his emails with an effort while feeding her the muffin.

Checking his phone, he held out his palm with a bit of the granola and almonds. Beside him, Harper murmured, her breath coming out in short pants of arousal. Xander rested his hand on her hand as he finished his coffee. He ate his yogurt, and when he was almost done, he offered the spoon to Harper.

"Lick it for me, pretty sub."

Her body lurched forward. Xander grinned.

"You're such a good slut."

Her eyes, big and glossy, briefly met his, and his hand lingered on her neck. Damn, there wasn't a better way to start his day than this.

She made the sweetest sound, grinding against his leg, a cry, a half moan. Her sound that told him this was turning her on. He fisted his hand in her hair, about to give her his bowl. A song about being alive and loving every minute blasted from the speakers."He needs to learn I like quiet in the morning," Xander mumbled.

Harper giggled. "Oh, it's funny little sub?"

"Yes Sir."

He brought her cheek against his leg and traced her lips with her fingers, feeling her grin.

"Good morning! That is one comfortable bed, Xander."

Xander glanced at Logan, shooting the sunshiny bastard his darkest stare.

"Oh, I interrupted, did I? Maybe we need a morning schedule."- "Can you turn that off?""I figured out how to work your sound system," Logan grinned but tapped his phone, and the music turned off.

He walked behind Harper, took her hair in his hand and pulled her head towards him. "Good morning, Kitten."He leaned down and kissed her deeply, and Harper's hand rested on Xander's knee.

"Mind if she comes up?"

"Nope, I got to respond to this email," Xander grumbled.

Logan pulled out a chair, sat down, and pulled Harper on his lap, nuzzling her neck. His hands swept over her breasts, and he kissed her.

"Try to cheer up dark lord over there. I see you guys found the muffins. They are packed with protein from Josie. Harper, you need to keep your calories up. How long is your rehearsal tonight, six hours?"

"Something like that," Harper said.

Xander smiled as they locked lips together. He finished his emails and closed his tablet.

"We have hours until you have to be at the theatre. Any ideas of what we can do, Logan?"

"I got a few."

"I think I want our sub on the table."

"Good place for her," Logan agreed.

Xander stood and lifted Harper onto the table. She giggled.

"Lay down, Angel. I want to look you over."

She laid back, spreading her legs. "Good girl."

Starting at her feet, Xander ran his hand over every inch of her, noticing the bruise on her thigh.

"You need a wax. Make an appointment as soon as I am done with you.""Yes, Sir." She closed her eyes, her hips rising off the table.Xander hummed with satisfaction, loving how his order brought her pleasure.

He flicked her pussy, and her knees drew up.

"None of that now."

"Gotta get some fuel. This show is making me hungry," Logan said.

Harper brought her legs back down.

His hand continued over her belly, under her breasts. "Your nipples would look so pretty pierced. What do you think?"

She licked her lips, searching his eyes. "If you want them pierced, I'd love that."

"Logan, what do you think?" Xander stepped out of his pants.

"Yeah, she can use some new jewelry." Logan pulled a chair out. He put a foot on his knee, eating his cereal.

"Yes, she can," Xander agreed.

His hands trailed down to her pussy. He parted her labia. She cried out, and his mouth was on her in the next breath, his tongue pushing hard on her clit.

She bucked under him.

Knowing the table would hold, he climbed on. Her eyes, so dewy and heavy with desire, made the blood roar in his ears. He parted her labia, then put his tongue to her sweet cunt and sucked, lifting her legs on her shoulders.

"Please, Sir," Harper cried out.

Xander grazed her clit with his teeth, slapping the insides of her thighs

"I need in you," he growled out. He lined up his cock and, with one thrust, seated balls deep in her hot heat.Damn.

Yes, this is what he needed. As she lifted on the table, her eyes glowed with pleasure, reaching for his shoulders.

Xander pounded into her, biting the hollow space between her shoulder and neck. His spine tingled, and his balls got heavy.

"Yes!" Harper cried.

Forever. He wanted to stay inside this beautiful cunt forever. Her pussy tightened around him. Blazing heat raced up his spine. He ached to release in her this instant.

"Angel, now," Xander ordered, kissing her mouth so hard he felt the burn. He felt her pussy clamp around him, and her orgasm rolled through her. Her eyes closed, and she cried out as his cum shot deep in her. He held her as she shuddered, not wanting to leave her. Xander looked across at Logan. The man smiled at him. Xander kissed their sub's forehead.

"God, I loved waking up to this," Logan said. He joined them, placing a finger along Harper's lips. "Perfect, do you agree, Kitten?"

"Yes, Sirs. I love you."

"Love you too, Kitten."

"I love you, Angel," Xander's voice broke on the word.

Logan slapped him on the back. "See? That wasn't hard."

Xander growled, but he smiled in complete agreement with his friend.

35

CHAPTER THIRTY-FIVE - HARPER

Harper smiled right into the front row under the stage lights. Her heart hammered frantically, and she took a deep breath as she waited for the host of *Canada's Best Dancer* to reveal the top five results.

These past weeks, through doing the competition, she got to reclaim a piece of her past and a part of her heritage, but it was the future she was looking forward to.

She took a deep breath and smiled towards where she knew Logan and Xander were sitting. No matter what happened here tonight, she could be happy knowing she had given it her all.

"Here we go," the host, Mindy Lewis, said. The lights darkened above as Harper felt the spotlight's glow on her. If the spotlight went out, she didn't make it.

"And the next dancer into our top five is...Eliza Sommers!" The audience applauded loudly as the spotlight darkened on Harper's spot. Her throat got tight. She had hoped just a tiny bit that maybe it would have been her.

"Congratulations, Eliza!" Mindy said. "Harper, we are so sorry to see you leave the competition!"

Harper crossed centre stage, and Mindy slung an arm over her. "You are a talented dancer, and we wish you all the best. Any parting words?"

"Thank you to the judges," Harper said to the panel in front. "And to the fans who voted for me. This was awesome! You guys are the best!" She waited for a moment until the applause ended. "I also need to thank my two pillars of support. You are everything to me, and I wouldn't be standing here without you."

"Let's give a round of applause to Harper Blake!" Mindy said.

Harper waved at the crowd and exited stage left.

"Sorry, Harper!"

"We thought it was going to be you!" The other dancers patted her shoulder, giving her quick hugs.

She smiled through it all. It had been years since she had danced, and to get to the top ten was an impressive accomplishment, she told herself as she walked down the hall into the dressing room. She changed out of her costume, hung it on the wardrobe rack, and then changed into yoga pants, a sweater, and a pair of kitten heels. She wiped the make-up off her face and slung her bag around her shoulder.

She just wanted to be in the arms of her men.

They met her at the stage door. Xander stood with his hands behind him and Logan, with his arms crossed in front of him.

"I demand a recount," Logan said with a warm smile playing around his lips. "You are so talented, Harper."

"Angel, how are you?" Xander took her hand, kissing her cheek. "We are so proud of you."

"Those people voting obviously don't know how good you are," Logan said, kissing her cheek.

"I'm okay," she said, smiling at them.

"You are?" Logan's eyebrows raised, and Harper's smile widened. For her giant being okay with not being in first place was a hard concept to understand.

"Yeah. Less time at the show means more time to spend with you, Sirs."

Each of them linked their arm through hers, making her giggle.

"We thought we would take you out to the fancy dessert place if you won," Logan opened the door to his Jeep for her.

"Can we still go?"

"Of course," Xander said, settling in the back seat.

On the way to the restaurant, Logan changed the music so many times that Xander finally turned it off. Harper laughed.

"Here we are, Angel."

She loved going places with her Sirs. Logan kissed her as he took her hand. In a flash, Xander kissed her, and for a moment, she wasn't sure they would let her leave the parking lot.

"Just remember, you are our dessert later," Logan said. Xander took her arm. Logan placed a hand on the small of her back. She couldn't stop smiling. She knew there was a cast party later, but she wanted to be with them. This was the perfect way to celebrate her success on the show.

They opened the door to One Dessert for her, the noise of the busy restaurant making Xander's shoulders tense. She reached for his hand.

"We'll just take the table in the far corner in the other room if it's empty," Xander said to the hostess.

"Of course, Mr. Montague. This way," the hostess led them to a quiet table, leaving them with menus.

Logan brought out his phone, “Social media is screaming that you got eliminated.”

Harper grinned. “That’s okay. I still get to go on tour with them this summer.”

“I guess we will travel across the country this summer, Marrock. You up for it?”“Hell yeah. If my boss will give me the time off.”-Xander shook his head. “I think it’s a perfect reason.”“How will I explain the two of you on tour?”

“You’ll think of something,” Logan said, his hand on her thigh.

“Ready to order?” a server said.

“Just coffee, please,” Xander said.

“I’m going to order the walnut hot fudge sundae with whipped cream,” Harper said. “And I’m not going to share.”

“You’re welcome to it,” Logan said. “Do they have anything not soaked in sugar here?”

“Logan.” Xander kicked him under the table.

The server smiled at them, collected their menus, and walked away.

“Listen, Kitten, we thought we might go look at houses this weekend.”

“Is Ares feeling cramped?”

For the past few weeks, they had been living at the Montague home, and it had worked out for everyone. She’d tried her best to balance the show’s busy schedule, Xander’s exacting demands and Logan’s needs, and it made her head spin, but it was nice having all of them together in one place. She promised Xander she would come into Axis Management and sort it out, though she didn’t know if she wanted to continue as his executive assistant. It would take time to train someone new.

"No, we just thought it would be nice to have our own place." Xander's eyebrows drew together.

"There's plenty of room," Harper said.

"I told him that, Kitten," Logan said, punching Xander's shoulder. "But he's convinced we need our own space."

The server set down Harper's colossal sundae.

"I brought extra spoons just in case you decided to share after all."

"Thanks," Harper said. She took a massive bite of walnut ice cream and whip cream. "You can't share everything but a mega-size house? You can share that. That was my first home for a long while, and I like having Ares around."

Ares's good humour and mild demeanour gave her a break from her demanding Doms.

"If you're happy there, I won't disrupt it," Xander said with a sigh.

"Yeah. And sometimes, if you're really lucky, you find out sharing is exactly what you needed." Logan slid down off the booth, kneeling in front of her.

"Logan, what are you doing?" Harper asked. Cold shivers raced along her arms, and her nerves fluttered.

"Will you honour me by being my wife? My wife, who I share with this non-sentimental fool," Logan said.

Xander stood by his side, shaking his head.

Tears ran down her face.

"Oh, God! Yes. Yes, Sirs!" she said.

Logan stood up and crushed his lips against hers. He made her feel adored with the heat of his kiss.

"Look at this." Logan opened the jewelry box to reveal a titanium band, one black band and one gold band, circling a diamond. He slipped it on her ring finger.

"It's perfect," she breathed.

"We're glad you like it, Angel. We can't wait to share the rest of our lives with you and make every dream you have come true." Xander pulled her over to him. "Now, I'm going to ask you another question. And I would like you to kneel."

She glanced at Logan. He gave her a small smile, encouraging her. Xander raised his eyebrows. She sank to her knees on the hardwood floor of the restaurant, with her head bowed.

"Damn, she's lovely," Xander said.

"And she's ours," Logan said.

"I want to offer you my collar, Harper, and with it my deepest vow that I will honour and protect you and treat you like the most cherished possession you are. And that I will share you in love and joy with Logan. Will you wear it, knowing I will always give you what you need and most of what you want, agreeing to respect and obey me as your Master and to respect and obey Logan?"

"Yes, Master," Harper trembled with excitement. "Yes, Sir!" she said to Logan.

Xander settled a black metal collar on her neck. It was cold on her skin and the perfect weight.

"Rise, Angel," Xander said.

His mouth crashed into hers, and Harper breathed in his familiar scent. Logan embraced them, nuzzling her neck and then his mouth was on hers, hot and needy, and Harper knew she was home.

"I love you, Harper," Xander said. "Never doubt it."

"I love you, too," Logan said. "And I can't wait to show you off. Let's go home, Xander."

"I love you both. You're my world, my home," Harper said.

They held her hands, walking her out of the restaurant, and Harper couldn't wait to see what came next with her Doms by her side.

Want to read a bonus scene from Flame For Two? Click here

36

ACKNOWLEDGEMENTS

Thanks to my mate and cubs for giving me space to write as I wrangle the words, and to my dearest, just put it on my tab.

Thank you to my beta and ARC Readers! I appreciate you so very much.

Thank you to the Critq Chicks! You're all amazing!

Many thanks to fellow authors, K.S. Ellis, Morgan Elliot and Ivy Whitaker, you got me over the finish line with this book, and it's better because of you.

And thank you for reading! You can keep up with Raleigh and find out when *Flame Again*, book three in the Bandit Brothers Series, is out by visiting the links here: https://linktr.ee/RaleighDamson

www.ingramcontent.com/pod-product-compliance
Lightning Source LLC
Chambersburg PA
CBHW031316280626
47169CB00019B/1635